C^{the}HRYSALIS

the CHRYSALIS

A NOVEL

HEATHER TERRELL

BALLANTINE BOOKS
New York

Published in the United States by Ballantine Books, an imprint of The Random House Publishing Group, a division of Random House, Inc., New York.

BALLANTINE and colophon are registered trademarks of Random House, Inc.

ISBN 978-0-345-49466-5

Library of Congress Cataloging-in-Publication Data
Terrell, Heather.
The chrysalis : a novel / Heather Terrell.
p.   cm.
ISBN-13: 978-0-345-49466-5 (hardcover : alk. paper)
ISBN-10: 0-345-49466-0 (hardcover : alk. paper)
ISBN-13: 978-0-345-49467-2 (pbk. : alk. paper)
ISBN-10: 0-345-49467-9 (pbk. : alk. paper)
1. Art treasures in war—Fiction.   2. Cultural property—Repatriation—Fiction.
3. Art thefts—Fiction.   4. World War, 1939–1945—Destruction and pillage—Europe—
Fiction.   5. Europe—Fiction.   6. New York (N.Y.)—Fiction.   I. Title.
PS3620.E75C47 2007
813'.6—dc22
2006034422

Printed in the United States of America on acid-free paper

www.ballantinebooks.com

2 4 6 8 9 7 5 3 1

FIRST EDITION

Book design by Casey Hampton

For my boys

ACKNOWLEDGMENTS

The Chrysalis could never have emerged from its prolonged pupal stage without the assistance of many people. First, I must thank Laura Dail, my wonderful agent who took the book on, in so many ways. Next, I want to express my gratitude to the incredible people at Ballantine Books, beginning with Paul Taunton, my extraordinary editor, who gave *The Chrysalis* a chance. I am so very fortunate to have the backing of the amazing Ballantine team: Libby McGuire, Kim Hovey, Brian McLendon, Jane von Mehren, Rachel Kind, Cindy Murray, the art department, the promotion and sales departments, and the managing editorial and production departments.

Countless friends and family members helped along the way: some with the manuscript itself, and some in other fashions. Among the many are Illana Raia; Ponny Conomos Jahn; Jennifer Kasmin Miller; Laura McKenna; Elisabeth Dyssegaard; Maureen Brady; my parents, Jeanne and

Coleman Benedict; my siblings, Coley, Lauren, Courtney, Christopher, and Meredith, and their families; my grandmothers; my aunt Terry; and my in-laws.

Yet, without my husband, Jim, *The Chrysalis* would still be in its cocoon. His love and support encouraged its metamorphosis. And, our little son, Jack, gave it the final inspiration to take flight.

the CHRYSALIS

one

BERLIN, 1943

THE TRAIN BOUND FOR MILAN SNAKES INTO THE BERLIN STA-
tion, sending billows of steam high into the station's skeletal rafters.
Its whistle pierces the night once and then recedes. Silence reclaims the
cavernous space, broken now and then only by the slow, steady scraping of
a sweeper's broom.

The sweeper has learned not to stare openly at the horrors that pass
through the station. He knows to keep his own counsel and inhabit the
shadows. Yet he watches, head bowed, from beneath the brim of his cap.

Track by track, click by click, the train comes to a stop. In the last car,
a couple sits facing each other. They wait without moving, framed like
portraits by the window's ruby curtains. Their incandescence defies the
heavy, quiet darkness, and the sweeper slows his pace.

He considers the woman first. A station lamppost throws her proud
profile into bold relief against the dark cabin corners. The low light catches

the folds of her silk persimmon dress and the ermine trim of her traveling jacket and cloche hat. He shakes his head at the decadence of her clothes and calculates the loaves of bread her ensemble could fetch on the black market. Then the sweeper shifts his attention to the man, whose overall deportment seems more respectful of a wartime journey than the woman's. He has a naturally engaging round face, but he is dressed somberly in a charcoal suit, simple black overcoat, and fedora. His right hand clutches a worn brown envelope so tightly his knuckles shine white, and the jagged points of a yellow star peer out from his coat. The sweeper supposes that both must understand the precariousness of their travel.

Suddenly, the door to the compartment swings open with a jolt, and the man and the woman spring to their feet. The sweeper steps back into the safety of the shadows.

Flaxen boy-soldiers swarm around the couple. Their black uniforms gleam with gold buttons, and every jacket boasts the slash of red swastikas. The sweeper knows that these are not the usual station militia, and he jumps when their gloved hands cut across the compartment to take the man's tickets.

Then the boy-soldiers part to let a decorated officer come forward. The official leans closer to address the couple. He hands over a document with a fountain pen and demands the man's signature; the officer wants the man to surrender something. Lowering his eyes, the traveler shakes his head. Instead, the man relinquishes his precious envelope, his hand trembling as he presents it to the officer.

The officer holds the envelope up to the cabin light, then slashes it open and scrutinizes the letter within. He stuffs the letter back into its envelope and returns it to the man. The officer and his soldiers pivot and depart, shutting the cabin door sharply behind them.

The train whistle cries out again, and the couple returns to their seats. A cautious smile curls on the corner of the man's mouth, but the sweeper turns away in despair. He has seen the boy-soldiers hard at work. He knows that when the train pulls away from the station, the last car will remain.

two

NEW YORK CITY, PRESENT DAY

MARA TAPPED HER FINGERS ON THE BAR AND CHECKED her watch again. Her new client was nearly an hour late, and the butterflies in her stomach danced ever more restlessly.

To calm her nerves, she took another sip of her tonic and lime, wished again that it were a chardonnay, and looked around Maggie's. The restaurant was once a speakeasy and rumored to connect to a maze of underground tunnels that ferried booze during Prohibition. Although the alcohol now flowed freely, the smoky jazz-era décor hadn't changed. The embossed tin ceiling and burnished plank wood floors reflected the crackling fire. Couples nestled into chocolate-brown leather banquettes that were lit by low votive candles. Strains of Ella and Louis rose over the hubbub of the bar; surely no music born later than the fifties ever played here. It felt safe, anchored in a simpler time Mara felt sure must once have existed.

As she turned back toward the entrance, Mara caught a glimpse of herself in the mirror over the lively bar. She smoothed the skirt of her fitted suit and looked down at her high heels, feeling, not for the first time, as though she had squeezed herself into someone else's skin, a bit like a duck wedged into the glossy-feathered costume of a swan. She wished she were roaming the aisles of her neighborhood bookstore in her favorite broken-in jeans and turtleneck sweater instead of waiting for Michael Roarke—the in-house counsel of her law firm's intimidating new client, the venerable art auction house Beazley's.

When Mara glanced again at the door, she was just in time to watch a cab pull up.

The outline of a tall, broad-shouldered figure emerged, his face in shadow. He crouched down to the passenger-side window and handed the cabbie some money. The glimmer of a street lamp illuminated a smile and the crinkle of laugh lines around his eyes. A joke passed between the two men. He tapped the top of the cab twice in a friendly farewell and turned. Although the man was neither paunchy nor slightly balding, as most in-house lawyers she'd worked with were, Mara somehow knew he was her client.

He crossed the threshold of the bar, but the street lamp behind him kept his features obscured. All that Mara made out were the tweed of his blazer and the knife-edge crease of his charcoal pants.

When his face finally did come into focus, she saw that a dimple on his chin softened his square jaw; his sandy brown hair was cut close except for the longer, cowlicky front; he had celadon eyes, like a cat, and sinewy muscles on his hands. She hadn't expected him to be so handsome or to elicit a nagging sense of familiarity.

Then the din muted. The bustle slowed. She tried to stifle her reaction, but a blush spread across her cheeks, and she gazed down in embarrassment.

He slowed his step as he approached. "I know you," he said as she looked up. "Georgetown."

"The Art of Byzantium," she answered.

Michael Roarke had once sat next to her in the Byzantine art history class, by chance at first, and then later by choice. They used to have long conversations about iconography and the fall of Constantinople as they walked to the library across campus. She remembered his effortless courtliness: how he always walked on the street side, how he always stood when she sat. But there was Sam then. So when the class ended, their time together had ended as well. Now here he was, her new client from Beazley's.

As he apologized for his tardiness, a hostess took them over to a corner booth that seemed better suited for a date than a business dinner. At first, she liked the twist, perhaps because their meeting conjured up her original attraction toward Michael, and because she found him just as appealing as she remembered. Then she chided herself for the unbidden thoughts, so improper for an attorney toward a client—especially one she needed to secure in order to have any shot at partnership later that year.

Still, Mara wondered how he now saw her. Did he see what she had been told others see: a tall, slim force, with dainty features, neat auburn hair, and professional poise? Or did he see the person she used to be before she had fashioned herself into a self-possessed city lawyer: the gangly bookworm of their college years, the young woman harboring aspirations of the scholarly life with an angular jaw and an uneven sprinkle of freckles?

They started with a bottle of Cloudy Bay, a practice she usually avoided with a client, and talked haltingly, uncertain at first how to navigate the surprise of their acquaintance. The script she'd prepared to discuss with and impress her new client—based on Beazley's research she'd undertaken earlier that day—suddenly seemed silly and false, too obvious and pushy to trot out. Robbed of her dialogue, she was unable to perform with her normal self-confident flourish and instead felt like a stage actor who had forgotten her lines.

After an awkward silence, Michael took the lead and began asking gentle questions about Mara's life since college. He asked her about her decision to settle in New York when her prominent political family lived in Boston, about finding her way alone through the minefield of big New York law firms, and finally about Sam, the question to which Mara felt sure Michael had been building all along. The wine helped loosen her tongue, as did his mild yet pleasantly teasing manner, and she answered most of his personal questions without hesitation, quite against the grain of her typically guarded self. But when he touched on Sam, her boyfriend of nearly six years, who had broken up with her a few years ago, the catlike hairs on Mara's self-protective back stood up, and Mara turned the questions onto him. There'd been no one serious in her life since Sam, and despite the time, the wound was still fresh.

"What about your move back to New York after law school?" she asked. "Your family must've been thrilled with your return." She recalled that he was from the area—Queens, she thought.

"Sure, they were happy—at first. But my return to New York was also the beginning of my tour of duty as an associate at Ellis & Broadhurst. After I'd spent six years slaving away there, my friends had drifted away, and my family had learned not to count on me. They're all regular people with normal work schedules; they couldn't understand my long hours and unpredictability." He paused and then rotated the conversation back to her. "I'm guessing you know what that's like from working at Severin. Am I right?"

Mara nodded. Minus the references to Sam, she enjoyed this conversation; she rarely had the chance to talk with someone who understood the thrills and the sacrifices of being a young lawyer who was in a large firm but wasn't currently in the firm's throes. But she was also conscious of the reason for their meeting: the plum *Baum v. Beazley's* case, which her boss, head of Severin, Oliver & Means's litigation department, Harlan Bruckner, had just conferred upon her as a final test of her suitability for partnership.

Before she could force the conversation back on track, Michael continued. "That's part of why I left Ellis. I looked out from the pile of work I'd been buried under for years, and I didn't like what I saw, what I'd been forfeiting friends and family for. I didn't like the people who'd be my partners, mostly men and women who'd been kicked around in the sandbox as kids and couldn't wait to wreak their revenge on the incoming class of first-year associates. I didn't want to play with such a vicious lot." Mara smiled; he could be describing her boss, whom she long suspected had been an ostracized youth who rose to success by sacrificing any and all relationships and who now demanded the same surrender from his associates. And usually got it.

Michael interrupted her thoughts again. "Do you remember those talks we used to have about what we were going to do with our lives?"

"Yes," she answered. As soon as she had recognized him, their conversations came back to her in a rush. They used to talk naïvely about becoming archaeologists or art historians, uncovering some long-hidden secret or artifact critical to unlocking the past. Mara and Michael had shared a passion for discovery and a kinship she hadn't experienced with anyone since her late grandmother, her father's mother, who passed her own Irish love of legend and lore and mystery on to Mara. They used to spend countless evenings before the fire in her grandmother's little sitting room in the rectory where she lived and worked, a warm sanctuary away from Mara's chilly home, reading faerie tales, Agatha Christie, classic mythology, Irish fables, saints' lives, Arthurian legend, *The Chronicles of Narnia*, always seeking the "aha" moment of clarity, as they called it. After Nana died in Mara's junior year of high school, Mara carried on the search for "aha" moments with her college major in medieval history, archetypes, and symbols. After her walks with Michael stopped, Mara's fantasies continued. She applied to Columbia's medieval studies graduate program during her senior year at Georgetown, but her father had vetoed it: too impractical, too frivolous, too unlikely to yield material success, and not the stellar trajectory he'd charted for his only child. She had let the veto stand, and here she was, ten years later, all but convinced that her father's dreams were her own.

"Well, over the years, I've thought about those talks. I still think about them," Michael continued, "and they began to make me think that the firm's goals—papering the latest, greatest takeover—didn't have enough worth, at least for me. I started to think back on what I wanted to be before the law locked onto me, *who* I wanted to be."

His statements mirrored Mara's unvoiced doubts, the secret uncertainties that she kept even from Sophia. Mara didn't allow herself the time to second-guess the choices she made. It was not part of the plan, and it certainly wouldn't help her make partner. Yet, almost unconsciously, she whispered, "I know exactly what you mean." As soon as the words escaped from her lips, she wished she could swallow them back into the abyss where they normally resided. They might be perfectly acceptable sentiments coming from a friend, but from the lawyer you've hired to champion your cause? They couldn't be more inappropriate. She stammered, trying to regain what she perceived to be lost ground. "I-I didn't mean that. I meant—"

Michael interrupted her backtracking with a laugh. "Mara, it's okay. I know what you meant. I still think you're a bloodthirsty New York litigator fully geared up for winning us the *Baum* case."

She was relieved and thought they might segue into the case, but he seemed determined to continue with his confessions.

"I guess the thing I didn't like most about my years at Ellis was who I became personally." He paused to take a sip of his wine.

"I'd spent six years at Ellis not doing some very important things," he said. "Not developing new friendships, not pursuing any outside interests, and not forming any relationships. So I decided to get out—of the firm, at least, if not the law. I thought that working for a company connected with history and art might help rekindle some passion for my job and maybe free up more time to work on the other stuff. Like a girlfriend." He paused then asked again, casually, "Is that what happened to your relationship with Sam?"

Mara was increasingly nervous about the intimacy of their conversation. She felt curiously close to him, almost as though they'd fast-forwarded past the small-talk stage of a relationship to comfortable familiarity. Whether this stemmed from their past connection, his natural ability to draw her out, or the wine, she didn't know. But this rapport, so unusual for the seemingly open and self-assured yet actually private Mara, was not at all the one she had planned for her new client.

Despite her hesitations, she felt compelled to respond. So she took a bolstering sip of her wine and answered the persistent question. "Well, Sam and I stayed together through law school and even into my first couple of years in New York. I'd pack up a pile of cases and take the train down to D.C. where he worked, nearly every weekend. Then the State Department offered him a job in China, and he took it. His true passion always was politics."

"I see," Michael said, with a note of sympathy in his voice. She glanced down suddenly, uncharacteristically shy, and saw the manila folder on the *Baum* case sticking out of her bag.

Mara counted to ten and looked back up. Her poised, professional demeanor was in place, and she asked about *Baum v. Beazley's*. This new conversation did not go as smoothly as the more personal one, almost as though Michael resented her return to the topic that had brought them to Maggie's in the first place. He withdrew into the banquette and spoke in a much more clipped tone. He even pushed away his wineglass and folded his napkin on top of the table. Mara ignored his tinge of disappointment and listened intently.

Michael explained that a former client, who wished to remain anonymous, had hired Beazley's to sell a painting—*The Chrysalis* by Johannes Miereveld—as part of a prestigious Dutch art auction timed to coincide with the Metropolitan Museum of Art's much-anticipated Dutch exhibit.

Once Beazley's circulated the auction catalog with its photograph of *The Chrysalis,* it received a barrage of calls and letters from the self-styled true owner, Hilda Baum, who claimed she had been searching for the painting for decades. She asserted that the Nazis had taken both *The Chrysalis* and her parents' lives. Specifically, they had labeled her Catholic parents Jewish, shipped them off to a concentration camp, and then stolen their art collection. Beazley's explained its practice of investigating a painting's lineage and shared *The Chrysalis*'s crystal clear provenance with Hilda Baum, but she was not appeased. She wanted *The Chrysalis* back. The suit soon followed, and Beazley's was forced to pull the painting from the auction pending the outcome of the case. Mara's job was to keep *The Chrysalis* from her.

Michael signaled for a waiter and paid the check, though Mara protested. "Can I walk you to a cab?" he asked. Clearly he was ready to leave, and Mara feared that she'd upset him somehow but knew it wasn't the time to indulge her feelings. They both had a lot of work ahead of them in order to win this case.

As they crossed the street to catch a cab going downtown, a livery car ran a red light and screeched to a halt at their feet. Michael reached for her hand to steady her. For that moment, the warmth of his grip felt completely natural; at Georgetown, she'd often wondered how it would feel to hold his hand. But when he slid his hand away, Mara pulled herself back into the present moment.

After Michael closed the door of a cab behind her, he leaned through the open window and asked, "Are you free next Thursday?"

"I think so," Mara answered hesitantly.

"I'd love it if you could come to the auction." She thought she saw a flirtatious twinkle in his eye but dismissed it as a trick of the light, perhaps a projection of her own feelings. After all, he had given her no real reason to think he shared her attraction, except for initiating their personal banter, which could easily be explained by his affable manner. "We'll even call it business, meet with some people beforehand. Will you come?" He waited for her answer.

"Yes, of course," she said, knowing that whatever else she had penciled in on her calendar she would erase the next day.

THE FOLLOWING MORNING, MARA HEARD THE FAMILIAR TREAD
of Sophia's step before she heard the knock on her closed office door.
Mara shut her eyes. She wasn't ready yet to dissect her meeting with
Michael, least of all with Sophia, the one person who could pierce through
any barrier Mara erected in the way of full disclosure. Still, she knew that
silence would only make Sophia more curious. So, removing her reading
glasses and tucking a misbehaving strand of hair behind her ear, Mara
crossed the little room and let Sophia in before she knocked a second
time.

Sophia entered, closed the door behind her, leaned against a bookshelf
in Mara's minute but tidy office, and cocked one eyebrow. On the outside,
Sophia embodied composure, but Mara knew that inside, Sophia was in
constant motion, like a hummingbird. Her poise was a sleight of hand
from her arsenal of tricks.

When Mara resumed her seat but failed to respond to the interrogat-
ing expression, Sophia's deportment gave way, and she slumped into the
chair across from Mara's desk. "Come on, I can't believe you're making
me work so hard to find out about the dinner meeting with your big new
client. How'd it go?" Sophia asked in her soft southern drawl, a disarming
device that belied her sharp intellect like cotton candy wrapped around a
blade.

Mara paused for a long moment before answering. "It went well."

"Why so hesitant? Aside from the hell of working for Harlan, you
should be thrilled with the opportunity he's giving you." Sophia knew the
torment that Harlan had inflicted on Mara in past assignments with his
manipulative games and general meanness, yet, better than anyone, she
understood that Mara must endure his machinations if she really wanted
to progress. The bottom line was that Mara's advancement to partner
hinged on his approval. Sophia had been slightly more fortunate in that
the senior partner of her department was not as overtly power-hungry and
controlling as Harlan, but she also maintained that Mara was particularly
susceptible to Harlan's maneuverings because his mercurial standards
and blatantly conditional approval reminded Mara of her larger-than-life
politician father. It was no secret between the two friends that Mara had
gone to law school and joined this particularly competitive firm as much
to please her father as to please herself. But Mara claimed to have embraced partnership at the world-class firm as her own goal and said that

Harlan's tricks took a toll on her only because she endured them so frequently.

"I *am* thrilled," Mara reassured her, knowing that Sophia wished one of her own corporate partners would select her to be the point person on the initial assignment for such a sought-after, high-profile client. Sophia, too, was up for partnership that year and would love the positive reinforcement of such a project. Mara believed that Sophia, with her boundless appetite for long hours and slavish adherence to the rules of the game, deserved partnership even more than she did.

Yet Michael crept into Mara's thoughts again, and she felt her cheeks grow warm and flushed.

Sophia stared. "Mara, if I didn't know better, I'd say you're blushing. What's going on?"

"It turns out that I know the client from college."

"Aw, Mara, you didn't date him, did you?"

Mara shook her head. "No, nothing like that. We were friendly; we had a class together."

"Then why are your cheeks as red as an apple? Don't forget what happened to Lisa." Lisa Minever's very public failed relationship with a powerful client had led to the loss of millions in business for Severin and an ongoing legal malpractice suit that named Lisa, a law firm classmate and acquaintance, as a defendant. More than once the night before, Mara had indeed thought of her, and she understood why Sophia felt the need to threaten her with Lisa's demise. Sophia envisioned that, years down the road, the friends would become the grandes dames of Severin, and so she needed Mara to share her ambition, required the strength she drew from their mutual efforts to advance, and feared any misstep that Mara might make on that path. Sophia had risen far from the poverty of her small-town Carolina upbringing, and Mara served as Sophia's lifeline in her new existence.

Mara started to open her mouth. She would love to reveal the emotions Michael had stirred up, to laugh with Sophia and strategize together. But in her play-by-the-rules striving for success, Sophia had turned the yearning part of herself off and would not understand. So Mara sealed the near fissure and tucked her secrets more deeply out of view. This one she'd work out on her own, and, anyway, she needed to quash her feelings toward Michael. "It was just really strange seeing him after all these years," she said, "especially as a client."

Eyes askance, Sophia took a long, hard look at Mara, but she didn't probe any further. She wanted to believe Mara's assurances; there was no room in her plans for alternatives. So Sophia adjusted her tightly wound blond braid and said, "I hope so. I wouldn't want anything to spoil this opportunity."

three

LEIDEN, 1644

THE BUBBLE FLOATS TOWARD THE COTTONY SKY. HE GIG-
gles as he sees the clouds catch it in their vaporous arms, tossing it
back and forth in a merry game. He dips his hollowed-out scallop shell
into the bowl and blows another bubble. The sun joins in the sport, en-
snaring the iridescent orb in its rays and turning it from vermilion to ultra-
marine to verdigris. He knows the colors from his palette.

The bubble pops.

For the first time, he realizes he is alone by the canal. He cranes his
neck to make sure Judith is not keeping watch over him. Then, with silent
steps, he creeps down the cobblestone walk, toward the little bridge over
the canal.

His eyes cannot help but see how the lines of perspective converge on
the arched bridge. His instructors are teaching him the mathematical
method for creating three dimensions out of a mere two on a page, though

they need not. He knows it without schooling, a fact they find curious. The cobblestones, the steps near the water, even the boats on the canal—all conspire to produce orthogonals, diagonal lines that recede and meet at a single spot on the horizon, just below the bridge's center arc: the vanishing point.

The lines hook him like a lure and reel him in. Riding them over the crests of the canal's wake, he nears the vanishing point and reaches out to grasp it. Yet it disappears the closer he draws.

He hears his name being called. It is Judith. "Johannes, what would the townsfolk think of your father if they saw you unattended?" she chides. She marches toward him, her meaty hand outstretched, her corpulence spilling out from the tight leather laces of her shift. Her advance cuts through the orthogonals, disrupting the order.

A shaft of sunlight reaches deep into the corner of her wimple. It reveals her florid cheeks, normally hidden from view. They are as doughy as the bread she kneads every dawn. As scrumptious as her *boterkoek*, her almond butter cake.

His hand securely lodged in her fleshy palm, they return to the whitewashed archway of his home. Cobalt light streams through the leaded glass windows of the back door. The light washes the scurrying chickens in the kitchen courtyard periwinkle and stains the drying laundry indigo. Judith drags him past the gleaming copper pots and the glazed earthenware to the *voorhuis*, the formal living room used to receive visitors.

Judith cries out for his mother. Punishment must be meted out for his wandering, for the inevitable judgment of the neighbors.

The gentle tinkle of the harpsichord stops. Peering around the corner, he glimpses the landscape painted on the underside of the virginal's raised cover. He catches Mother's eye in the convex mirror that faces the instrument. Before she fashions the admonishing expression expected by Judith, she smiles at him, at her Johannes—her conspirator.

They wait until Judith leaves for the market. Canvassing the lane for familiar faces, all dangerous, they slip out the back door. Mother's story for traveling the way of scullery maids is at the ready. But mercy provides an empty path.

He knows the way by touch, for they have traveled it after nightfall on holy days, with nary a candle to light the way. Testing himself, he closes his eyes and runs his hand along the uneven brick walls of the narrow alleyways. His fingers memorize the undulations of certain corners, the roughness of particular stones, and the end of the passage. He wonders how to capture the texture of the mortarwork with his paints, settling on hues of white over reddish brown with brushstrokes of different widths and concentration.

He opens his eyes. The illuminated windows of a diminutive house blink at him with wide-eyed innocence. Only the initiates know the truth: The smallness of the exterior masks a subterranean expanse that billets a banned Catholic meetinghouse. Here, far from the Calvinist sight of Father, far from the condemning view of the townspeople who pretend to practice religious tolerance but, in truth, see themselves as foot soldiers in the battle against the remnants of Spanish Catholic tyranny, Mother furtively worships.

Pushing aside a rough-hewn wooden door, they descend a steep staircase. Though it is Monday, the hall teems with familiar faces, all of which greet them with nods. Like so many Catholics, Mother attends Calvinist service on Sundays—as marital vows dictate—then repents on Mondays.

They wait in silence for Mass to begin. Except for the paintings of Jesus and the saints that adorn the walls and altar, the whitewashed, vaulted interior and rows of wooden pews remind Johannes of the Calvinist church they attend with Father. Mother says the pictures are meant to help achieve a prayerful state, to bring them closer to God. Yet he learns in Sunday school that Catholic worship is heresy and idolatry, that the Word alone should be used for spiritual meditation. Johannes pities his Calvinist teachers, that they cannot feel the sacred power of the art.

The procession to the altar begins. The priest leads the pageant, resplendent in robes embroidered in gold and silver thread, and incants the Introit and Kyrie at the foot of the altar. He welcomes the congregation: "*Dominus vobiscum.*" Of his own volition, for Mother does not demand participation, Johannes greets the priest in reply: "*Et cum spiritu tuo.*"

During the Mass, the priest places his left hand on his chest and lifts the censer to incense the altar. As the censer swings like a pendulum, candlelight catches on its golden surface, irradiating dark corners and shadowed faces for a moment before arcing to brighten others. It gives all the chance to share in the light.

The incense rises. Johannes inhales the heady, sweet-smelling perfume, as exotic as his cimarron paint or perhaps the Indian yellow. He watches the smoke ascend high in a pleasing offering to God, an emblem of their prayers.

four

NEW YORK CITY, PRESENT DAY

JUST BEFORE 4:00 P.M. THE FOLLOWING THURSDAY, MARA PAUSED at the entrance to Beazley's. She had passed the mansion before and marveled at its design, a fanciful construct of its former owner, a nineteenth-century coal baron. But she had a different appreciation for its grand scale now that she stood on its steps, poised to enter the massive front doors.

Once inside, she found her way across the festooned lobby by weaving through the bevy of female assistants in charge of setting up the auction and festivities. Almost all of them sported pin-straight, shiny hair, pearls, the latest Manolos, and headsets. They were preoccupied and utterly oblivious to her. Mara had chosen a black Calvin Klein sheath with a figure-skimming jacket for the event, but she felt dowdy compared to everyone else.

After checking in with a formidable receptionist, Mara sat down on one of the scattered chairs covered in blue brocade. She eyed the collection of auction catalogs that were fanned out expertly on the marble coffee table. Though wary of disrupting the display, she slid out the Dutch auction catalog.

The glossy publication contained painting after painting of vast light-filled churches, serene domesticity, minutely crafted still lifes, and bucolic scenes of villagers: all the subjects that made the Dutch artists famous and their artwork coveted. Mara recognized certain pictures and artists. The night before, she had pored through her musty college art history books, trying to refamiliarize herself with the golden age of Dutch painting so that she could speak intelligently to Michael about the auction's artwork. Her crash course reminded her why the seventeenth-century Dutch artists once captivated her: Their exquisite, unprecedentedly realistic paintings were rife with symbols and puzzles, something Nana would have loved. She had scoured through her textbooks trying to determine where *The Chrysalis*'s creator, Johannes Miereveld, primarily known as a gifted portraitist, belonged amid the pantheon of artists, but his approach didn't fit into any of his contemporaries' molds.

As Mara perused the catalog, fragments of a hushed conversation drifted into her awareness. The conspiratorial tones piqued her interest, and she strained to see the speakers without being seen herself. She leaned forward to replace the catalog on the coffee table and glanced over at two men waiting on a nearby couch, with their backs to her.

"I hear that Masterson's is being accused of putting up a Hebborn for auction," she heard one man whisper to the other. Though she was unfamiliar with what she assumed was the artist's name, Mara had become acquainted with the art auction house Masterson's over the previous few days. The firm was Beazley's fiercest rival.

"Let me guess. A Hebborn that looks like a Corot?" the other man murmured back.

"Who knows? It could be a Hebborn that resembles a Mantegna or a Tiepolo."

Suddenly, Mara realized that the two men must be talking about a master forger.

"Well, I know that I wouldn't want anyone looking too closely at the 'Castigliones' we've sold in the past."

Mara listened to the two men chortle at the thought. Engrossed in their tête-à-tête, she jumped when Michael tapped her shoulder. She looked up and noticed that his cowlick dipped down as he stooped to greet her and that the corners of his eyes crinkled when he smiled. Mara admonished herself. The evening before, she had given herself a stern talking-to: She acknowledged her attraction to Michael, but she reminded herself that she had a clear line to walk and a professional relationship to build. She knew she couldn't strike that balance if she allowed herself a physical reaction to him.

He shepherded her into his office, which was aglow with the afternoon sun. His antique captain's desk of gleaming wood and brass fittings sailed on the waves of a richly hued Aubusson rug and cast its sights on a panoramic view of Central Park. The walls were buttery suede and covered with art. On a prominent wall closest to his desk hung several black-and-white sketches of a man in robes. The subject seemed familiar to Mara, and when she asked Michael about them, he told her they were drawings of Saint Peter by a Renaissance artist with whom she was unfamiliar.

Arms crossed, Michael rested against his office door; he was clearly awaiting her reaction. Mara had given up her romantic delusions of a book-lined, mahogany-paneled lawyer's office long before, and she was having a hard time imagining the luck of working in this richness. As she ambled around the room, running her fingers along shelves and tabletops, the compliments tumbled out one on top of the other.

He beamed a charmingly sheepish smile. "Thanks, I'm almost embarrassed by it sometimes, especially after six years behind that banged-up metal desk at Ellis. Unlike my former white-shoe partners who found it appropriate for the associates to work in squalor, my patrons here expect to see us surrounded by exquisite objects . . . even if they're just on loan."

Michael launched into the day's schedule, and Mara noted, with both relief and a hint of disappointment, that his tone was friendly but businesslike. He informed her that her day would culminate with a meeting with the Provenance Department chief, Lillian Joyce, a woman he characterized as prickly. She served as Beazley's ultimate gatekeeper: It was her job to guarantee the untainted pedigree of all the artwork that passed through the institution, and she would assure Mara of the purity of *The Chrysalis*'s title.

Michael's words faded into the background as Mara's eyes cast about for any clues that would help her read this man. The snoop in her longed to study the bookshelves, examine the photographs, and paw through drawers. Was there a story behind the jade Fu dogs that served as bookends or the richly carved teakwood elephant collection on an end table? Where and when had he acquired such beautiful exotic objects? Had he done a lot of traveling? Did he travel alone? Or did all the items come from Beazley's coffers? She realized that, in fact, she had learned very little about the adult Michael over dinner, then told herself that two professionals having dinner *should* learn very little about each others' personal lives. If anything, she had perhaps learned way too much.

"If you're not too tired after all that," she heard him saying, "I'm hoping you'll join me at the cocktail party and the auction?"

Mara nodded. In spite of herself, she was happy that he hadn't forgotten his original invitation.

After brief, futile meetings with the operations and auction departments, Mara rejoined Michael for their appointment with Lillian. They entered a conference room, unlike any meeting space Mara had ever encountered. Three walls covered with priceless carved antique cherry paneling enclosed a phalanx of French doors that opened onto a flagstone terrace looking over the park. A John Singer Sargent portrait of a well-dressed man who had to be Beazley's founder presided at the head of an impossibly long boardroom table, while Impressionist paintings, a Cassatt, a Seurat, and a tiny Renoir adorned the remaining walls.

Mara held out her hand to greet Lillian, who wore an immaculately tailored navy skirt suit that was somehow au courant and classic at once. If she overlooked the severity of the tight chignon of thick, silvery hair and the harsh slash of deep red lipstick, Mara found Lillian attractive, particularly her piercing, nearly turquoise eyes. She certainly looked younger than what Mara had assumed, given her years at Beazley's. But she very quickly understood Michael's "prickly" label. Lillian's terse welcome and brusque handshake conveyed the fact that she both begrudged the time spent away from her research and resented the implicit challenge to her work.

In contrast, however, Lillian bestowed a grandmotherly kiss upon Michael's cheek and even allowed him to snake his arm around the back of her chair in a protective nonembrace once they settled at the table. Mara understood now why he had deemed it necessary to attend this meeting as opposed to the others: His presence was a peace offering to Lillian.

Lillian began with a primer on the provenance search. "A provenance is the history of ownership of a prized object." Lillian spoke as if reading from a textbook, her accent clipped in the mixed British and New England manner of the stars of Hollywood's golden era. "A completed provenance search results in a document, which enumerates the known owners of the object. Sometimes this document is combined with a list of the scholarly literature where the object is mentioned and the exhibitions where it has been displayed."

"How do you create a provenance?" Mara jumped in. She wanted to manage this meeting in her standard take-charge fashion.

Lillian, however, refused to fall back in the face of Mara's attempt at control. She paused for a moment, and then, when she resumed, her voice dripped with condescension. "Let's not be hasty, Ms. Coyne. That's a very difficult question. I'll answer it as best I can, in my time, in a simple way that you will surely be able to understand."

Mara yielded to Lillian and listened without further interruption. She settled into her chair and folded her hands in her lap. Lillian, meanwhile, sat up more erectly and returned to her practiced presentation. Mara felt as if she, not just Hilda Baum, were the enemy. "We have here at Beazley's one of the world's most extensive collections of documents dedicated to provenance outside of certain world-class museums and universities. We deliver to our clients a guarantee that our artwork's lineage is clear, and this is among the reasons we are considered one of the country's premier auction houses. That's the goal of my research team, all of whom I require to have Ph.D.'s in art history. Their job is to ferret out all references to a piece of artwork that are available. I know it may sound rather peculiar to you, but our researchers must love combing through all types of historical documents, no matter how obscure, to find clues to the art's earlier whereabouts." She paused, waiting for a response from Mara that ensured she understood the magnitude and intricacy of the work they performed.

Mara weighed her next remark carefully before speaking. "Ms. Joyce, it doesn't sound odd at all. It's very similar to how we lawyers prepare for a brief or an argument: We, too, pore through countless documents—in our case, legal decisions and treatises—hoping to find that one key piece of support for our proposition. Rummaging through historical documents, I must admit, sounds a lot more interesting."

Lillian softened a bit as she enumerated the categories of documents in which the history of an artwork's ownership might be found: home inventories, dowry lists, auction sale catalogs, bills of sale, museum provenance files, indexes to paintings in public collections, governmental records, collectors' files. Michael registered in Mara's peripheral vision from time to time, though she locked in on Lillian's lesson by sheer dint of will and a certain fear of her instructor.

Lillian finished and indicated that she would hear Mara's questions.

"Ms. Joyce," Mara began, "would I be wrong in assuming that you have a computer index of some sort, that you wouldn't have to look through each and every document in a particular category?"

Lillian nodded. "Your assumption is correct. Each category of documents has its own word-searchable index, which is organized by type of artwork, owner, country, time period, artist, title, subject matter, even size of the painting and color of the paint."

"Are many of the documents comprising the index loaded onto a database?"

"Yes, we call it PROVID, for Provenance Index Database. We are just finalizing it now."

Lillian moved the conversation into the historical realm of the Baums. "With the Nazi-era artwork, the process of documenting provenance becomes much more complicated, particularly since the Nazis may have confiscated approximately 20 percent of the world's Western artwork. But I've probably jumped ahead a bit. Do you know what I mean by Nazi-era artwork?"

"No."

"It is artwork acquired after 1932 and created before 1946 that changed hands during those years and was, or could have been, in continental Europe during that time. But before we go into the provenance process for the Nazi era, you need to understand the historical context." Her voice quavering a bit, Lillian described Hitler's obsession with the arts and the resultant Nazi art lust. A failed artist himself, Hitler believed that, as the ultimate leader of the "superior" Aryan race, he needed to involve himself in even the smallest aesthetic details of his domain. He dreamed of a Germanic empire, in which all "degenerate" artwork—including such modern movements as Impressionism or works created by artists who were either religiously, politically, or racially "incorrect," such as Jews or Catholics—was purged and only Aryan dogma displayed. For Hitler, the only art that counted was the brown, varnished Germanic art or art celebrating "proper" ideals, such as domestic tranquillity or the heroic Germanic past of the Valkyries.

Lillian shuddered as she talked. "As the Nazi war machine swept through Europe, the primary branch charged with confiscating art, the Einsatzstab Reichsleiter Rosenberg, or ERR, was never far behind, plundering artwork wherever it went. In the beginning, the ERR—with Nazi Party leader Alfred Rosenberg, for whom it was named, at its head—limited itself to taking artwork from the libraries or museums belonging to its conquered political enemies. But as time went on, the power of the ERR and its local counterparts expanded, and so did its looting, especially from the Jews. Interestingly, though, the ERR wasn't permitted simply to march into a Jewish home and rip the art from the walls. No, the Nazis set up an entire body of law governing this thievery: 'Confiscation' they called it. According to the regulations, which differed a bit from country to country, the ERR and its local equivalents could take Jewish goods only if the owners voluntarily relinquished them or the owners 'abandoned' them by fleeing, being deported to camps or ghettos, or dying. So, though the ERR created lists of prominent Jewish art collections and marked them for acquisition, if it couldn't get the Jewish owners to sign over the art, the ERR would mark their owners for the ghettos or the camps."

Lillian rose and wandered over to the French doors, where she peered out over the terrace topiary and caught sight of the start of Central Park's simmering fall foliage. "Once confiscated, the art was sent to a central location, oftentimes the famous Jeu de Paume Museum in Paris after France was conquered, to be categorized as either 'suitable' or 'degenerate.' If the painting was deemed 'degenerate,' the Nazis used the artwork as currency. They brought in collaborating art dealers who'd either buy the painting, usually at a low price, to resell it on the free market, or exchange the painting for several Nazi-appropriate ones. If the piece of artwork was 'suitable,' then Nazi leaders would descend on the site like carrion birds to decide which of the spoils they wanted for their own walls."

She fixed her eyes on Mara. "The methodical Nazis had a penchant for meticulous record keeping of their booty; they believed they were divinely decreed to take ownership of their plunder so had no shame in recording their spoils. This means that with Nazi-era art provenances, my researchers are hoping to prove a negative: that the artwork does *not* appear on any of the Nazi lists of looted art, such as the ERR inventories, or in declassified intelligence reports from American agents operating in Europe just after World War II. These latter documents, reports by art historians working for the Art Looting Investigation Unit of the United States Office of Strategic Services, contain detailed interrogation reports of those involved as well as records of the stolen pieces. Why do my re-searchers hope *not* to find the piece of artwork listed in these documents? If the art appears on the Nazi lists or in the intelligence reports, it means that the Nazis looted it—which, in turn, means that Beazley's cannot pos-sibly provide a clean provenance for the art."

Standing up and startling Mara, Michael interrupted. "Lillian, I hate to stop you before you even get to *The Chrysalis*'s provenance, but Mara and I have to head to the auction. Would it be possible for her to set up an-other appointment with you?" Michael gifted Lillian with a disarming grin.

She could not suppress a return smile, though she tried. "Oh, Michael, you know I've never been able to say no to you." Mara wondered how Michael had managed to forge such a warm relationship with the thorny, bureaucratic Lillian.

When she turned to Mara, Lillian's tone iced over once again. "Ms. Coyne, just call my assistant to set up a time. I'll be in Europe all next week." Head held high as if it were bearing a crown, Lillian exited the room.

five

NEW YORK CITY, PRESENT DAY

A TRAY OF CRYSTAL CHAMPAGNE FLUTES FLOATED BY ON THE arm of a tuxedoed waiter. Michael grabbed two glasses, pressing into Mara as he handed her one. He raised his glass. "Cheers. To seeing you again."

She clinked her glass with his. "Cheers." Mara took a healthy gulp to calm her nerves, though she knew she needed to keep her wits about her.

He lifted his drink again. "And to working together."

Their flutes chimed one more time.

Mara scanned the party, luminous with the glow of the city's elite. She smelled the perfume of the fresh-cut flame roses that filled the blue-and-white porcelain vases all around the entryway. The ballroom sparkled from the suspended chandeliers and the jewels worn by the guests. A constant, seamless flow of champagne and hors d'oeuvres sustained the room, though the rail-thin female patrons paid the delicacies no heed. She thought how Sophia would soak up every detail of the event.

Michael touched her hand. "I'm sorry about Lillian. She droned on much longer than any other time I've heard her give that spiel. She must've wanted to impress you. I thought we'd be able to duck out and join the party a while ago."

"Michael, please don't apologize. You have no idea how much more interesting this case is than my usual work on securities fraud."

He chuckled. "Oh, I have a pretty good idea. Still, I don't want Lillian's off-putting manner to make the whole Nazi-era provenance process sound more daunting than it really is. She has a big team of people who do nothing but ensure that contaminated artwork doesn't pass through Beazley's doors out into the world."

"Don't worry. That's precisely the impression that I got." Mara took a long sip of champagne and then owned up. "I also get the impression that Lillian doesn't much care for me."

"Not at all. That's just the prickliness I told you about; she'll warm up. Okay, let me show you around."

Removing her jacket to reveal her sheath, Mara maneuvered through the room on Michael's arm, brushing up against society mavens and corporate moguls she had read about in magazines, and watching the auction's behind-the-scenes staging as the crew prepared to unveil the breathtaking paintings to the room. Michael explained to her that the lavish party was just one small attempt to woo art collectors and win over prospective consignors and estates. Dealing in glitz as much as art, Beazley's threw elaborate dinner parties, organized all-expense-paid trips to exotic locales, employed collectors' children, sponsored black-tie balls on its premises, and made donations to patrons' favorite causes as part of its ongoing battle with Masterson's. At the end of each season, the competitors tallied sales and designated collections to determine who dominated as the market leader and then used that nugget to garner ever more collectors and consignors.

A gong sounded. On cue, the luminaries shifted their glow from the ballroom and lit the pathway to the auction theater. While no less exquisite than the ballroom, the theater, with its serious, hushed tenor, reeked of commerce.

Mara sat down in a reserved seat next to Michael. She was giddy from the three glasses of champagne and the room's palpable sense of anticipation. The lights dimmed, and a hush descended upon the audience as they awaited the first painting. A *Merry Company*, a rare work by Pieter de Hooch, the second most important painter in the Delft school after the master Johannes Vermeer, took the stage. Set in a tavern filled with sunlight, the painted scene showed a red-robed serving girl pouring wine for three revelers, two of whom vied for the attentions of the young maiden. The painting's radiance and scarcity transfixed the audience and upstaged the priggish auctioneer and his officious underlings for a moment. Then the bidding began.

Hands rose, heads nodded, paddles flashed. As the bids climbed, so did the auctioneer's voice and tempo. Mara glanced at the auction catalog and then stared in wonder at Michael, who laughed. The bids far exceeded the catalog's preauction price estimates. The gavel slammed.

"Sold. For $3,250,000."

Bucolic tavern scenes; tranquil domestic visions; dark historical paintings and portraits; whitewashed, expansive church interiors; Saenredam; van Ruisdael—the goods flew on and off the stage. They went for twice the estimates, three times, again and again. Each painting competed with the next for the highest bid at the already legendary auction.

Afterward, Michael and Mara made their way across the auction theater to the receiving room, the scene of the private postauction gathering. A miniature of the ballroom, the space flowed with champagne, though the bubbly was of an even more extraordinary vintage. Self-congratulatory backslaps and air kisses surrounded them. The mood was euphoric, not just among the new owners of the Dutch masterworks and their previous possessors but also among the recently richer Beazley's principals and senior executives. For a moment, a tiny voice imbued with her grandmother's familiar lilt whispered in Mara's mind, cautioning her against the scene's artifice, but she banished it.

A few minutes into the party, Michael murmured in Mara's ear, "Do you mind if we leave? I've made plans for us."

She was shocked. It was a huge night for Beazley's, and based on their earlier conversation, she understood it to be a critical evening for Michael to mingle and share the success with his colleagues and their patrons. Moreover, it was her chance to meet more of the players at Beazley's. But he was the client, and she was intrigued, so she agreed.

They made their way through the throngs. Just as they neared the polished door, a meticulously manicured male hand clamped down on Michael's shoulder. Its ageless owner was similarly well maintained, with a full head of thick, skillfully cut silver hair and a custom-made navy pinstriped suit. Mara felt Michael's entire body stiffen.

The man looked straight at her. "Michael, aren't you going to introduce me to your pretty friend?"

"My apologies, Philip. May I introduce Mara Coyne? She is the Severin lawyer who will be representing us on the *Baum* case. Mara, this is Philip Robichaux, the cochairman of Beazley's. The success of this auction can be attributed to him."

As Mara and Philip shook hands, he demurred at Michael's comment, a bit unconvincingly. "Michael, there's no need for flattery. The success of this evening belongs to Beazley's as an institution." Michael and Philip spent the next few minutes reveling in the evening's sales and laughing over the fact that Beazley's had acquired many of the paintings for the auction—beating out Masterson's—because one keen intern had combed the obituaries, found the estate containing much of the art, and then wooed the bereaved, vulnerable widow away from the family's long-standing relationship with the rival house. Mara found their gloating over the underhanded but seemingly standard scooping a bit distasteful.

Philip interrupted their self-satisfied banter with an abrupt change of topic. "So, Miss Coyne, you'll be defending us on the *Baum* case. As a lawyer at a firm of Severin's magnitude, I'm sure you'll be able to swat away Baum's flimsy claims with ease."

"I certainly plan on it, Mr. Robichaux."

"Please, call me Philip."

Before they could discuss the case further, Michael announced their imminent departure. Philip raised an eyebrow. "So soon, Michael? You know how important these events are. There are many people here that I'd like you to meet. People that your uncle Edward would've wanted you to meet."

"I'm sorry to disappoint you. But I promised Mara we would take some time tonight to discuss the lawsuit. I hope you understand."

"Of course I do. Well, you'll be missed; as will you, Miss Coyne. It was lovely meeting you. I hope to see you again very soon." His eyes glanced adeptly at her legs, chest, face, and ring finger.

They said their farewells, and Michael ushered her through the door.

Outside, they walked past a caravan of limousines to a Town Car that Michael had waiting for them. Though the night air was bracing, it felt oddly heavy to Mara, weighted down with her disappointment at Michael's whisking her away from the party—just as she had the opportunity to make an impression on one of Beazley's leaders. She was thinking about the best way to broach the subject when the car pulled away from the auction house and Michael brought it up himself.

"I'm sorry for the half-baked introduction to Philip Robichaux. It's just that I wanted us to be able to go, and nothing less would satisfy Philip."

"Please, Michael, there's no need to apologize." She was still frustrated, but the fact that he had addressed his caginess placated her.

His eyes met hers. "Anyway, I'm looking forward to us spending the rest of the evening together."

Mara didn't know how to respond and wasn't sure she should take his comment as the suggestive remark it seemed. He hadn't been overtly flirtatious before, so she averted her eyes. But she caught herself smiling in the dark. She reminded herself that he was a client, first and foremost, and one critical to her success at that.

He interrupted the quiet hum of the car. "There's something I thought you might like to see. In private."

"Really?"

"Really."

In a block and a half, Michael directed the car to pull into a back entrance to the Beazley's mansion. They got out of the car in a dark, narrow alleyway, and Mara stood tensely by while Michael fished around in his pocket. Finally, he pulled her toward a nondescript door, where he slipped an identification card into a disguised security panel and tried out a number of the keys. When the door opened, he gestured for Mara to step inside. They made their way down a long, pitch-black hallway, following the low red lights that ran along the walls. Michael advanced, mumbling to himself, as if trying to remember directions, and Mara grew more apprehensive about the "plans" he had in store for their evening.

Then he stopped in front of a door. He turned toward her, his eyes eerie in the red light. "This is it," he announced. He slid another key into the lock and held open the door.

There stood *The Chrysalis*. Alone, in a room as dark as midnight, it was illuminated from above, as if from a single beam of starlight.

A rapturously, indulgently beautiful woman commanded its center. With an enigmatic, otherworldly face and a small, involuntary smile, she stared out at the viewer with turquoise eyes, directly, invitingly. Her open arms and hands stretched out ever so slightly. Her hair encircled her head, a mellifluous halo crowned with tiny leaves. Mesmerized by the woman's face, Mara failed to notice her garments or setting for some time.

When she did, she saw that they were equal to the woman's face. She wore a sumptuous, pure white, long dress. A cloak of cerulean blue and crimson sinuously wrapped around her and draped down to and around the slight, mysterious swell of her belly. Pellucid rays of sunlight pierced through an oval window to her right, irradiating her, washing over her. The listless head of a dead serpent lay under her foot, the only jarring image in the otherwise perfectly serene scene. In a dark corner of her room, on a rough-hewn wooden table, the flame from a single candle was reflected on the petals of an alabaster lily and illuminated the silhouettes of a crucifix, a chalice, and a terrestrial globe.

Finally, in the woman's left hand, a yellow butterfly burst forth from a ruptured cocoon: *The Chrysalis*. Mara wondered what it all meant.

Surprising, inexplicable tears welled up as Mara met the woman's eyes and saw the woman's inscrutable smile turn empathetic. Mara felt as if the woman were telling her that she stood at some crossroads and was inviting Mara to transform, like the golden butterfly emerging from the pupa in her palm. She wiped away the unprofessional tears as inconspicuously as she could, then twisted back toward Michael. "How can I begin to thank you for this?"

Michael's smile lit up the dark. "I thought you'd want to see her alone."

Hours and many, too many, mojitos later, Mara found herself burrowed deep in the brocade pillows of the corner booth in a sexy little tapas restaurant, so tiny that it felt like a secret. Michael's hand began to brush against her knee and on her arm and in her hair, and she realized that he had meant his earlier comment to be as suggestive as it sounded. Mara extricated herself from the hazy allure of his touch to stumble to the bathroom. There, the mirror said it all: her tousled hair and disheveled dress, her failure to walk the tightrope of her attraction and her professional responsibilities, her disregard for her career.

When Mara returned to the table, Michael moved toward her to draw her in for a kiss. But her resolve had been restored when she looked in the mirror, and she backed away into the nubby tapestry of the banquette. When Michael continued his steady progress, Mara grabbed her bag and stood up. "I-I'm sorry, Michael," she stammered. "I can't do this."

six

AMSTERDAM, 1940

H E WALKS ACROSS THE STUDY, HIS GAIT DELIBERATE BUT
not hurried. A man of fixed habits, he is determined to experience
the fullness of his nightly ritual, to savor this last evening with her.

He reaches for a crystal glass and the bottle of Duhart-Milon, 1934. He
pours the last drops of the precious liquid into the glass, thinking that he
could never find another bottle, even on the black market. Knowing this,
he has saved the vestiges of the liquor for this night.

Glass in hand, he sighs with pleasure as he looks around his study, his
refuge from the Victorian-era clutter of the rest of his home. His wife and
daughter decry the room, decorated in the new Art Deco style, as too stark,
too modern, even cold. Yet the room's clean, fluid lines soothe his restless
spirit and create the perfect spare backdrop for his treasure.

He walks toward the fireplace, which blazes and crackles with a freshly
made fire. He holds the glass up to the light, admiring the rich reddish

brown hue of the liquor as it gleams through the facets of the crystal. He settles down into his black leather club chair, positioned before the fire and mantel just so, and situates himself as precisely as the chair.

He stretches out his legs and crosses them at the ankles. He looks down into his glass and takes the smallest of sips, relishing the wonder of the wine's taste on his tongue and the slow burn as it makes its way down his throat. He readies himself to look over the mantel, at her. The series of motions is his private genuflection, a veneration of her and her message.

Just as he is about to lift his eyes to her, he hears the clip of fast steps approach the study door and then hesitate. After a moment heavy with apology, a knock sounds at the door.

"Yes?" he asks, as if he does not know who it is and what the unwelcome caller wants. He wishes he did not.

"Mr. Baum, sir, they have packed the rest of the paintings and loaded them onto the truck. They are ready for the last one, and they say they have very little time left."

"I see, Willem, I see. Can they give me just a few more minutes?" Erich Baum understands the haste, though he begrudges it. The transporters, whom he refuses to think of as smugglers, have a narrow window through which they can sneak his precious paintings across the Belgian and French borders without alerting the authorities, and Erich cannot afford to delay the shipment to Nice by complying with the complicated snarl of import laws. Though many of his countrymen insist that the Netherlands will remain neutral through this war just as it did through the last, he will not ignore the letters from his daughter, Hilda, in Mussolini's Italy, warning him that the Nazi invasion is imminent. He must get his paintings to France for safety or sale, depending on the piece; he will not allow his cherished possessions to end up on the office walls of Göring, Himmler, or some other Nazi dignitary, and in any event, he needs the money.

"I am sure that can be arranged, sir."

"Thank you, Willem."

Erich closes his eyes and inhales deeply, pretending that this interruption has not occurred. The loss of his other paintings saddens him, but nothing like the visceral pain, the grief he feels at parting with her. So he imagines that he is experiencing his ritual as if it were any other evening, takes another sip of the wine, and finally raises his eyes.

She is as breathtaking as the first time he laid eyes on her, all those years before at the Steenwyck auction. With her outstretched hands and turquoise gaze, she summoned him from the jumble of portraits for sale; the rays of light illuminating her from within the painting seemed to pierce through the auction throngs, warming him to her message. As others bid furiously on Miereveld's signature works, he held his breath and waited for her number to be called so he could take her home: *The Chrysalis.*

A knock sounds at the door again. Erich knows he will not be granted another reprieve. He cannot bear to witness the savage separation of her from the wall that has served as her home since the Steenwyck auction more than three decades ago. So he says his farewells to her and then opens the door, signaling Willem to send in the transporters.

seven

NEW YORK CITY, PRESENT DAY

MARA AWAKENED IN A COLD SWEAT JUST AS THE GRAY light of dawn trickled in through the slats in her living room window. The daylight first touched the heather-gray pinstriped couch on which Mara lay, then the painted brick fireplace flanked by glass-enclosed bookshelves and topped by black-and-white photographs of Mara with her grandmother. Finally, it eased down the long, dark hall to the kitchen.

She was still in her clothes from the previous night's auction and dinner, though her sheath was rumpled beyond recognition. The remnants of a memory teased her, pushing themselves into her consciousness despite the way her head pounded from all the champagne and mojitos. The recollection took firm shape, and she caught a vivid flash of sitting close, too close, to Michael in the booth of the tapas restaurant. "Oh God," she thought, "he tried to kiss me." Mara's stomach churned at the thought of what had almost happened.

Groaning, she changed into pajamas and crawled into bed. She tried to fall into the escape of sleep, but her stomach would not allow it. She tried a shower, hoping to wash away her shame and concern. Mara scrubbed her already aching skin raw, but she winced more at how she had allowed herself to get into a compromising situation with a client. How had she permitted herself to concede her professional boundaries? How had she let Michael believe that she'd be receptive to his advances? She knew the answer, of course: his undeniable physical draw and her past attraction to him, mixed with her years of solitude and far too many drinks.

After she dressed, Mara decided to walk to work. It was an indulgence she usually denied herself since a cab took half the time, but she needed to clear her head and formulate some sort of plan. The sun seemed particularly bright, so Mara put on her sunglasses and stopped off to get a large coffee, heavy on the milk and sugar. With each step, a new, troubling thought occurred to her. What if he tried to continue the relationship, despite her initial rebuff? Mara was not sure how long she'd be able to resist him. But even worse, what if he were angry about her rejection, so angry that he wanted her off the case? She saw her chance at partnership, so dependent on her rapport with the new client, Beazley's, disappear before her eyes.

As Mara passed the normally padlocked Gramercy Park, the only private park left in the city, she noticed that the gate was ajar, and she stepped in. Autumn had begun to transform the little sanctuary into an extravagant montage of fiery orange, brassy gold, apple red, and rich chocolate; the morning sun set it aglow. Mara slowed to a saunter. Fallen leaves crunched underfoot, and a crisp smell permeated the air. When she sat on one of the park's ancient wrought-iron benches, a leaf danced down and landed on her shoulder. Mara felt totally alone. She imagined that Michael weren't a client and that she were sitting beside him. The fantasy brought a short-lived smile to her lips, but then her cell rang. It was her secretary, reminding her of a departmental meeting over which Harlan Bruckner would preside, among other appointments. She tore herself from the park, reentered the bustle of the city, and rushed the remaining blocks to Severin in a cab.

Mara felt the eyes of impressed passersby upon her as she pushed the massive, always spotless revolving doors of Severin's colossal tower, though they seemed heavier than normal this morning. After passing through security, she rode a mercifully empty express elevator to her floor, her ears popping as the car raced upward as if it knew that its passengers charged by the tenth of an hour. She walked down the long hall toward her office, passing through the hum of computers and fax machines, long conference calls and slamming file drawers, bursting meeting rooms and smart people doing difficult work. Even now, with her misstep with Michael weighing upon her, the buzz of the Severin halls boosted her.

Before entering her office, Mara, still foggy, armed herself with a second large coffee. Her office seemed the essence of organization, a relatively clear desktop, much-referenced papers in standing folders, and cabinets for bulky case files. Yet, like her apartment, the drawers hid wayward articles, and the under-desk panel secreted mountains of shoes.

Leafing quickly through her morning mail, Mara spotted a message slip from Michael. He had called first thing. Regardless of the course he wanted to pursue and her own feelings, she knew that she needed to reestablish the proper order between them as quickly as possible. But she feared that she would weaken when she heard his low, gravelly voice; after all, that was how she had gotten into this mess. Sophia would help her to get back on the safe track, though Mara would have to brave a blast of condemnation first.

Mara headed down the narrow hallway to Sophia's office, barely nodding to any of the fellow associates she passed, and pushed open Sophia's closed door. An eager smile greeted her. "I was wondering when you'd work your way down here," Sophia exclaimed. "How was the big shindig?"

Mara hesitated. She knew that she had to tell her everything to get what she needed from her friend. She took a deep breath and spread the evening out before Sophia, moment by moment.

"Good God, Mara. What the hell were you thinking?" Sophia unleashed the full force of her disapproval of Mara's behavior—as unwise, as unethical, as murderous to any impending advancement. She repeated all the details of Lisa Minever's disgrace, her potential financial and professional liability under the suit, her ostracism by former friends and colleagues, and her inability to find other work in the face of the publicity.

Mara offered no response, nor did Sophia really desire one. Sophia wanted an excuse to vent her anger at Mara. Clearly, she thought that Mara's gaffe reflected on her as well and jeopardized Sophia's plans for their shared future.

Sophia started demanding more information. Why had Mara yielded to Michael when she had been so strong in rejecting the overtures of other clients and even partners? "Why didn't you just nip this in the bud by telling him about the 'boyfriend'?" she asked, referring to the elaborately detailed stories about significant others that Mara and Sophia concocted for just such situations. Without blinking, they could evoke busy investment bankers whose demanding travel schedules both prevented them from minding the women's long work hours and kept the "boyfriends" from attending all firm functions.

"Because I like him, Fee. I know it was stupid, but my feelings got in the way of my better judgment." It felt good to admit the truth out loud, even though she knew she risked further outbursts from Sophia.

To Mara's surprise, Sophia's stony stare softened. "I'm sorry, Mara." She squeezed Mara's hand. But then Sophia quickly and efficiently closed the door back over her heart and refocused her sights on success. "But you know the rules. If he's still interested in pursuing you, you have to draw the line for him as politely, but as firmly, as possible. Because if you don't and you decide to continue with him, you know what will happen if it all blows up. Do you really want to throw away all your hard work?"

"No." At least, the self-protective, ambitious, Sophia-like parts of Mara did not. "Anyway, I'm probably making too much out of this. He's probably regretting last night and calling to ask if we can forget it happened." She half hoped he felt that way, since it would make everything easier. Then again, she half hoped he didn't. "I just pray he isn't so furious that he wants to pull the case from me."

"I doubt that very much. How would that look for him? How would he explain that to Beazley's or Harlan?" Sophia urged, "Mara, you've got to do the right thing."

Mara nodded, squared her shoulders, and returned to her office. Before she even sat down, she checked the number on the message slip and reached for the phone, firm in her resolve but with her heart racing. "Michael Roarke, please," she stated clearly.

"May I ask who's calling?"

"Mara Coyne."

"Just one moment. He's on a call, but he asked me to interrupt him if you rang."

Mara almost hung up, but she willed herself to wait. Her stomach, however, continued with its backflips, not soothed at all by the Mozart hold music.

"Mara," Michael answered, his voice conjuring up images of them in the booth. It challenged her determination for a brief moment, and Mara held her breath, letting him speak first. "I'm so glad you called back. I've been thinking about you all morning."

"You have?" The question escaped. Despite the echo of Sophia's admonishments and her own commitment to maintaining an attorney-client relationship with him, she couldn't stifle her instinctive reaction.

"All morning. I'm sorry if I came on too strong last night. But I want to see you again, and not just as your client. Can I?"

The word *yes* formed on her lips, but she forced the *no* to take its place. "Michael, I want to, but I can't."

"What do you mean, you can't?" His voice brimmed with surprise, with disappointment, with anger.

"It's against the rules, Michael, though I really wish it weren't. But I will be here for you on the *Baum* case, working day and night to win it for you. Do you think that we can do that together?"

He paused for what seemed to Mara like forever. "Yes, Mara, I do. I just wish it could be more."

eight

NEW YORK CITY, PRESENT DAY

FOR THE NEXT FEW WEEKS, MARA RETREATED INTO HER WORK. She marginalized her other cases—tender offer litigation, a securities fraud action, a fiduciary breach class-action suit—and plunged into *Baum v. Beazley's* with single-minded intensity, almost as a way of apologizing to Michael, as if offering him a victory would serve as an ample act of contrition for what she withheld.

Michael aside, the *Baum* case was unusually demanding because of the intricacies of replevin law, the archaic civil law that governed the return of stolen property. The only way Mara could understand and detangle replevin's latticelike web was to hole up in the law library, neglected by most associates since the advent of computer research, and pore through its disused treatises. Ignoring the firmwide paging system bellowing out her name from time to time, she studied the dusty tomes, learning that the most straightforward way for her to win a replevin case would be to find a gap in Hilda Baum's title. Although Mara hoped that she could gather enough material from Lillian to challenge the plaintiff's claim to title, she worried about her ability to create an entirely impenetrable defense on the title issue alone, given the staleness and unavailability of old wartime records.

After midnight one night, as she was downing her third cup of coffee and willing her eyes to stay open, she stumbled across a promising footnote in a treatise. It explained that, while replevin law stated that neither a thief nor any subsequent good-faith purchaser of a stolen piece of artwork could have legitimate title to it, certain cases placed restrictions on owners' abilities to get their artwork back by providing defendants with a particular type of defense called laches. Those cases required that owners hunt ceaselessly for their art before bringing a replevin suit, or the courts would deem the suit time-barred by the statute of limitations. Mara was elated. If she could persuade the judge to follow these cases, and if she could establish that Hilda Baum had waited too long to search for *The Chrysalis* or hadn't searched hard enough, and that this prejudiced her client, Mara could have an unassailable case.

But she needed to make sure the cases were as strong as the footnote implied. Mara tracked down the primary cases cited in it, *DeClerck v. McKenna*, a 1958 case from the New York appellate court. In *DeClerck*, the father of the German plaintiff had had a substantial art collection that included a Cézanne. The plaintiff inherited the Cézanne in 1925 and kept it in her home until 1942, when she sent the painting to her sister's estate in Austria for safekeeping. In 1945, an American soldier was quartered at her sister's, and after he left, the Cézanne vanished. The plaintiff immediately contacted several authorities, as well as her insurance carriers, to no avail. After these initial attempts, the plaintiff did not undertake any further efforts to locate the painting.

In the meantime, the Cézanne made its way onto the American art market, where a well-known American businessman purchased it in 1948 from an esteemed Boston gallery at a highly publicized auction. The businessman displayed the painting in several exhibitions in major museums around the country, each of which had glossy exhibition catalogs with pictures of the Cézanne.

When the plaintiff eventually brought suit, ten years after the painting surfaced, the court gave the painting to the businessman, on the grounds that the plaintiff had failed to exercise reasonable, timely diligence in trying to locate the painting. The plaintiff should have looked for the Cézanne in the decade following the war, especially through such obvious, readily available sources as the exhibition catalogs.

Though she realized she faced a serious challenge convincing the judge to adopt *DeClerck*, with the additional burden it would impose on Holocaust victim Hilda Baum, Mara was overjoyed with *DeClerck* and its progeny. Until she found the *Scaife* case.

In 1964, a Seurat painting was stolen from the Scaife Museum of Art in New York. The Scaife neither publicized the theft nor informed the authorities of it. In 1969, fully believing that they were good-faith purchasers of the painting, the Laurel family bought the Seurat from a prestigious New York art gallery. In 1986, when the Laurel family placed the Seurat up for public auction, the Scaife Museum discovered the painting and demanded it back.

Following along with the reasoning of *DeClerck*, in 1987, the lower New York court denied the museum's arguments in *Scaife* and granted the Laurels dismissal of the case. The court adopted the reasoning of *DeClerck* and found that the Scaife Museum did not act with reasonable diligence in trying to locate its stolen Seurat. But several months later, the appeals court reversed this decision by utilizing the unusual "demand and refusal" rule. The appeals court determined that a time limit for an action for the return of stolen property did not begin to run until the former owner located the stolen property, demanded its return, and was refused; it did not matter whether the former owner had exercised due diligence in searching for the property, only whether he or she did so in demanding its return once the property had been located. Since the Scaife Museum had just demanded the return of the Seurat and the Laurels had just refused, the court found the Scaife's suit timely.

The Laurels did not further appeal to New York's uppermost court, which meant that the judge Mara faced would have his choice of appellate decisions: *DeClerck* or *Scaife*. The burden would be on Mara to guide him toward *DeClerck*.

As she wove together her argument for *DeClerck*, Mara continued to review all the other related replevin cases she could locate. She hoped to marshal as much legal precedent as she could to protect her position against any unexpected holes. Technically, the cases she studied assured her that she did indeed have a strong argument that wouldn't unravel under either her opponent's attacks or the judge's scrutiny, and for the most part, her confidence and excitement grew. But the cases also detailed the human stories that underlay all the legal posturing, the tragedies that had spawned the lawsuits. Mara read about the sacrifice of Alphonse Schwarz, who suffered through repeated Nazi interrogations and permanent disfigurement in order to protect the secret location of his family's extensive Flemish art collection, only to learn eventually that the paintings had already been looted by the Nazis and his brothers killed. She read about the bankruptcy of Eva Blumer, who spent every mark of her family's fortune trying to recover just one of her father's treasured Tiepolo sketches. Eva never had a single one returned to her, despite the fact that they were on public display in a small museum in Nice. Mara learned about the harrowing journey of Otto Stern, who survived the war years in and out of concentration and refugee camps only to discover that the Renaissance engravings he had so painstakingly secreted in a French friend's wine cellar had been scattered across the world by the Nazis; he spent decades futilely trying to locate even one engraving before eventually dying of heartbreak.

These personal stories unnerved Mara and brought her back to the moment when she had first reviewed Hilda Baum's complaint and felt a pang of empathy for her. Before, she had experienced elation at being selected for the assignment. As she worked into the dark, night after night, the only thing that kept her from lingering on the pathos of the plaintiffs' stories was the technical complexity of her argument. In her best imitation of Sophia, Mara forced herself to go over and over her points and counterpoints. The intensity fueled her concentration and sense of gamesmanship, so Mara kept her strategies secret from Michael during the fact-finding meetings he arranged and their daily e-mail and phone exchanges. She wanted her argument to be seamless when she finally revealed it to him, and she could almost taste the triumph she'd feel.

Early one afternoon, Mara was engrossed in *DeClerck* when she heard Sophia banging on her door. "Come on, Mara, I know you're on some kind of crusade with that *Baum* case, but you've gotta eat."

Mara looked up and actually had to think hard about whether she had already eaten lunch that day; over the previous few days, she had lunched at her desk elbow-deep in cases in about six minutes flat. Her stomach grumbled, so she reluctantly left her work and joined Sophia. They made their way to the weekly attorneys' lunch, a lavish catered affair designed as much to impress visiting clients as to provide the firm's lawyers with a social forum.

As they filled their plates, various classmates passed by, and everyone exchanged polite hellos, but no one invited the two women into their conversations or to their tables. Mara and Sophia had an ostensibly cordial, though actually icy, relationship with their contemporaries in the firm. Their classmates resented the preferential treatment the attractive friends received—assignments with client exposure or court appearances, attendance at dinners designed to lure in business, invitations to any social minefield requiring a finesse that the often awkward partners couldn't muster—and they often gossiped about what the friends did to procure it, though nothing was further from the truth. So, without other options, Mara and Sophia sat down at a table of corporate partners, even though they knew it would only fuel the rumor mill.

Sophia quickly joined the conversation about a hotly contested takeover battle, but Mara could barely follow. Her mind kept returning to the cases she had left on her desk. Just then, she spied Harlan. Not that Harlan was easy to miss, of course, with his huge body and the begrudgingly extinguished Cuban cigar he carried between his fingers like some nefarious magic wand.

Harlan usually dined alone in his office, so Mara was both surprised and more than just a little curious about his presence. But then she saw Michael trailing behind him, and her stomach lurched. It wasn't the mere sight of Michael that churned her gut. She'd grown used to seeing him, had even become accustomed to demurring tactfully to his ongoing entreaties and flirtations. It was seeing Michael in *her* territory that unsettled her.

She wondered what had brought him here and why she hadn't been invited to meet with the two men. They settled at a table in her line of vision but outside of their view of her. She studied the way they interacted, fascinated by Michael's ability to draw Harlan out, even to make him laugh. No one made Harlan Bruckner laugh. She recognized the same charisma that, despite her resolve, she still found so attractive.

As she watched, someone approached the men's table. From the back, all Mara could see was a tightly belted plum wrap dress and the swivel of hips. But she recognized that particular saunter. It was Deena, a fellow senior litigation associate one year behind Mara in seniority with a penchant for powerful, married partners. Deena leaned toward the men, her attention clearly directed at Michael. Mara watched Michael warm to Deena's banter and caught his smile when Deena gently touched his jacket sleeve. Even though she knew the display couldn't possibly be done for her benefit, she couldn't stand the exhibition any longer. She pushed back from her table, apologized to a confused Sophia for forgetting an imminent conference call, and raced from the room.

THAT EVENING, MARA LEFT FOR HOME MUCH EARLIER THAN usual. For a change, she didn't feel driven to labor on the *Baum* case long into the night. Instead, she convinced herself that an engrossing video and popcorn would help calm her agitation. But after she flipped on the balustrade lamps in her living room, Mara proceeded immediately to the kitchen and poured herself a glass of wine in the tallest glass she could find.

As she drank it, she changed into sweats, peeling off her uncomfortably close work suit. The wine further softened her and allowed her to recognize that her loneliness was of her own making. If she was alone with only work and Sophia to keep her company, there was no one to blame. She had made all her own choices, including the decision to gun for partner at any cost. Finally, the tears came.

nine

LEIDEN, 1646

S HOUTING ROUSES JOHANNES. THE VOICES REVERBERATE
through his drafty loft, muddling the words and masking the identity of the speakers. He shoves off the sheets and strains to understand. Risking a beating, he slides out of bed and crawls to the top of the stairwell.

He peers through the spindles. The voices belong to his parents. Mother is on her knees. She begs Father for forgiveness. She pleads for Johannes's freedom. She offers herself in exchange.

Father refuses. He has learned their secret. The path to the Catholic meetinghouse was not as empty as they had thought. Judith spied them on it and followed.

Mother beseeches him. She has kept her promise. Johannes has taken none of the Catholic sacraments; he is pure Calvinist.

Father's voice cracks like a whip. "How can I leave Johannes in your charge? The one child God saw fit for us to steward to the next world?" Her leniency with Johannes's games and her soft affection seemed harmless folly, but he sees now that they marked her lack of care for the child's soul. No, Johannes will stay under her supervision no longer.

The house grows silent, except for the howling winter wind. "Where will he go?" Mother whispers.

"To the studio of Nicholaes Van Maes."

"The painter?"

"Yes, the court portrait artist. His faith is beyond reproach."

The stairs creak as Father begins the steep ascent. Johannes scrambles back to bed. Feigning sleep, he feels the edge of his bed bow as Father lowers himself down. As he tries to quiet his breathing, a lock of his hair rises with each labored inhalation. Father brushes the lock from his forehead, the first time Johannes recalls his touch, and begins explaining that God's will for Johannes has changed. He now desires Johannes to develop the talent He gave him and apprentice at the studio of a man with the patronage of their very own burgomaster and even members of The Hague. This man will shepherd Johannes well, Father promises, and places his cheek on Johannes's.

Judith hands him one last parcel as he climbs into the barge. Father secures the trunks and orders their departure. With his pole, the boatman breaks the ice gripping the barge and then signals for the barge to push off from the landing. Johannes turns back to etch his home in his memory and sees Mother in the turret window, a handkerchief to her eye. Seeing Johannes's lip quiver, Father forbids the tears, reminding him that this is a test of his faith.

Johannes shapes the passing silhouette into a landscape in his mind. Redbrick buildings and orange tiled roofs sail by, their reflections on the mirrorlike surface of the water joining the journey. Clouds, azure, slate, and ocher, color the tarnished pewter sky. The spire of the vast church, where he worships with Father, and the towered city gates darken the canal before them. They must pass through the brackish liquid before they can get under way, out to the open waters.

·   ·   ·

The surprising jolt of the boat's arrival at their destination interrupts his mind-painting. When Johannes alights from the boat onto the stairs, he feels moisture about his feet and ankles. He looks down. The boat has begun to fill with freezing water. The wetness accompanies him to his new master.

ten

NEW YORK CITY, PRESENT DAY

SATURDAY ARRIVED LIKE EVERY OTHER DAY, AND MARA AUTO-matically got up for the office. The only difference in her routine was that she put on jeans, a sweater, and boots rather than a blouse, suit, and heels. As she neared her office building, her favorite bookstore, her Saturday luxury, pleaded for her attention, its storefront displays seeming to dance frantically to catch her eye. She knew she should ignore the store today, since work summoned her just as loudly, but she pushed open the door anyway.

The familiar jumble of books and crowd of eager readers soothed her restless mind. She made a beeline for the art history and archaeology section, where just opening the books, cracking the new spines, smelling the fresh print, always thrilled her. Here time faded away, and she forgot to measure in tenths of an hour.

She moved from art history to biography: Although she rarely had any time to read, she gathered heaps of books on lives she doubted she'd ever be brave enough to live. Mara bent down to add one more book to the basket she'd have to have delivered to her apartment and then stood just as a fellow browser stepped back and accidentally knocked her to the floor. A hand appeared before her and apologies spilled out before Mara could even get to her feet. The voice was Michael's.

Standing face-to-face, without a conference table and piles of paper between them, Mara noticed that his eyes twinkled and his dimples flashed. Though the bookstore was equidistant between their two offices, she was astonished to see him in the Midtown store on a weekend. After all, his apartment was downtown, and she thought Beazley's didn't demand his presence on Saturday and Sunday. "Michael," she managed to say, "what are you doing here?"

"Looking for a good book, just like you, I assume. Although maybe not quite so many good books as you," he answered coyly, glancing down at her basket.

"Sorry, I meant, what are you doing in Midtown? I thought you didn't work on weekends."

He explained that he had needed to stop by the office to pick up a few contracts to review over the weekend, and since he had no plans for the day, he decided to stop in the bookstore. "How about lunch?" he asked.

She begged off, although she was tempted on many levels. "I've got too much work."

"But aren't I part of your lawyerly duties? You can bill me." His logic proved both irrefutable and irresistible.

Lunch turned into a walk in Central Park. The walk in the park developed into cocktails. Cocktails grew into dinner at a favorite Japanese restaurant near his apartment. Throughout the day, Michael was friendly but surprisingly businesslike. Mara expected to feel wary and on guard, but instead, she found herself wondering whether he had fallen for someone else. Deena? She shook her head at her own silliness and tried to feel relieved by the prospect of relating to Michael solely as a client, without the specter of a relationship constantly throwing her off course.

Over fresh sushi and warm sake, Michael enticed Mara into presenting her strategy. She felt nervous about the fact that it was merely a legal sketch awaiting animation by the facts and her performance, and her heart fluttered like a butterfly's wing. "I want to invite the judge to make new law," she said.

Michael raked his fingers through his hair. "Make new law? Are you sure we should gamble this case on the chance the judge will 'make new law'?" Her daring didn't impress him. Nonetheless, Mara remained confident; this was her domain, and she knew exactly how to proceed.

"Let me back up a second to explain the landscape of replevin law. Typically, triumph for a defendant in a replevin case hinges on proving that there is a chink somewhere in the plaintiff's chain of ownership—for instance, that the person from whom the plaintiff obtained the property didn't have title to pass. While I know that I'll be able to pull some evidence together along those lines from Lillian—after all, I'm sure she would never have approved *The Chrysalis* for auction if its title weren't airtight—I don't want our success to depend on that argument alone.

"So I have developed a second avenue that we can pursue. I unearthed a line of cases, starting with an old New York appellate case called *DeClerck*, stating that if the claimed 'rightful owner' in a replevin action hasn't taken reasonable steps to find the stolen article, then the suit's dismissible as time-barred. Based on the rough timeline Hilda Baum sets out in the complaint and simple reality, I think it's improbable that Hilda sleuthed enough in the past sixty years to meet *DeClerck*'s standards. I'm going to try to prove that in the discovery phase of the case—in Hilda's deposition, to be exact." She paused. "What do you think?"

Michael looked at her, impressed. "I like it. Especially that second path, since we'd be able to avoid getting into the Baums' tragic history. It'd be all about what Hilda Baum did or didn't do afterward—her failure to search. We'd get to turn the tables on her, making it her problem. But just how viable do you think it is? How strong is your *DeClerck* precedent?" There was an unnerving excitement in his voice and a cold calculation in his eyes that Mara had never heard or seen before. She was taken aback, and she suddenly thought about the plaintiffs from all the replevin cases she had read: Alphonse Schwarz, Eva Blumer, Otto Stern, even Hilda Baum. She struggled to respond.

After a few moments, she composed herself and assumed the poise she had learned as an attorney. "Pretty viable," she answered. "But we have two major hurdles to overcome. The biggest barrier is another New York case: *Scaife*. In that one, the court used an entirely different standard, basically holding that it doesn't matter whether a replevin plaintiff exercised due diligence in searching for his or her property. But *Scaife* is another appellate case, just like *DeClerck*, so neither case will automatically govern.

Our judge will have the ability to choose between them, and I'll have to persuade him to adopt *DeClerck*, or some harmonization of the two that mandates investigation on the plaintiff's part."

"How will you convince him?"

"Public policy, I think. *Scaife* pretty much absolves former owners from any efforts to locate their stolen property, but this makes New York vulnerable to ancient claims that plaintiffs may have allowed to languish for years—even decades. If our judge were to follow *Scaife*, New York would be left without an effective statute of limitations on replevin cases and could become a magnet for stale, questionable litigation over stolen art. Given that New York is the hub of American art commerce, it could chill trade, driving galleries and auction houses elsewhere, to states that are more protective of them. What judge would want that on his conscience? Or on his record?"

"I sure wouldn't, but then no one would appoint me to a judgeship. You mentioned two hurdles to *DeClerck*. What's the second?"

"The facts. At this stage, I've no idea how dedicated Hilda Baum was to the task of finding this painting. The complaint doesn't have to be very detailed, and the facts in it are all we have to go on at this point in terms of her search. If Hilda let her claim languish for years, as I'm only guessing may be the case, we could have a powerful argument and—"

She froze. Deena had entered the restaurant, dressed in black leather pants and a skintight black sweater. Mara felt a surge of jealousy at the memory of Deena and Michael's flirtatious exchange, but the emotion was quickly supplanted by a wave of terror at the lightning-fire gossip that would spread through the firm if Deena saw them.

Michael was speaking, complimenting her on her creativity, but she could not respond. "Mara, what is it?" he asked.

She blushed, realizing she'd have to admit to spying him at the office in order to convince him of the situation's gravity. "You were at the attorneys' lunch at the firm this week?"

"Yes. Did you see me? Why didn't you come over and—?"

She interrupted him. "Do you remember talking to a tall, dark-haired woman in a purple dress?"

He looked down—a little guiltily, Mara thought. "Yes, but—"

"Never mind. That woman, Deena, just walked into this restaurant."

Michael followed her gaze and craned his neck toward the entrance, muttering, "Oh my God, I think I mentioned to her that I come here."

Mara grabbed his arm before he turned around fully. "Stop, don't turn around. I don't want her to spot us. This may sound histrionic, but we really need to get out of here." Mara scanned the narrow room, realizing that they would have to pass directly by Deena's table to leave. She grabbed the jacket of their waiter. "Is there a back door to the restaurant?"

"Yes." The waiter pointed to a metal door in the front area of the kitchen. It exited onto the side street. He tittered, assuming one of their spouses had wandered in unexpectedly. "Follow me."

Michael gaped at her. "You've got to be kidding me. We're going out through the alleyway? What's there to hide?"

"Michael, here we are, on a Saturday night, miles away from either of our offices, but very close to your apartment. This is not so easily explained as a work dinner, innocent or not. Besides, her gossip about this dinner will be all over the firm by Monday morning. And you can be sure that the story won't be limited to the associates—it will reach the partners as well. Deena's on her second or third affair with a partner." Mara held steady. "It'll compromise not just me but *Baum v. Beazley's*. This has been my fear all along. There are very strict rules about relationships between lawyers and clients. I'm sure you've read about the case of Lisa Minever?"

She needed to say nothing more. Michael laid out far more cash than the bill and seized their coats from the waiter. As he shielded Mara from the front of the restaurant, they hustled after the waiter toward the back.

Michael and Mara dashed by the startled gazes of the busboys; straddled the bags of garbage that blocked the entrance to the rear door, no doubt a fire hazard; and finally stepped into the alley. After weaving their way through abandoned boxes and piles of refuse, Mara and Michael emerged onto the street. They walked quickly without speaking for a few blocks, until they reached a local pub. Michael pulled Mara inside, strode to the bar, ordered a Guinness for himself and a glass of sauvignon blanc for her, and then joined her in a booth.

They raised their glasses in a toast and exploded into hysterical laughter.

Wiping away the tears, Mara apologized. "I feel so ridiculous. I'm so sorry to have made you do that."

He downed his beer. "Are you kidding? That might be the closest thing to espionage that I ever experience."

She gulped her wine, hoping to stop her heart from racing. "Another?"

Glass after glass later, after a long stroll, he walked her to her apartment door. She protested that such chivalry was unnecessary, but all the wine had made her foggy and vulnerable, and when he insisted, she acquiesced.

She fumbled for the apartment keys in her bag. He turned her toward him and reached for her free hand. He pressed each one of his fingers up against hers in a kind of embrace. She resisted folding her fingers into his.

"Mara, I'd like there to be something between us for Deena to gossip about."

"Oh, Michael, I don't know. There's so much at stake."

He whispered. "Please take it down, Mara."

"Take what down?" She was confused.

"This barricade, this wall, whatever it is that stops your hand from folding into mine."

"It's not that I don't want to, Michael, it's just that I'm scared."

"Of what, Mara?"

"Of what will happen to me if things don't work out. You know how Severin would deal with me."

"What if I promise you that things will work out?"

She knew he could make no such promises, but she was so tired of loneliness. Nor did she want to close herself off completely and marry herself off to Severin, Oliver & Means like Sophia. Michael pressed up against her, backing her into the apartment door. He kissed her, and his fingers began sliding up her sweater. As she wriggled away from him to open the door, he leaned into her back, nibbling her neck, breathing into it, breathing into her. He ran his hands slowly down her back and around to the insides of her thighs. He reached between them and then up. Mara froze. She stopped fumbling with the door and put her forehead on it, letting him touch her. She didn't care if her neighbors could see or hear. For once, she let herself go.

eleven

NEW YORK CITY, PRESENT DAY

MONDAY MORNING, AN ASSISTANT SO FLINTY SHE SPARKED led Mara deep through Beazley's labyrinth to meet with Lillian. Their appointment had been canceled and rescheduled more times than Mara could count due to Lillian's travel demands, and Mara was both relieved that it was finally to happen and apprehensive about its outcome. She had gone as far as she could with the case on her own; now Lillian's cooperation and information were vital. While Mara had no reason to doubt that Lillian could provide her with all the supporting documentation she needed, she sensed that she would have to work pretty hard to earn Lillian's full assistance.

Now, sitting in an uncomfortable wooden chair facing Lillian, Mara felt like a wayward student called in for a reprimand by her headmistress. Lillian sat behind her commanding desk and glowered out at Mara through her pince-nez. Mara had chosen a favorite Armani suit in hopes of running into Michael, but she still felt cheap and flimsy in Lillian's scrutinizing presence.

Mara knew that she should be paying very close attention to Lillian, but Michael was all she could think about. He was right here in the building, just a few floors above her, just a short elevator ride away. She could almost feel the warmth of his breath on her neck, a residue from the morning, and it sent shivers through her. When they had first awoken on Sunday, entangled in each other's arms, however, she had felt differently. Dread had filled her veins like lead, and she could barely breathe. All she could envision were the faces of her coworkers, Sophia, and Harlan. But over brunch and dinner, and later in bed, Michael had reassured her again and again of his deep feelings for her and of his determination never to allow their relationship to jeopardize her standing at Severin. His promises alone assuaged the romantic in her, but the pragmatist in her had insisted on absolute secrecy for at least as long as she was working on *Baum*. He had readily agreed to anything and everything, and so, in a very different way, had Mara.

Lillian jumped up and disrupted Mara's reverie. She adjusted the equestrian-themed Hermès scarf at her neck, flattened her pressed heather-gray skirt, and marched out of the room without even glancing to see if Mara was following.

Mara scrambled to gather her belongings. After they had passed down a series of winding hallways, Lillian nodded to the two security officers guarding an old oak door sized for a giant. "This is PROVID," she announced as the guards unlocked the door.

Mara stepped into the jewel-box library of her bookworm dreams. Rows of French doors looked out over Central Park on the west wall, while the other walls boasted sumptuous paneling, leather-bound books, and stepladders. The ceiling arched high above them, airy with the gilded mural of a blue sky and wispy clouds. Four long worktables, dotted with computers and flanked by upholstered chairs, dominated the center of the room. Another similarly goliath barricade guarded the back, east wall. Mara wondered if Michael had ever been so lucky as to work here.

Lillian poured herself a cup of steaming tea from a silver service and begrudgingly offered one to Mara. Then she headed to a work area near the French doors. She gestured for Mara to sit beside her and commanded, "Come on, Ms. Coyne, enough staring. Let's get you what you came here for—*The Chrysalis* provenance."

Mara nodded and surrendered to the subordinate role she knew she must play. With great flourish, Lillian handed her a document.

JOHANNES MIEREVELD

The Chrysalis

Oil on canvas

45 x 35 inches

Signature lower right

Provenance

Johannes Miereveld, Haarlem, the Netherlands (1660–61)

Jacob Van Dinter, Haarlem, the Netherlands (1675)

Erich Baum, Amsterdam, the Netherlands (1908)

Albert Boettcher & Co., Zurich, Switzerland (1944)

Blank (1944).

Exhibitions

New York, New York, National Museum of Catholic Art and History, "Northern European Painting from the Time of the Reformation," October 14, 1970–April 20, 1972, No. 34, illustrated

Boston, Massachusetts, Museum of Fine Arts, "Sixteenth- and Seventeenth-Century Dutch Art," November 24, 1985–February 22, 1990, No. 12, illustrated

Washington, D.C., National Gallery of Art, "De Hooch and His Compatriots," May 18, 1993–August 31, 1993, No. 28, illustrated

Literature

Arthur Childs. *Vermeer.* London, 1968.

Charles Harbison. *Delft Artists around 1640.* New York, 1975.

Lois Magovern. *Dutch Painting.* The History of Art. New York and Toronto, 1979.

James Alexander. *Dutch Genre Painting and Portraits of the Seventeenth Century.* London, 1983.

Natalie Pollard. *The Dutch Golden Age: Popular Culture, Religion, and Society in Seventeenth-Century Holland.* New York, 1991.

Goerdt Kopf. "The Artist's Religion: Paintings Commissioned for Clandestine Catholic Churches in the Netherlands." *Gerontius* 42 (1998).

Lillian sipped from her delicate porcelain cup as Mara reviewed the document. "Now, you understand, of course, that The Chrysalis's provenance was first assembled by Beazley's in the 1940s, when we initially sold the painting to the current owner. Since The Chrysalis has not changed hands since that time, updating the provenance for the Dutch art auction was relatively simple. We needed only to add recent references to The Chrysalis from publications and exhibitions and do some general double-checking through any newly surfaced documents. So that you can fully understand the provenance I have just handed you, I want you to see how a provenance is done. You have to be familiar with the process in order to prove just how clear The Chrysalis's title is, don't you?"

Lillian walked Mara through the work behind the title portion of the completed Chrysalis provenance and then interpreted the final document for her. "As far as we know, The Chrysalis began its long, quiet life in the studio of Johannes Miereveld and Nicholaes Van Maes, in the burgeoning commercial and artistic center of Haarlem in what is now the Netherlands. We know little about the life of the artist Miereveld, except that he and Van Maes were the favored portraitists for politicians and prominent Calvinist families in their region in the mid-1600s. While Van Maes's portraits are attractive, they are quite typical for the day, with standard poses and symbolism. Miereveld's paintings, on the other hand, are ground-breaking. Not only are they masterful renderings of his subjects' features and dress, but they also use revolutionary color, brushstrokes, and iconography to capture his subjects' essences." She sighed with obvious respect. "His portraits are really quite extraordinary.

"In any event, we think that Miereveld finished The Chrysalis in the early 1660s, although this is only an educated guess based on scientific dating techniques and the evolution of his style: Virtually no contemporary documentary evidence of The Chrysalis exists. Then, in about 1662 or 1663, Miereveld painted a group portrait for the Brechts, an established political family in the region. Afterward, he seems to have disappeared, not painting again before his death three years later, in 1665."

"Why didn't he paint again?"

"We really don't know. I have my own theory, though. The iconography of The Chrysalis is very Catholic; whether this reflects Miereveld's sentiments or a client's, I don't know. While Catholicism was tolerated in the seventeenth-century Netherlands, it was frowned upon, even scorned, in the devoutly Calvinist upper-class circles in which Miereveld traveled. If his patrons learned of *The Chrysalis*, perhaps they ostracized him because they couldn't fathom his painting their portraits by day and religious Catholic paintings—banned by their own religion—by night. If so, they might have lodged grievances with the artists' Guild of Saint Luke, which controlled all art commissions and could have prohibited him from working. But so little documentation from the artists' guild survives," Lillian confessed, "that we don't have any specific evidence supporting my theory."

Lillian returned to the provenance. "After Miereveld's death, many of his paintings languished for hundreds of years in the attic of the ancestral home of the Steenwyck family of Delft. It seems as though one of the Steenwyck ancestors went about the region purchasing the portraits in the years after Miereveld's death. This explains why most of his paintings survived. When the few extant portraits began to surface and gain in popularity in the late 1800s, the Steenwycks unearthed their cache of moldy paintings and held a large auction in 1908. Not surprisingly, at this time, *The Chrysalis* was rediscovered. Interestingly, it was found not in the attic of the Steenwyck family home but in that of the Van Dinters, an old Calvinist Haarlem family." Lillian pointed to the printout.

"Do you think the Van Dinters commissioned *The Chrysalis*?"

"While I can't say for certain, I think it's unlikely. The Van Dinters were a prominent Calvinist family, so *The Chrysalis* would have been anathema to them. But while it's a mystery as to why the Van Dinters had *The Chrysalis* in their possession, it's certain that the painting was in their custody for hundreds of years. *The Chrysalis* is listed on the 1675 death inventory of the Van Dinter family patriarch, Jacob."

"And the Van Dinters put up *The Chrysalis* for sale along with all the other Miereveld portraits in the 1908 auction?"

"Yes. It seems our Erich Baum bought it at that auction, often referred to as the Steenwyck auction. *The Chrysalis* found a home—for a while, at least."

The two women deliberated the critical wartime journey of *The Chrysalis*, starting with Hilda Baum's version. According to Hilda, as the war escalated, her father's painting sailed to Nice, France, in early 1940 to the safekeeping of a now-deceased family member, as evidenced by a cryptic note from her father. Somehow, she claimed, after the Nazis reigned victorious over France in the summer of 1940, the ERR stole *The Chrysalis* from her family's care, trading it as currency until it ended up in the hands of Swiss art dealer Albert Boettcher. In Hilda's tale of *The Chrysalis's* travels, it then made its illicit trip from Boettcher to Beazley's, and then to Beazley's anonymous client in the American art market.

Lillian shared her opinion that Hilda's account of *The Chrysalis's* World War II expedition was pure confection. It was gossamer spun sugar that dissolved under the weight of related provenance evidence uncovered by Lillian—namely, that Erich Baum sent the painting to Nice not to family but to his longtime art dealer Henri Rochlitz. Lillian maintained that Baum must have authorized Rochlitz to sell *The Chrysalis* to Boettcher, a rare-art dealer with a squeaky-clean reputation, making Beazley's title, and therefore its current owner's title, clear. Mara grew more and more enthused about the strength of the *Baum* case, even on the title issue, which she had previously perceived as a possible weak point.

"Is the provenance finished?" Mara asked, believing the lesson had reached its end.

Lillian brimmed with superior knowledge. "Yes, the provenance is complete. However, there is some additional documentation I uncovered in a box of recently declassified reports that isn't useful for the provenance per se but that you might find interesting." She typed with great alacrity, screens flying through the Postwar Art Restitution category.

Lillian read aloud from the screen. "In a statutory declaration, Hilda agreed to the following:

> I have submitted no other applications for compensation for the artistic works which are the subject of the reimbursement proceedings before the Restitution Offices of Berlin, be it on my own behalf or through any institution, organization, or authorized agent, nor will I do so in the future against this entity or any other.

You see, Mara, in the late 1940s, Hilda filed applications with the Dutch and German art restitution commissions, seeking the whereabouts of her family's collection. As it did with many of the applicants, the German commission proposed that the parties enter into an agreement to 'completely settle' the claims for fifty percent of the artwork's stated value. Hilda agreed."

Mara was stunned. Her success with this case was beginning to seem inevitable, and she began to devise ways to use this new information.

Mara needed the papers for discovery, so Lillian led her toward the blockade at the back of the library. She input a code into the security panel, then pulled from her inside blazer pocket a set of keys of varying shapes and sizes, some of which looked medieval in their design and weight. Lock by lock, she unsealed the heavy door.

Before they crossed the threshold, Lillian turned back to Mara. "The documents we have in here are unique. Some are priceless, some highly private, and some so old they must be stored in certain conditions in highly controlled temperatures."

Mara noted that the air seemed cooler, thinner, and she felt that she had entered a treasured room. The single entrance belied the vast space within. Nearly twice as big as the library, the room mimicked the library's décor, with arched ceilings glistening with murals, richly paneled walls, and glossy wooden floors. In place of the long worktables in the room's center stood numerous rosewood cabinets to hold the valuable documents. The delicate appearance of the cabinets masked their functional purposes. Mara saw that they were hardly ordinary: Inside, they resembled storage units for scientific materials rather than bookshelves.

Lillian scurried around the room, gathering book after book, paper after paper, and assembling them on one of the few desks. Lillian explained their unique coding system and showed Mara critical references to The Chrysalis in each of the documents, some of them yellow with age.

"We'll take these materials, seal them in airtight bags, marking on the bag the pages to be copied, and insert them in that slot." Lillian gestured to a wide opening in the far corner of a paneled wall. "Copies will be ready in the morning." She hastened toward the door.

Mara interjected, "Why are such elaborate duplication measures necessary?"

"The condition of the documents means that they must be copied very gingerly and with special equipment. The confidential nature of some means we need to have security measures surrounding the copying."

"What about the fact that, in discovery, we're going to have to produce the documents you just copied to Hilda Baum?"

"As long as we subject the copies to a confidentiality agreement, so they can be used only for this case, we will give you the necessary copies. With the current owner's name redacted, of course."

Mara assured her that this was possible.

Lillian's posture slackened a touch. "Wonderful." She motioned for their departure. "Shall we? We still have to run through the rest of the provenance."

As they returned to the main library, Lillian explained further the process of assembling all references to the artwork in the scholarly publications and the exhibitions presenting the piece. Mara recognized that the exercise would prove indispensable for her *DeClerck* argument that Hilda was obliged to search for her lost painting. If Mara could prove that the whereabouts of *The Chrysalis* were easily ascertainable, then Hilda's failure to hunt for the painting would become obvious. The developments began to banish the ghosts of Alphonse Schwarz, Eva Blumer, Otto Stern, and the many others like them, which had been haunting Mara's conscience. After all, how could *The Chrysalis*'s title be anything but flawless with Lillian at the helm? Still, she suspected that the defendants in all those other replevin cases had believed their titles were impeccable, too.

At day's end, the two women retired to Lillian's office. As the warm glow of the sunset filtered through the window, Mara sipped a cup of tea.

"Ms. Joyce, it's amazing that you know *The Chrysalis*'s history by heart, given all the artwork you deal with every day."

Lillian puffed up at the flattery. "Please, call me Lillian."

"Thanks, Lillian. And please, call me Mara."

"I-I guess the painting does hold a special place for me. As does Johannes Miereveld," Lillian continued, but her speech faltered a bit—with embarrassment or some other emotion, Mara couldn't quite tell. "*The Chrysalis* was the first painting for which I prepared a provenance, among other reasons."

Mentally calculating Lillian's age, Mara's jaw dropped. "Really? You were working here in 1944?"

Lillian chuckled. "Yes. I was nineteen years old and right out of finishing school. I had studied art history, and so Beazley's hired me."

Mara contemplated whether she should raise the question with which she'd been privately struggling. In all her reading, Mara hadn't come across a satisfying discussion of the painting's symbolism, though she'd formulated some theories. She asked, "What do you think *The Chrysalis* means?"

Lillian invited Mara over to her side of the desk and paged through the Dutch auction catalog to the picture of *The Chrysalis*. The photograph of the ethereal woman encircled by sacred objects was breathtaking but did not compare to the splendor of the actual painting that Michael had shared with her. "Here," she pointed. "I believe that these limpid rays of light penetrating the beautifully rendered oval window over the woman's right shoulder were meant to be the rays of God's light piercing the woman's symbolic womanhood: her virginity."

"So the woman is the Virgin Mary?"

"Yes, of course."

"The blue and red cloak, the lily . . . It seemed fairly obvious, even to an art history college minor who hasn't studied her iconography for years."

Lillian smiled. "Well, you're right. The woman irradiated by the light of God is the Virgin Mary. The blue and red cloak, the halo of hair, the lilies lying at her feet: They are Mary's hallmarks. As God passes through Mary, God gives the gift of Jesus, of rebirth through death, of resurrection, as symbolized by the chrysalis—or pupa—in her left hand. But the God of *The Chrysalis* is a specific God: the God of the Catholics. The crucifix, the chalice, and the terrestrial globe in the darkened left corner of the room tell us this, as does the single illuminated candle, an attribute of faith personified. The vanquished serpent under her foot represents the defeat of false religions, such as Calvinism." Her turquoise eyes turned to Mara. "I believe *The Chrysalis* tells the story of the power of resurrection, the possibility of redemption for us all, but only through the Catholic faith."

The door flew open, and the women jumped. Michael sauntered in, smiling at the snug scene. "Can I take my two favorite ladies to dinner?"

⎯⎯⎯

CLUTCHING HER SIDE IN LAUGHTER, LILLIAN GAVE MICHAEL A playful slap on the arm. "Stop, stop. You're giving an old woman a stomachache with all those impersonations. And all this wine." She drained her sparkling glass. An air of camaraderie had descended over the three during the long, formal French meal; they were the last remaining patrons at the only Michelin-ranked restaurant in the city. With Michael as a buffer, any vestige of edginess between the two women disappeared. Mara felt particularly relaxed and, with a smile, asked, "Should I tell you guys my latest theory for the Baum case?"

"Do tell." Lillian tilted toward her.

Michael caressed her thigh under the table. "Yes, Mara, please do."

Despite a hazy sense of hesitation whose origin she couldn't define, Mara explained to Michael how she could use the documents that Lillian had recently uncovered, particularly Hilda Baum's agreement with the German Art Restitution Commission. The agreement's language, she pointed out, could be used as a release from all further actions to recoup *The Chrysalis*, including *Baum v. Beazley's*.

Lillian and Michael beamed across the table. As she downed the remainder of her port, she caught Lillian nodding in Michael's direction, almost maternally. Mara gave a small shake of her head, dismissing it. Surely she was mistaken. Lillian didn't know about their very new personal relationship. The wine must have made her cloudy.

twelve

HAARLEM, 1652

JOHANNES HOLDS A SECRET TIGHT TO HIS CHEST. ONE HE dare not utter aloud, for fear of hurting Pieter Steenwyck or, worse, committing the deadly sin of pride. Only at night, when the loneliness descends, does he unwrap his secret like a present, like a salve: He is the master's best student.

The boys—young men, really—rise while evening still holds sway. In the pitch dark, they race to the studio along a path they know even without daylight's guidance. The first to arrive gets to mix the paints, the prized daily task. Johannes prevails.

After they light candles, Johannes gazes at the paint table, long and gleaming with lustrous pigments like the jewelry cabinet of a great lady. He checks to ensure that his staging area has the proper tools. With the mortar and pestle, he grinds the pigments to a fine powder: lapis lazuli, ruby shellac, gum arabic, wineskin, and malachite. Measuring out the ideal amount of linseed oil from its flask, he blends it with the precious colors, liquefying the gems. The boys do not speak until Johannes finishes the crucial chore.

Dawn arrives, revealing the cavernous studio in measures. Windows of leaded glass to the north, designed to admit even light, are unveiled. Contrasting flooring, paint-splattered wood planks for work and black-and-white tiles for the honored subject, is exposed. A table is uncovered, groaning with the weight of portrait objects: a leather-bound Bible to proclaim the subject's devotion, a globe to announce the expanse of his holdings, a medal to declare his valor. An immense easel, cradling an unfinished canvas shrouded in linen, makes a final, dramatic appearance.

They hear the clip of boots and scramble to their other chores before the master's assistant, Lukens, enters. The boys clean surfaces, sharpen metalpoints, lace canvases onto stretchers, bind brushes, and prepare copper plates for etching. To displease Lukens is to forfeit the chance to paint that day, so they hurry.

Lukens runs a gloved hand along the surfaces and rearranges every item according to his own private plan before giving leave for the master's two journeymen, Leonaert and Hendrick, to enter. Gifted painters, the journeymen stay on with the master only because they have no funds for their own studios. They begrudge the boys' daily instruction; moments away from painting the finery and landscapes of the master's portraits are money lost. Yet the position demands it, as the master has not the time to train.

The long day ends like every one before. Weighed down with leaden pork dumplings and the day's exertions, the boys crawl up to the attic and get ready for bed. Eyes heavy, they cast their petitions to the heavens. Pieter prays that the master might procure a mystical camera obscura, a darkened box admitting one focused ray of light through a convex lens that projects a detailed image of the scene in front and lets the painter see an image the naked eye alone cannot. Johannes once asked God for visits with his parents beyond the allotted Easter and Christmas, but now, as his parents seem more and more like distant memories, he prays for more of the master's time. He longs for schooling from the master's own hands, not the hands of the journeymen.

. . .

Having cleared the hurdles set by the artists' Guild of Saint Luke for progression in their craft—rigorous instruction in drawing, endless repetition of brushwork, constant tutoring on Calvinist religious texts, particularly those needed for symbolic effect in portraits—the boys enjoy the privilege of copying the master's own works as practice. Pieter, however, is temporarily denied this dispensation, for he has recently displeased Lukens. So, in the anteroom off the studio, Johannes struggles alone in the dying light, wrestling to re-create a pendant, a pair of paintings of the husband and wife Van Dalen. The dynamic magistrate and his much younger, graceful spouse taunt him from the master's canvases.

"Why is the brushstroke so different on each pendant?" a voice commands from the back of the anteroom.

Johannes turns round. It is the master, and he is studying Johannes's reproductions of his work. Having never seen him so close, so still, Johannes stares at the intricate web of lace that flops over his inky silk overcoat, at the tremendous brim of his hat. Words refuse to come to his mouth.

"I was told you speak. Was Hendrick wrong?"

"No, Master."

"Then did Hendrick err in telling me that the time had come for me to see your paintings? To weigh your readiness for the master test?"

"Hendrick said that, Master?" Johannes blurts out, unable to imagine a single compliment issuing from Hendrick's tongue. Perhaps Hendrick hopes that premature evaluation will ensure Johannes's ejection from the studio.

A tiny smile emerges on the corner of the master's mouth. "You seem surprised, Johannes. The time must come for all artists to stand and be judged, whether by a master, the guild, or God."

"Yes, Master."

"Then perhaps you should answer my question. Why is the brushstroke so different on each pendant?"

"Master, I am not sure how to explain."

"Not sure? How is that possible? You chose the *nette* brushstrokes for the magistrate's wife's lace collar and gold earrings, even her skin. I can barely discern those strokes, you've blended them so completely. Yet you used such bold, *schilderachtig* strokes for the magistrate himself. You've not mixed them at all; I can differentiate the layers of glazes and opaque paint, even the lines of color. It is curious, Johannes. Most painters have one style, one stroke. As I have."

Johannes cast his eyes down; he knows the master will not like his response. "The subject tells me what brushstroke to use," he says.

"The subject tells you?"

"Yes, Master." Johannes does not lift his eyes.

"Well, it seems as though Hendrick was wrong about one thing—failing to inform me that one of my students is a half-wit." He pivots toward the heavy curtain guarding the exit.

Johannes rushes to the door, blocking it. "Master, please don't leave. I can explain."

The master turns, arms crossed.

Johannes tries to describe what he intuits. "You see, the wife, she seems so genteel, so serene. She calls out for a gentle touch, a refined hand. But the magistrate appears so physical a presence, delicacy will not do. He cries out for a brushstroke to match his vigor. This is how the subjects speak to me, Master."

Johannes realizes that the master has grown still. He stops.

"Who taught you this? Leonaert? Your childhood instructors?"

"No, Master." Johannes stutters, "I-I have always known this."

The master's brow furrows. "Johannes, where do your allegiances lie?"

"Master, I don't understand."

"You sound as though you believe God empowers the paintings through you, as some sort of medium. That's a dangerously Catholic sentiment."

Johannes rushes to reassure him. "No, Master, that is not what I meant."

"I hope not, Johannes. Remember verse 5:8 of our Lord's disciple Pieter: 'Like a roaring lion your enemy the devil prowls looking for someone to devour. Resist him, steadfast in your faith.' Be careful, Johannes. I do not want to lose your talent to the enemy."

———

THE MASTER IS WORKING ON A FAMILY PORTRAIT COMMISSION much envied by his fellow guild members: the new burgomaster Claesz and his brood. The burgomaster is dependent on the province's upper-class regents for the longevity of his position. He strives to impress them with their choice by planning lavish festivities where the portrait will be shown.

The studio casts aside all other projects to complete the work. The burgomaster plans on unveiling the painting at his celebration, and it must be well received, for both the burgomaster and the master. The death of the prior burgomaster, long the master's patron and advocate, jeopardizes the master's standing and endangers his future stream of commissions. This painting could change the situation.

Johannes sits by the master's side as he outlines the family members with his metalpoint. The master insists that Johannes see firsthand the interplay of light from the subjects' skin with their lush clothing and jewels, if he is to capture those accessories. Hendrick and Leonaert protest Johannes's assignment, one more fitting to artists of their stature and experience, but the master dismisses their remonstrations and points to Johannes's skill in calming the burgomaster's restless lot of six children during the long hours of posing—a task the journeymen abhor.

Johannes regrets his newfound elevation. Each time Pieter enters the room to deliver a freshly mixed paint or a newly assembled brush, he keeps his eyes down, and Johannes sees that his position pains his friend as well. The boys are no longer compatriots, no longer racing to the studio, no longer chatting in solidarity, no longer flinging prayers to the Lord like coins into a fountain. The nights are silent, each drifting off to sleep with the other nearby, yet completely alone.

Halfway through the painting, illness strikes the master's house, incapacitating his wife and infant son and necessitating his attendance. He leaves off completing the faces and hands of the burgomaster's children and instructs the three to finish their parts: Hendrick, the curtain draping behind the family; Leonaert, the black-and-white tile floor; Johannes, the coveted pearls and lace handiwork. During the long days of jostling for a place at the canvas, Johannes withstands upturned paints, missing brushes, and malignant mutterings from Hendrick.

One day, Lukens bursts into the studio, breathless. Disease has taken the master's wife and son, leaving an afflicted master in its wake. What shall they do? It is a tragedy, of course, but only three days remain until the burgomaster's celebration.

Johannes knows what must happen. He alone has studied the children's faces; he alone has formed a kinship with them. He makes his proposal.

Hendrick erupts at Johannes's audacity, at his disregard for the master's reputation. Painters of the master's ilk did not pass off the work of a lowly apprentice as their own, never mind the guild repercussions to Johannes for painting portrait likenesses before qualifying for the master test or the inevitable blow to the master's guild standing.

Lukens disagrees. Perhaps Johannes has a point, and there is more at stake than this painting alone. After all, what are the alternatives?

Lukens leads the children and nursemaid into the studio. Johannes greets the gaggle as usual, tickling the youngest two and playing sleight-of-hand tricks for distraction. Johannes informs them that the master will arrive shortly, and Lukens queries as to whether Gertruyd, the nursemaid, would care to view some of the master's other works in the main house while they wait.

She declines, though her eyes signal acceptance. "Mistress would never like the children to be out of my sight."

Lukens clucks. "Too bad. You would be one of a very few to have regarded them."

Gertruyd's eyes widen at the thought of the marketplace gossip.

Lukens purrs. "It will be for but a moment."

Blush floods her cheeks at the unexpected attention. "Well, if it will be only a moment. Johannes, will you be able to mind the children on your own?"

"A pleasure, Gertruyd." The unlikely pair saunters off, arm in arm.

Johannes places the children in the exact spots they had occupied days before and then disappears behind a screen secured around the easel. It is large enough to mask his identity, but it is angled such that he can see the subjects. He places the master's usual hat upon his head, its wide brim peeking out from the top of the screen.

Johannes claps and announces from behind the screen, "Places, children, the master is ready to begin."

The children remain remarkably still as Johannes rushes to capture their likeness: the cherubic infant docile on the obedient eldest daughter's knee; the defiant toddler dressed like a miniature lady with her hand locked in the palm of a compliant middle daughter; the soulful young son caressing a lute; the eldest son with his hand gripping a spear, a lion in wait. Johannes lets those whispers guide his brush: *nette* strokes for the placid baby; bold strokes edged with controlled outlining for the reined-in toddler; an even blending for the obedient older girls; a misty cloud of color for the middle son; strong diagonal lines, jumping from the page, for the eldest.

A bowl clatters to the floor, startling Johannes. Frozen with fear, he hears a voice. "Not to worry, children, I'll clean up around your feet; you just stay in place." It is Pieter. Johannes peers through a crack in the screen and watches Pieter tumble in a somersault toward the children, in an effort to soften the mood and garner laughter. Johannes smiles at the antics of his friend.

"Many thanks, Pieter," Johannes bellows from behind the screen, in his best attempt at the master's voice.

"You are welcome, Master. I thought you might need assistance."

A feigned love interest by Lukens and copious quantities of mulled wine help distract Gertruyd the next day as well. Johannes spends the nights in a feverish trance of work. The third and final day, the celebration day, he gathers together Lukens, Leonaert, Hendrick, and Pieter. Standing in front of the easel, he pulls back the fabric safeguarding the canvas.

The revelers cut a wide berth as Johannes helps the master to his seat. The master's hollowed-out face speaks of his loss, and his body tells the tale of the ravaging power of the disease. A different man than ten days before, he looks out of place amid the merriment of the burgomaster's celebration, yet he has insisted on attending.

The guards grant the uninvited Johannes access to the festivities only because of the gravity of the master's illness and circumstances; no other member of the studio is permitted entrance. Johannes takes a place standing behind the master, in the event of his need, in the long line of servants flanking the wall. Admiring the banquet table resplendent with platters of savories, porcelain vases of decadent tulips, and guests uncharacteristically colorful in saffron and crimson, Johannes longs for his easel to dissect the scene into genre paintings, portraits, still lifes.

The burgomaster stands, his hand curling around a jeweled chalice. He lifts the cup and toasts his guests the regents with particular flourish. He announces his special commemoration of the occasion, the commission, and then pays heed to the master's recent tragedy.

The burgomaster strides toward a wall where a painting enshrouded in plum velvet hangs. Johannes's stomach lurches as the burgomaster reaches for a golden cord and draws back the curtain. The portrait is unveiled.

A hush descends among the celebrants as they await the burgomaster's pronouncement. Johannes hears a sharp intake of breath from his wife, followed by a whisper. "It is unearthly. My children, they look so . . . so themselves." The burgomaster steps back from it, staring at it from this angle and that, then issues his judgment. "Master Van Maes, you have outdone yourself."

As the crowd returns to its gaiety, relieved, Johannes hears a clamor. The guards scuffle into the room, trying to hold back an intruder. The man breaks free of their grasp. It is Hendrick, shouting that Master Van Maes has misled the burgomaster. The painting was finished not by Master Van Maes's hand but by the hand of his apprentice. Hendrick lunges toward Johannes.

The burgomaster yells out to his guards to take the imbecilic man away, to put him in shackles. They seize Hendrick and whisk him toward the exit.

The master rises on unsteady feet. Johannes rushes forward to assist him but is brushed away. "Burgomaster, please order your men to let him go. He is one of my journeymen. He tells the truth—at least, in part."

The burgomaster raises a hand, staying the guards for a moment but not signaling Hendrick's release.

The master explains, his voice strong in conviction but weak in intensity. "My Lord, I apologize for the intrusion of my journeyman into your celebration; he has stolen from me the ability to make a planned announcement at a more opportune time. As you so graciously acknowledged, illness recently came to my family home. It took my wife and baby boy and felled me for a period . . . before I could finish the portrait. A gifted painter from my studio, fresh from his master test, completed the unfinished portion—the likenesses of your children—in time for this evening. I had hoped to introduce his work tonight and to present him as my partner."

"This is the man here? This boy?" The burgomaster gestures to Johannes, his brow arched quizzically. Johannes freezes in fear, in disbelief.

"Yes, his name is Master Johannes Miereveld." The master bows his head, surrendering to his sentence.

A long pause ensues while the burgomaster considers the master's fate, weighs the impact of it on his own. He settles on acceptance. "Master Van Maes, I shall consider myself fortunate to be the first recipient of Master Miereveld's work; I am certain I shall not be the last." The burgomaster welcomes Johannes to the table.

thirteen

NEW YORK CITY, PRESENT DAY

OVER THE COURSE OF THE NEXT SEVERAL WEEKS, MARA
    spent her days at work and her nights with Michael. Their relation-
ship moved forward with an intensity she had never known before. For the
first time in a long time, Mara felt joyous. Although she'd dated since Sam,
the men always seemed two-dimensional: the clever banker, the brooding
artist, the humorous marketing executive. She had neither the time nor
the inclination to animate those possibilities. With Michael, such investment wasn't necessary: He was fully, immediately enfleshed.

The impulse to share her delight tugged constantly at her. Despite all
her earlier reservations, Mara wanted to introduce Michael to her friends
and colleagues—especially Sophia, with whom she'd shared nearly everything for years and with whom silence felt like a sacrilege. She wanted her
father to meet him; wished her grandmother were alive to approve of him.

But she knew better than to act on her whims. Once she opened the door and fully welcomed Michael into her life, even if it were just to family and friends, her professional goals would be jeopardized. For at least as long as the *Baum* case continued and he qualified as a client, their relationship needed to remain a secret.

In the nighttime hours, Michael pursued her, forcing her to come out of hiding, even from herself. She told him stories she'd kept locked away even from Sophia, saying them aloud in the cocoon they created for themselves, a private hibernation made easy by the cold winter nights. She toppled the myth of her father, the successful politician. She revealed his shady connections, forged in his desperation to bury his South Boston, Irish roots in political success. She disclosed the story behind his marriage to her mother, the prize daughter of a family with means substantial enough to launch his career, a woman willing to forgo her own ambitions to provide her father with a Junior League wife and a Ralph Lauren life. She divulged the pressure her parents had felt to produce children. For the first time, she revealed the way her father had pushed her mother to the periphery once she was born. Mara had been the picture-perfect trophy child pursuing success whom he pressed forward into the light as her mother retreated into the shadows. Her father needed Mara's legitimate achievements to wash clean the taint of his own political rise. Mara shared how she had learned to become whomever her father needed her to be, a skill she now wielded at work.

Not that her father didn't love Mara, in his way. It was just that his love, such as it was, was won by tangible accomplishments: grades, Ivy League schools, advanced degrees, name-brand positions, mammoth salaries, and an advantageous marriage—the one area in which she'd disappointed him. She told Michael how, whenever she set her target sights wrong, she would retreat to her grandmother, her father's mother. Her father ran from this relationship, but for Mara, her grandmother's simple rooms at the parish rectory where she lived, worked, and had raised her son always felt like a warm embrace, where all of her accolades and awards didn't matter. Nana inhabited a world where plain, meaningful work meant far more than public recognition or remunerative jobs. In her role as rectory housekeeper, her grandmother served as confidante, intercessor, helpmate, friend, and surrogate grandparent for the Catholic congregation, and Nana could envision no greater honor. Michael, who had been raised in a similar Catholic environment, could understand her grandmother's world. Her death in Mara's junior year of high school had created a void that Mara could not imagine anything would ever fill.

But as much as Mara revealed at night, she stashed away during the day. She could not risk candor or self-disclosure at work, particularly with Sophia, so a double life became her daily fare. To her friends, to work, to her family, to Sophia, she was as she had always been: an attractive, hard-working lawyer fulfilling grand ambitions for her career. And as always, she remained entirely, inexplicably alone. What no one could see was that now she could tolerate their pity, because her life included Michael.

In the deep hours of the night, she awakened to Michael stroking her hair. Lying on her side encased in his arms, she struggled to turn around. Then, nuzzled against his chest, she fell back asleep.

But increasingly, Mara's sleep was full of dreams about *The Chrysalis*, and not the serene smile of the painting's subject or the tranquil touch of its light. These dreams were filled with disturbing images of its wartime journey. Mara saw it passing from pitch-black crates to murky train cars, from skeletal hands to the gloves of soldiers in swastika'd uniforms. The dreams woke her. They lingered, and she didn't want to be alone with them in the dark. "Are you awake?" she whispered to Michael one night.

"Not really," he murmured.

"I've been dreaming of *The Chrysalis*."

He wrapped her up, like ropes around a cargo chest. "Good dreams, I hope."

"Not really. It was more like a nightmare. I pictured it during wartime."

"It's only a dream, Mara."

"I know, but I can't shake it."

He yawned. "Tell me about it, if it'll make it go away."

She described *The Chrysalis*'s voyage as she had seen it in her dream. She compared the painting's travails to the passage of looted art from other wars, to the famous four horses decorating the façade of the Venetian Church of San Marco, for instance. A creation of the ancient Greeks, the horses had journeyed with military campaigns from Constantinople to Venice to France and back again, as part of the Crusades, the Napoleonic Wars, and World War II—whoever won them in battle carried them as a victory banner. But, really, she wondered aloud, who rightfully owned them?

She felt Michael disentangle his sinuous arms from her body. "You sound as if you're thinking twice about our case."

"No, not at all," she rushed to reassure them both. "The research I've been doing just churns all this up. *The Chrysalis* is different—clean." She pulled his arms back around her and tightened them.

"Really?" She heard the unease in his voice, sensed it in the slackness of his limbs, and felt it echo in the corner of her own mind.

"Really," she insisted, and initiated a more intimate embrace, involving their whole bodies. Afterward, delicious, protected sleep.

"Mara." Somewhere she heard a whisper. "Mara, honey, I don't want to wake you, but I need to leave. I don't want to, but I have to."

She knew he had to leave. He was scheduled to meet with friends she had never met to travel to the bachelor party of his last bachelor friend. From there, he had a business trip to Europe, where he'd be for weeks. She feigned sleep, as a way to savor the last few moments.

"Mara, honey, I don't want to leave without saying goodbye."

She opened her eyes to the morning light and stretched to the very tips of her toes. "I know. I don't want you to leave with saying goodbye either." She shut her eyes again.

He kissed her closed eyelids. "It's okay, baby. I'll call you every day."

She unraveled herself from the bedcovers and appropriated his T-shirt, wrapping herself into it to cover her nakedness. They padded to the door.

Stooping down as if to kiss her, he instead rested his head in the curve of her neck.

"I'll be thinking about you. Missing you." He encircled her. She breathed him in. His musky morning aroma was so different from his crisp day smell, the scent of pressed Thomas Pink shirts and money.

"Me, too. Travel safely."

After he left and she secured the door behind him, Mara put her back against it for a moment, eyes closed. Then she buried herself deep under the tangle of sheets he had left behind, hoping to recapture some of the gift of sleep he granted.

With Michael gone, Mara allowed her day life to take over. She longed for him at night, but she felt his presence in her work, and her hours were spent endeavoring to win him his victory and secure her advancement. She formulated lists of information that she needed to procure from within and without, she crafted a roster of witnesses and testimony, and she spent day after day foraging and scavenging in Lillian's sacred library of provenance, amassing defensive and offensive weaponry.

If she were diligent, and very, very lucky, she might be able to build an impenetrable barricade to Hilda Baum's attack on the painting. Mara knew firsthand that Hilda's personal story had a strong emotional appeal, and she did not want the judge to hear too much of it. So she outlined a summary judgment motion to make at the close of discovery, to prove to the judge that the undisputed facts warranted final judgment for Beazley's, thereby obviating the need for a public, damaging trial. She hoped her motion would become a blockade, forcing the judge to one conclusion only, no matter how unpalatable—that Hilda Baum should lose her war for *The Chrysalis*.

Mara made the first move and served a series of document requests and interrogatories to Hilda Baum's lawyer. She hoped to gather additional admissions that would help her cause. Hilda Baum produced the expected papers, not the roomfuls of discovery Mara handled in her typical cases but a few critical boxes. Alone, they told a tragic, compelling tale, but Mara knew how to combine them with Beazley's documents to cast a less sympathetic light on her story.

A date was set for Hilda's deposition. Mara knew that the war could be won or lost on Hilda's tale of *The Chrysalis*'s lineage and her recitation of her long quest. But in the days before the deposition, a calm descended on her. Unlike any deposition she had taken before, there was little more she could do to prepare; everything rested on her performance at the deposition and before the judge at the summary judgment argument. She would lurk like a panther as Hilda's story unfolded and, in the subtlest way, pounce to elicit the testimony she needed to defuse the compassion.

The day finally arrived, and when Mara awakened, her heart was racing. Her hands and mind, however, were steady, like a soldier ready for battle. She selected a light gray suit, with an ice-blue sweater underneath. The sweater highlighted her eyes and made her look younger and, she hoped, deceptively vulnerable. She wore only the simplest of jewelry and makeup and tied her hair in a barrette, low at the back. She wished Michael could see her.

Mara arrived in the conference room first and took her time settling in, arranging notepads of questions, manila folders of documents, and a paralegal at her side. Then she sat and waited for her opponent.

A grandmotherly woman toddled in on the arm of a stooped, elderly gentleman. She was dressed in an A-line plaid skirt with a sweater set and a tiny pearl cross. A near halo of fluffy white curls encircled her face. Her eyes sparkled as she stretched out her hand to Mara. Her English was perfect, but the cadence different, a staccato punctuated with crescendos. The accent was European and somewhat British, but not otherwise placeable.

Pleasantries completed, Hilda Baum and her lawyer took their seats, and Mara signaled for the court reporter and videographer to begin. The battle commenced: *En garde*.

"Ms. Baum, isn't it true that your father, Erich Baum, often used Henri Rochlitz of Nice, France, as his agent to sell paintings on his behalf?"

"Yes, Ms. Coyne, that is true."

"And, Ms. Baum, isn't it correct that, in the late 1930s and early 1940s, your father actually sent several paintings to Henri Rochlitz to sell on his behalf?" Mara spread out exhibits, bills of sale procured by Lillian from the bowels of Beazley's, in front of Hilda Baum. "These paintings?"

The older woman reached for the documents with a withered, sunspotted hand and perused them with care. "Yes, Ms. Coyne, that is correct."

For a moment, Mara felt buoyant. She was poised to prove her argument that Erich Baum had sent *The Chrysalis* to Nice not for safe storage with a family member but to his longtime agent, Henri Rochlitz, with authorization to sell it to Albert Boettcher, from whom Beazley's had procured it. But before Mara could ask her next question, Hilda Baum parried, doing her best to protect the detail that Mara sought. "But, of course, the letter my father sent me stated simply that he had forwarded certain paintings, including *The Chrysalis*, on to Nice. It does not say anything about sending the paintings to Henri Rochlitz for him to sell. That is how I know they were sent to our family in Nice—my father's aunt—for safe storage. In fact, he told me during Christmas of 1939 that if the war situation worsened, this is what he would do." She paused for effect. "Surely you've seen the letter? We produced it as part of our document production." Indeed, Mara had seen the handwritten note, more like a scribble, from Erich Baum to his daughter stating that he had sent certain paintings, including *The Chrysalis*, to Nice. She had spent long hours pondering it, as the note was a problem with which she'd have to contend. But Mara hoped that the exhibits helped establish that it was Erich Baum's pattern to send his paintings to Nice for sale, not storage.

Each time Mara tried to question the nature of *The Chrysalis*'s journey to Nice and beyond, Hilda cut Mara with the sharp edge of her own story and that of her parents. She reminded Mara over and over that *The Chrysalis*, the devotional portion of her father's renowned art collection where he honored his family's conversion to Catholicism, was a painting for which the Nazis had killed her parents.

As the two women jousted over the topic of *The Chrysalis*'s significance to Erich Baum, Hilda turned to her lawyer, as if she'd just remembered something. "Bert, could you hand me that envelope I found last night?"

Her gnarled knuckles scraping over the tabletop, Hilda passed a large white envelope to Mara. "What is this, Ms. Baum?" Mara asked.

"Oh, I think the contents explain themselves. Why don't you open it?" Hilda answered, with the tiniest grin on her face.

Mara sliced open the heavily taped envelope, and curling yellowed photographs spilled out from it. She looked at them. In one, a delicate woman, overwhelmed by an elaborate coiffure, perched imperiously on a rococo side chair. Mara brought the picture closer, noticing the hesitancy of the smile on the woman's deeply colored lips and the direction of her gaze. The woman's eyes were fixed on the round-faced, dapper man at her side, who sported an infectious grin and a pomaded helmet of black hair. A young girl, blond ringlets escaping from a bow, stood between them, linking her hands with theirs. They formed this little chain for the camera again and again in the other photos, captured at Christmas holidays, birthdays, Easters. The innocence and immediacy of the young family transfixed Mara, and she could almost feel her fingers interlaced with theirs. This was precisely the human element that she had hoped to keep out of the case.

As she pored back over the photographs, trying to formulate questions that might defuse their emotional resonance, Mara saw that the surfaces of walls, tables, and mantels surrounding the young Baum family overflowed with paintings, sculptures, silver, and woven tapestries. When she looked closely at certain pictures, she saw *The Chrysalis*. The artwork started to morph into instruments of destruction. A silver chalice became the butt of a rifle. A striking sculpture turned into a blade. A richly embroidered tapestry formed a noose. A priceless painting depicted a gas chamber.

The Baums' smiles melted into screams, and the little girl between them cried.

Mara looked over at Hilda Baum's beaming face; the photographs had the desired effect. "These are pictures of your family," Mara pronounced somewhat hesitantly.

"Yes. With *The Chrysalis*, of course."

Mara felt blood seeping from her wounds. She needed to turn everyone's attention away from these sympathetic pictures as quickly as she could. If she didn't, she risked losing not only the case but also herself to the Baums.

It took all of her strength to try again with a different line of questioning. Mara needed to lance Hilda with *DeClerck*, make plain her failure to search, and then stab her with the German Art Restitution Commission release. "Ms. Baum, in late 1945 and 1946, the year following the war, what efforts did you make to find *The Chrysalis*?"

Hilda sampled her tea and then answered deliberately. "The year following the war. Let me see if I can remember, Ms. Coyne. I think I spent much of that time trying to find my parents. I confess my search for *The Chrysalis* really didn't start until I learned that the Nazis had killed them."

Again, Mara tried to steer away from the Baums' personal story. "Ms. Baum, I would request that you respond only to my inquiry about *The Chrysalis*."

"Can you please repeat the question?"

"In late 1945 and 1946, did you look for *The Chrysalis*?"

"No, Ms. Coyne, as I mentioned already, I focused on finding my parents. Other than that, I really have no memories of the last year of the war. It is as if on the first day of peace, I awoke. I went directly to the Red Cross, where there were lists of people who had survived the concentration camps. My parents' names were not on those lists. I went roaming throughout Italy, where I was living at the time, throughout any part of Europe I was permitted to enter, trying to find them—"

Mara broke in, "Ms. Baum, please just answer the question I asked. About *The Chrysalis*."

Hilda's lawyer struggled to stand up. "Ms. Coyne, I object to your last statement. You opened the door with your question, and my client should be permitted to answer, in her own words and in her own way."

Mara winced. He was right. Any attempt Mara might make to take Hilda's obfuscation up with the judge on motion or in a middeposition phone call would backfire: Mara would seem heartless and unreasonable. So she gestured for Hilda to continue.

"I spent late 1945 and 1946 combing through refugee camps, interviewing anyone I could find who might have crossed my parents' path as they made their way across Europe from the Netherlands. My parents thought they had been granted safe passage to Italy to see my husband, Giuseppe, and me where his connections could offer some kind of protection for them. They had to travel via Berlin, of course: All international trains had to pass through Berlin at that time." Tears formed in Hilda's eyes as she recalled her parents' innocent trust of the Nazi officers who'd showed up at their home early one morning with visas and train tickets, despite the fact that their own daughter had tried for months to procure those same tickets and visas without success.

"They so wanted to believe, because they needed to get out of the occupied Netherlands after they'd been classified as Jews. Father's grandfather, you see—an ardent Catholic, by all accounts—had been born Jewish but converted as a child. Somehow the Nazis managed to hunt down any weak link in someone's lineage. I continued to receive my father's letters, which arrived more and more sporadically due to the vagaries of the diplomatic pouch. While they were unfailingly pleasant, I knew that my parents' lives must have become a living hell—"

"Ms. Baum, you are straying very far from my questions. Let's refocus on your attempts to find *The Chrysalis*."

"Ms. Coyne, I am an old woman. You're asking me to recount events that happened over sixty years ago. To properly remember them, I must review them in order." Mara surrendered to Hilda's trump card. No judge in the world would let Mara cut off Hilda's litany if she claimed it was necessary for her full recollection of the facts.

"From Italy, my husband and I did what we could to protect them. We were able to get my parents a letter, signed by the reichskommissar of the Netherlands, Seyss-Inquart. I know what it said by heart:

No security or police measures of any kind are to be carried out against the Jew and Dutch citizens, Erich and Cornelia Baum, who reside in Amsterdam. . . .

We thought they'd be safe, that the letter would protect them. But Father's passion, his art, was too much of a temptation for the Nazis. I suspected they would want Father's art collection. Not the Impressionists so much. The Nazis' hatred for 'degenerate' modern art was well known, although they could not ignore its value in trade. No, I surmised the Nazis would covet those old masters and German portraits that my father had collected early on. The Nazis stalked my parents for those paintings, harassed them for them, deprived them of what few liberties they had as so-called Jews just to get to them. They threatened to arrest them if they left the house without the stars my parents often refused to wear, unless they handed the paintings over. The Nazis tried everything short of outright hauling them off to concentration camps. But the Seyss-Inquart letter put a stop to the harassment, and being good, obedient Nazis, they wouldn't dare defy Seyss-Inquart's letter. Not in the Netherlands, at least. So they staged the trip to Italy."

Liquid warmth spread across Mara's lip. She tasted blood. She'd been biting her lip throughout Hilda's testimony.

"In 1946, in refugee camps, I finally met some people who knew what had happened to my parents in the Berlin train station and beyond: a sweeper from the Berlin station and two concentration camp survivors, Jewish acquaintances of my parents from Amsterdam. When my parents' train pulled into Berlin, a Nazi officer presented them with a document, in which Father would agree to sign away his art collection and tell them its whereabouts. Father refused to sign, waving the Seyss-Inquart letter in front of them. But with my parents out of the Netherlands and actually before them with the loot nearly in hand, the letter did not deter the Nazis. They disengaged my parents' car from the train and then dragged my parents into Nazi headquarters in Berlin for interrogation. They tortured my parents. Father first, to get him to sign away the art collection. When he resisted, screaming that he would not, they whipped Mother in front of him. Father remained stalwart.

"So, they put my parents on another train, this one going toward Munich, to Dachau. When their torments yielded nothing, the Nazis shot my father to death in the public square in the center of the prison, in front of all the prisoners. After this, Mother had no value alive, so they killed her at Dachau. With the death of my parents, the Nazis were free to confiscate the rest of the art collection. Including *The Chrysalis*."

Silence. The cross-examination Mara had at the ready could not be asked. In the stillness that followed, Mara could almost hear her grandmother gasp.

Hilda stared at Mara, her eyes triumphant. "So, to answer your question, Ms. Coyne, I began my search for *The Chrysalis* after I learned all of this."

fourteen

AMSTERDAM, 1942

"WELCOME HOME, MR. BAUM, SIR."

Willem opens the door for Erich as he crosses the threshold to his home and then helps him off with his overcoat. His once elegant cashmere coat is now emblazoned with the garish yellow of a crude star, cut as if by the dull-edged scissors of a kindergarten child. Though labeled a Jew by the Nazis, Erich cannot quite think of himself as one.

As the coat lifts off his shoulders, Erich feels the weight of the star lift off him as well, allowing his stature to elevate and his shoulders to square. For this one fleeting moment, he can almost bear the day's humiliation of calling on old colleagues in hopes that they'll ignore Reichskommissar Seyss-Inquart's rules prohibiting Jews from working in the financial industry, a necessary exercise now that an Aryan "trustee" has taken over his insurance business, leaving him with no livelihood. He abides this shame every day during his long walk to and from the business district, as Jews are no longer permitted to ride in cars or on public transport.

"Thank you, Willem." Erich marvels that the servants have stayed, though he reminds himself that his house has been their home as long as it's been his, and he supposes they have nowhere else to go. No one is hiring help these days, not even the Nazis or their Dutch henchmen, and he and Cornelia can still provide the servants with meals and shelter, though cash is now scarce since the reichskommissar forbids Jews from withdrawing money even from their own bank accounts. Yet he feels like a fraud as the servants rush to minister to him. Outside these doors, he is the abomination unworthy of subservience, and they are pure Aryan gold.

"Erich, is that you?" He hears his wife's voice ring out from the parlor.

"Yes, dear. Who else?" These days they have no callers, so different from the halcyon days before the occupation. Their former friends are afraid to be seen in the home of Jews.

As Erich walks toward the parlor, he runs his fingers along the dark rectangular markings on the faded red silk damask walls, scars where paintings once hung. Not for the first time, he says a silent prayer of thanks that he listened to his daughter and removed his paintings to France before the Netherlands fell to the Nazis on May 14, 1940. Otherwise, Erich would have had to hand them over to the reichskommissar's local band of government-sanctioned art looters, the Dienststelle Mühlmann, in compliance with the ordinance requiring Jews to surrender all valuables to the Dienststelle Mühlmann's agent, the Lippmann, Rosenthal and Co. Bank. Though he turned over only the few, lesser paintings that remained on his walls when the ordinance was issued, the Nazis have heard rumors that he once had other treasures and now hound him for their location.

"A letter has come. From Hilda."

He hurries into his wife's rosy Victorian domain with its rococo murals of cherubs taking flight, so different from the austere décor and uncluttered surfaces of his study. The parlor's shelves and tabletops are littered with silver frames of every imaginable shape and size, capturing events from a life that has passed. Cornelia sits in her usual wingback chair near the fireplace with an envelope, rather than her usual needlepoint, perched on her tightly closed knees.

"What does she say?" Erich is almost afraid to ask. Their daughter Hilda's letters have grown increasingly rare and ever more filled with unwelcome news.

"I daren't open it, Erich. It is addressed to you."

"To me?" He is confused; Hilda's letters are usually directed to his wife.

"Yes, and it came by the embassy pouch."

He rushes to take the envelope from Cornelia's hand and then slices it open with an ivory-handled letter opener from the parlor desk. A second, sealed envelope flutters out onto the floor.

After reaching down to grab the fallen letter, he sits in the wingback chair facing his wife's. His hands shake as he tries to open the second envelope without breaking its ornate waxen seal. Only then does he pore over the two letters.

"What do they say, Erich?" Cornelia looks at him, her eyes brimming with expectation.

He hesitates, but there is no way to soften the news. "She cannot get us visas to Milan."

The hope pours out of her eyes in tears. "What will we do, Erich?"

"She did manage to get us this." He places the document enclosed in Hilda's letter into his weeping wife's hands.

Her cries stop for a moment as she dabs her eyes with an embroidered handkerchief and reads the missive. "So this will protect us from the reichskommissar's deportations and the other ordinances against Jews? From the Dienststelle Mühlmann's questioning?"

"So it seems. For now, at least."

"But what of your brothers and sisters and their families?"

"The letter does not safeguard them. And Hilda would have arranged protection for her dear Maddie if she could."

Cornelia's sobs resume. He rises and runs a consoling but preoccupied hand along her shoulder as he leaves the parlor. He wishes he could comfort her, but there is something he must do. Something he had hoped to avoid.

His body feels heavy as he climbs the stairs to his study. The once gloriously spartan room, which had brought him such peace, now serves as a stark, even barren, reminder of all they have lost—all they still stand to lose. He sits at his desk and begins to compose a letter of his own, a letter to his daughter.

fifteen

NEW YORK CITY, PRESENT DAY

I N THE TEN DAYS THAT FOLLOWED THE DEPOSITION, MARA
spent most of her time writing and assessing the transcript. She needed
a tourniquet in several places to stop the bleeding from Hilda's sympathetic deposition testimony. But she acquired a few spoils as well, not least
of all Hilda's concession about her failure to search and her admission
to the German Art Restitution Commission release. Out of these, Mara
wrote the summary judgment motion with which she could protect Beazley's claim to *The Chrysalis*. In truth, however, she had few illusions about
the motion's weaknesses. Even Sophia, ever her champion, acknowledged
the inherent sympathy of Hilda Baum's story.

Mara delivered the summary judgment motion to Harlan for his final
endorsement and sat alone with Hilda's condemning words and her grandmother's frowning judgments.

Within hours of Mara's dropping off the papers, the phone rang to summon her upstairs. She trudged to Harlan's office with leaden steps, certain of his reaction. Mara waited outside the door of his office, and as usual, the anteroom was filled with the stale odor of the Cuban cigars he smoked in flagrant but tolerated violation of the building code. The fact that his smoking was permitted irked Mara no end. It was an unavoidable reminder of the hierarchy of power that governed both the firm and her life.

A guttural sound emerged from behind Harlan's door. Mara knew that this was her signal to enter, so she steeled herself, glanced for a nod of confirmation from his secretary, the ubiquitous Marianne, and opened the door. As usual, Harlan's colossally wide body was ensconced in an enormous leather chair. A panoramic view of downtown Manhattan loomed behind him, but the way he positioned his chair and imposing mahogany desk deliberately blocked the vista. The room was arranged to remind anyone who entered of Harlan's authority, that he alone had earned the right to his view.

He gestured for Mara to sit in a small, stiff chair and then pretended to pay her no heed as he continued to examine the summary judgment papers on his desk. But Mara knew that he was scanning her as much as her words. He wanted to see how she held up under the pressure of the case and his inspection. His game had some value—Mara acknowledged that his scrutiny had a positive effect on her posture in the courtroom—but as much as it was educational, it was also manipulative and designed to keep her in obeisance. As with all his other power tricks, Mara had learned to look the other way.

Finally, he gave her a toothy grin.

"I liked the brief," he said.

Mara was flabbergasted. In her six years of working for him, she had never once seen him smile in her direction. She knew she should respond to the compliment, the only one he had ever bestowed on her, but she was shocked into silence.

"I said I liked the brief," he repeated.

The gruffness returned to his voice and prompted Mara to speak. "Thank you. I really appreciate it, but are you at all worried by Hilda's testimony about her parents?"

"I'm not too bothered by it. Sure, it's a tragic tale, but it doesn't change the law. What I am impressed by is that you took a pretty unwinnable situation and came up with some legal arguments that stand a chance. You handled the flaw in the title well, even turned it back on them. After all, she didn't really look for the painting, did she? Just as in *DeClerck*. But the waiver argument is the winner, I think. She signed away her rights to pursue *The Chrysalis* all those years ago and probably never thought that release would resurface. Let's call the client." He bellowed, "Marianne, get that guy at Beazley's on the line!"

They sat in awkward silence, not quite knowing how to deal with the changed dynamic between them. A frisson of excitement at the impact of Harlan's compliment pulsed through Mara.

"He's on," Marianne announced. Harlan hit the speakerphone button. "Michael? I'm here with Mara Coyne, whom you know."

"Yes, I've had the pleasure of working with Mara over the past few months. We all think that she has done a terrific job."

Mara's cheeks turned scarlet. Michael had returned from his European trip just an hour or so before, and since their evening had been planned over many transatlantic phone calls and e-mails, they hadn't spoken since he landed.

"Glad to hear it. You're about to see even better. We're sending over to you the summary judgment brief. As a rule, I don't assess our chances of success up front, but I think we have some powerful arguments here. If you like it, I'd recommend we file it within the day."

"If it's anything akin to Mara's work to date, I'm sure it is fantastic. Feel free to send it right over."

Without a goodbye, Harlan hung up. It was something of a relief to know that he didn't stockpile his brusqueness for the firm associates alone. "Marianne! Fax this to Beazley's." He tossed the brief on the floor toward the door and, without a word to Mara, returned to reading the documents on his desk. Her moment in the sun was over. She excused herself and hurried back to her office, descending staircase after staircase, past the flashy, light-filled floors where the senior partners tallied their hours in large, airy offices to the darker, dingier ones where the associates toiled shoulder to shoulder in barely delineated cubbies. She was jubilant about Harlan's favorable judgment and her "client's" public praise of her work. She was also elated at the thought of seeing Michael that evening, if a little nervous after their weeks of separation. She wondered if things would be the same between them.

She shouldn't have been anxious. When she walked into Michael's apartment that night, his delight flickered from the candles he had lit on every surface, bloomed from the bouquets of her favorite light pink roses spilling out of cut crystal vases, and steamed up from the stove, where he was putting the finishing touches on lobster tails. He pressed a kiss on her lips and a glass of sauvignon blanc into her hand. They toasted to her success and to their reunion. For the moment, Mara felt utterly at peace.

———

ON THE FINAL FILING DAY FOR ALL THE SUMMARY JUDGMENT papers, Mara's father announced an unexpected visit, an event that always filled her with an unsettling mix of excitement and trepidation. She wished she could invite Michael to dinner; she'd been awaiting the day when she could introduce the two men. But she and Michael wanted her father to think the best of him, and they could not expect a hearty welcome when they were dating in blatant disregard of her career. Their introduction would have to wait until after the case was won. Perhaps, she dared to imagine, they'd all celebrate Mara's partnership together.

So when the taxi reached the Four Seasons Hotel on Fifty-seventh Street, Mara alighted alone. Almost instantly, a bellhop appeared at her side and escorted her inside. With its enormous granite columns and regal staircase, the hallowed hotel was a large-scale, contemporary version of her favorite refuge, the Temple of Dendur at the Metropolitan Museum of Art. It was also the place her father always stayed when he visited New York for business, and Mara knew exactly where he'd be sitting with the paper, waiting for her.

After their initial, perfunctory embrace, he told her that he had just enough time to squeeze in a cocktail before a business dinner. Well, to be fair, he had enough time for two whiskeys, neat. A long line snaked out of the famed lobby bar, but Mara and her father were led right in to a prime center table. Her father heaved his corpulence into a signature maroon velvet chair and waved off some hovering politico courtiers. If he weren't so clearly Irish, with his ruddy cheeks, fair complexion, and graying red hair, an onlooker might have mistaken him for a don. He really was a lot like Harlan, Mara mused.

Of course, he was here without her mother. She was never invited on business trips. When Mara thought about her mother, she was blurry, out of focus. Mara tried to zoom in and sharpen the picture, but she never could. She could just make out the edges of her, but never the details. Blonde, petite, perfectly appointed, pretty, in sort of a pale, forgettable way, her mother was like a conch, retreating deep into a pleasing shell but nowhere to be found.

Mara recalled her as ever present and never present, all at once. Certainly, meals were prepared and presented, and car pools duly driven. School functions well attended, cocktail party chatter handled expertly, and events flawlessly orchestrated. But her mothering was offhand, even absent. She could sit at the dinner table and seem never to have been there at all.

In rare moments of animation, a light sparked behind her eyes. Mara had learned to recognize these moments as the result of more than a few predinner martinis or the infrequent attention of her father. A tall, hulking man with a tall, hulking persona, when he left a room, his presence lingered on for long hours. His expectations governed her mother's life as they did Mara's, who ran as far from the vapidity of her mother as possible, even when it meant modeling herself after her father.

Immediately, her father directed the conversation to her work: how her tenths of an hour matched up to the tenths of an hour of her competition. She told him about her new case and client but left out the personal part about Michael. She took a sip of her drink and looked up for his response: As always, validation was what she sought. After long years in the habit, she couldn't help herself, and she knew her news would please him.

"So, if this goes well, you could be the reason a big client comes back for more," he surmised.

"That's a big 'if.' "

"Still, that sounds promising. For your partnership chances, I mean."

"I'm hopeful."

"Good. I'd hate to see you passed over. " Her heart sank, but as he downed his drink and turned to order another, old eavesdropped words came to Mara, ones that had seemed blasphemous at the time but brought her a measure of comfort. She had once overheard her grandmother render judgment on her son: "Ah, in a rare while, a family tree bears a different fruit from all the rest. No matter that it's always fed the same water, no matter that the trunk and branches are all the same. The branch bearing Patrick grew a different fruit—fancy skin on the outside but no flesh, no seeds, nothing within." It was a verdict even her gentle lilt could not soften.

"Aha, I see my dinner dates." Her father waved to two pin-striped gentlemen. "Call your mother. You know she worries about you." He gave Mara a big bear hug and disappeared, leaving her alone with his fresh drink, her own half-finished wine, and the room's flickering candlelight.

sixteen

NEW YORK CITY, PRESENT DAY

SEVERAL WEEKS LATER, MARA STRODE UP THE WIDE EX-
panse of stone stairs leading to the infamous New York State Supreme
Court, flanked by Michael and Harlan. The court building was home to
the paparazzi-plagued trials of reputed mafioso bosses and fallen Wall
Street traders, the lair of famed commercial law judges, and the battlefield
for everyday New Yorkers' skirmishes, large and small.

It was almost a relief to arrive at the courthouse, even though it meant
she'd have to deliver the summary judgment argument in front of the notoriously mercurial and crotchety Justice Ira Weir. Mara had spent the day
with Harlan, running through the argument over and over again and sub-
jecting herself to his merciless criticism and ridicule. It was rare that he
surrendered the chance to present a summary judgment argument to an
associate, as he reminded her over and over. The harangue continued in
the limo ride to the courthouse, with Michael as a witness. At one point,

Mara nearly snapped at Harlan, but she had stopped herself, knowing that the opportunity to deliver the argument was critical to her partnership prospects.

Watching Harlan climb the courthouse steps, Mara realized she had never witnessed him move so quickly. By the time they reached the long lines of the security check, he was gasping for breath and dripping with sweat.

As she waited for the two men, Mara calmed her nerves by strolling through the lobby beneath the recently restored cupola. Standing on the intricate marble parquetry flooring, she gazed up at the mural. The cerulean blue ceiling was covered with gilded representations of renowned judges and lawmakers: Egyptian, Assyrian, Hebrew, Turkish, Greek, Roman, Byzantine, Frankish, English, colonial, and finally, American. They all testified to days when ideals rather than money were championed in the courthouse. Her grandmother would have loved the values emblazoned on the ceiling, if not the actual justice handed out in the chambers.

The fast clip of Michael's step reverberated across the floor, followed closely by Harlan's belabored shuffle. As he approached her, she reveled in the fact that she towered over him. She nearly chuckled at the fleeting, subtle shift in power, which went a long way toward alleviating his earlier belittling treatment of her, when Harlan's harsh tone had quickly restored order.

Together the three passed under an archway bearing the inscription "The true administration of justice is the firmest pillar of good government" and walked toward the courtroom of Justice Weir. Like most lawyers, Harlan and Mara had experienced mixed reactions when they drew his name. Weir was considered smarter than most of the supremes, a stickler for the clear letter of the law, and longer on the bench, but he was also known to have cantankerous flashes. So they prayed for a good-mood day.

Mara scanned the courtroom. The rich, dark wood floors, though scuffed and worn with use, were burnished bright. The tall windows let in little light, facing as they did the façade of another building; any illumination was left to several dim chandeliers. Ornate crown moldings bordered soaring ceilings. Stark white walls were emblazoned with the phrase "In God We Trust" in gleaming brass. And an American flag, topped with a golden eagle poised to take flight, presided over it all. She reveled in the room's distressed-leather luxury; it was like the worn pages of a much-beloved legal textbook.

Mara nodded hello to opposing counsel and Hilda Baum and then made her way to the counsel's table, a pewlike wooden bench set before the altar of the judge's desk and the jury box. She could hear an ancient clock ticking on the wall behind her. The butterflies in her stomach swirled to its rhythm. Once the judge entered the courtroom, she knew she could get through it, but until then, anticipation had her on edge. She swallowed hard, perused her argument, and tried to ignore the unnerving proximity of Michael and Harlan.

The court officer cried out, "Hear ye, hear ye. The Honorable Justice Ira Weir. All rise." A sense of dread chilled Mara's blood like ice, and she braced herself for the justice. His tiny frame emerged from his chambers. He climbed up the steps leading to his formidable bench, and his large hands and head commanded Mara's attention. For a second, Mara thought she saw the glimpse of a smile in her direction. Before she recognized the grimace for what it really was, she smiled back.

Pushing the blunder out of her mind, Mara assumed her place at the podium. She consulted her notes one last time and took a final breath.

When Weir spoke, it was like Oz from behind the curtain. "You are?" he asked in a booming voice that belied his minuscule frame.

"Mara Coyne, Your Honor, with the law firm of Severin, Oliver & Means. Here for the defendant, Beazley's."

"I understand we have a summary judgment motion on for today. In the case of *Baum v. Beazley's.* Is that correct?"

"That's right, Your Honor." Mara's voice cracked.

"This is the case in which the plaintiff alleges that a painting was stolen from her family—Holocaust victims—by the Nazis. Am I right?" His eyes glowed royal blue from the reflection of the computer screen on his desk.

"Yes, Your Honor." Mara's delivery strengthened.

"You may begin, Ms. Coyne."

Mara gulped. "Your Honor, I stand here today before you arguing for summary judgment in the case of *Baum v. Beazley's.*" Her eyes riveted on the judge's hands, clasped in the triangular shape of prayer. For a split second, Mara saw her grandmother's hands on a church pew, as if Nana had entered the courtroom to weigh Mara's arguments.

"Ms. Coyne, I think we've already established that. I told you that you can begin," the judge commanded.

Mara's heart thudded; she couldn't seem to shake her dread.

Justice Weir ordered her to speak. "Ms. Coyne!"

Somewhere behind her, she heard Harlan whisper, "Mara!"

"Your Honor, please don't interpret Beazley's application for summary judgment as a lack of sympathy for the plaintiff's plight. After all, a horrific fate befell the plaintiff's family in World War II." As if from a slight distance, Mara heard herself begin. She had planned a legalistic affair, full of persuasive, yet detached points of law designed to appeal to the judge's reputation for cold, hard logic. But the unexpected memory of her grandmother disturbed Mara's assurance, and new opening words spilled forth of their own accord. "From what we understand, the Nazis categorized the plaintiff's family as Jewish and stripped them of their liberties, their humanity, and their property. The plaintiff claims that *The Chrysalis* figured among the property looted by the Nazis as part of their art lust and Final Solution. In order to acquire it, the Nazis robbed the plaintiff's parents of their lives.

"So I come to you torn. Torn between, on the one hand, my sympathy for the plaintiff and her unimaginable family history and, on the other, my understanding of what the clear letter of the law requires. I won't lie to you, Your Honor, there have been times when I have been uncomfortable representing Beazley's."

Justice Weir looked startled. It wasn't every day that an attorney came into his courtroom and admitted that she was uneasy with the morality of her client's position. Mara imagined the expression of suppressed rage on Harlan's face. She took a deep breath and continued.

"But then I took a close look at the facts and the law. I came to understand what the law really says, what the law requires. And I became convinced that Beazley's obtained clear title to *The Chrysalis* when it purchased the painting and that Beazley's conveyed that clear title to the painting's current owner.

"The law says that the plaintiff's title must be pure to recover the property, but discovery revealed that the plaintiff's title isn't. In fact, it's anything but pure. Let me tell you the true story of *The Chrysalis*'s ownership, Your Honor." As Mara returned to her prepared remarks, her adrenaline quickened and her confidence returned. She knew that she could command the language and the legal facts. "No one disputes that Erich Baum, father of the plaintiff, legitimately bought the painting at auction from its original owner, the Van Dinters, in whose family home it had languished for over three hundred years. It's what Erich Baum did with the painting that brings us here today. The plaintiff will tell you that she has a letter from her father asserting that he sent certain paintings—including *The Chrysalis*—to Nice, France, and that he sent it to family for safe storage. And from there, the Nazis' ERR branch plundered the painting, passing it on to Albert Boettcher & Company in Switzerland. That's why no documents exist demonstrating the transfer of the painting to Boettcher, according to the plaintiff—because the painting was stolen by the Nazis in between. The plaintiff will then tell you that Boettcher sold his ill-gotten goods to Beazley's.

"But what the plaintiff will not tell you is this: That Erich Baum, unable to work in his insurance business once deemed a Jew, needed money to keep his family afloat. That Erich Baum sent *The Chrysalis* to Nice not to family but to his art dealer, Henri Rochlitz, on consignment for Rochlitz to sell. That, in the 1930s, Erich Baum shipped nearly twenty paintings to Rochlitz as his sales agent, and in early 1940, the very time frame in which he sent *The Chrysalis* to Nice, he shipped four other paintings to Rochlitz to sell. That France was far more war-torn than the Netherlands and swarmed with Nazis, making it an illogical choice for safekeeping. That Rochlitz routinely sold paintings to Boettcher, particularly during this time period. That no records exist of this transaction in either Rochlitz's or Boettcher's files because the war destroyed both Rochlitz's and Boettcher's businesses. That Boettcher had a squeaky-clean reputation of never trafficking in Nazi-plundered art. That, in fact, the Allied governments recognized Boettcher for his assistance in the French Resistance. Finally, that no Nazi records exist of *The Chrysalis*—and the Nazis were notoriously fanatical record keepers of their war spoils. If the Nazis had indeed taken *The Chrysalis*, as the plaintiff claims, we would see it in the Nazis' records. And the plaintiff has not provided us with one piece of evidence that *The Chrysalis* was stored in this so-called family member's home in Nice. All of this proves that Erich Baum authorized Rochlitz to sell *The Chrysalis* to Boettcher. And then, in turn, Boettcher legitimately sold it to Beazley's. As a result, Beazley's title, as well as the title of its current owner, is clear."

Mara punctuated her argument with dramatic enlarged visuals: large-as-life bills of sale demonstrating that Erich Baum sold paintings through Rochlitz many times over during this time period; voluminous military reports listing Boettcher as an "asset" to the Allied forces during their campaign; a video clip of Hilda at her deposition, detailing the dire nature of her family's financial situation.

"But, Your Honor, even if I'm utterly wrong about this, and the Nazis did pilfer *The Chrysalis* from the Baum family in Nice, there is a line of authority based on the *DeClerck* case that says a plaintiff must hunt down the stolen property to have it returned in a replevin action." Mara explained the facts behind *DeClerck* and its progeny. She highlighted the policy reasons for embracing *DeClerck* rather than the competing authority of *Scaife:* If the judge followed *Scaife* instead of *DeClerck,* New York would be vulnerable to long-stale replevin claims, potentially chilling New York art commerce.

"Your Honor, I invite you to pave new ground and adopt these cases. It is in your control. Following the *DeClerck* authority, if a plaintiff hasn't hunted down the stolen art, the plaintiff waives his or her claim to it. Discovery has shown that Hilda Baum did not scour for *The Chrysalis.*

"Discovery established that *The Chrysalis* has been on public display in the United States since the 1950s, in exhibitions and in museums." Mara gestured to the screen, which showed a series of exhibit and museum catalogs with color photographs of the painting. "Discovery also proved that *The Chrysalis* has featured prominently in numerous British and American art publications since the 1950s." The screen scrolled through the scholarly literature referencing the piece. "If Hilda Baum had been looking, she would have found *The Chrysalis.*"

Hilda materialized on the enormous video monitor, in a carefully edited deposition excerpt of her most damning confession. "However, as we can see, by her own admission, Hilda Baum gave up the search for *The Chrysalis* sometime in the 1950s and never considered trailing after it in the United States. She never even listed *The Chrysalis* as a piece of stolen artwork on the recently formed art loss registers. And who can blame her? The search churned up the memories of the evil done to her parents and broke her spirit. But by giving up the search, Hilda Baum relinquished her rights to *The Chrysalis.*"

Mara concluded with her trump card. "Finally, Your Honor, even if I'm wrong, even if the Nazis poached *The Chrysalis,* and even if Hilda Baum searched with reasonable diligence for the long-lost painting, the law says that once you've waived your rights to a piece of property, you can't later seek to recover it."

The screen displayed a magnified and highlighted version of her prize possession: the German Art Restitution Commission release. "Discovery showed that in the late 1940s, Hilda Baum filed a claim for her family's lost artwork with the German Art Restitution Commission, including *The Chrysalis*. When she received a payment from the commission, she signed a release, waiving all future claims based on those paintings. Take a look at the translation: 'For *The Chrysalis* . . . I have submitted no other applications for compensation . . . be it on my own behalf or through any institution, organization, or authorized agent, nor will I do so in the future against this entity or any other.' This waiver prevents her from pursuing a lawsuit now to regain *The Chrysalis*. The case law refutes any argument by the plaintiff that this release does not apply in the United States as well as any contention that the release applies only between plaintiff and Germany, not between plaintiff and defendant. And think about the impact of the release on her desire to ferret out *The Chrysalis*, Your Honor—if you've already been paid for a painting and you've released your rights to it, would you really invest a lot of time and energy searching for it?"

Mara filled in the broad outlines of her argument with the finer points of the law for nearly an hour. Exhausted, she finished and sat down to give the plaintiff a chance to reply.

Hilda Baum's ancient attorney struggled to stand up and then hobbled over to the podium. For a moment, his seeming frailness buoyed Mara's spirits. Until he spoke.

"Well, well, well, Your Honor. It seems that the defendant, Beazley's, wants to make my client, Hilda Baum, a victim of the Nazis once again," he declared, his voice surprisingly strong and commanding. "Let's see what Beazley's is asking Ms. Baum to give up."

He lifted his hand to signal a colleague, and the lights dimmed in the courtroom. He made another gesture, and new images appeared on the screen: the photographs of the young Hilda Baum and her parents, surrounded by art. "Your Honor, I think you'll agree that Beazley's is asking Ms. Baum to surrender more than just the painting you see on the wall of her family home. Beazley's is demanding Ms. Baum relinquish the only keepsake she may ever have of her parents."

He then launched into a response anticipated by Mara: strident claims that a gap in the title existed, which "proved" that the Nazis took the painting from Erich Baum's aunt in Nice. Desperate assertions that *Scaife* applied, and even if it didn't, *DeClerck* said a claimant must undertake a sensible investigation to find the painting—not an exhaustive one—and that Hilda Baum's quest, limited as it was to Europe and Russia through the 1950s, sufficed. Tortured arguments that the German Art Restitution

Commission release signed in the Netherlands did not apply in the United States or to Beazley's, and finally, heart-wrenching pleas to return *The Chrysalis*.

Mara stood up and took her last turn at the podium. She inhaled deeply and delivered an impromptu speech, an attempt to defuse the empathetic images imprinted onto the courtroom by Hilda Baum's counsel. The remainder of her extemporaneous reply was easier, as she had predicted the bulk of the plaintiff's legal argument. Then she rested.

The courtroom held its collective breath as Justice Weir pulled himself up to his full height, such as it was, and prepared to speak. He was known for delivering a forerunner of his final opinion at argument's end. "Ms. Coyne, I will not deny that I entered the courtroom today firm in my conviction that Beazley's motion for summary judgment should be denied, and certainly Ms. Baum's attorney made a persuasive presentation to that end. However, your argument, which took your written words to a higher plane, has caused me to question that conviction. My clerks and I will have work to do before I render judgment."

As the judge droned on about the procedures and timing—it would be three to four weeks—surrounding his decision, she averted her face from Harlan. Regardless of the judge's favorable forecast, she knew that Harlan would be furious; her argument deviated from the approved script. Not to mention Michael's reaction. Worse, it actually played to the sympathetic nature of Hilda Baum's loss, something they had worked hard to avoid. Yet, in that split second before she began her argument, Nana, the Schwarzes, the Sterns, the Blumers, and all the others like them loomed before her, and Mara felt compelled to make room for her conscience amid all her professional maneuverings.

But she was wrong. Once the judge finished and they all rose for his exit, Harlan slapped her on the back. "You had me scared there for a minute, Mara, with that new opening and all. But you really turned this thing on its head. Nice job, using the natural sympathy for the plaintiff as a weapon against her."

A wave of nausea assaulted Mara. She had expressed an empathy that any normal human being would experience in the face of Holocaust tragedies, and Harlan assumed she had simply been exploiting the plaintiff's plight. She could understand his fury at her script deviation, but she could not comprehend his utter lack of compassion for the people underlying the case. He seemed devoid of natural emotion altogether.

Watching Mara falter, Michael diverted the conversation. "I believe a congratulatory drink is in order."

The motley threesome ambled over to O'Neal's, the famous courthouse watering hole. Secure at a table near the bar, the three recapped the day's events. Their analysis of Mara's argument relaxed her. Harlan was well pleased. So was Michael. She tried to let her courtroom victory, with its attendant prizes, triumph over her disgust at Harlan's reaction.

A voice bellowed across the bar, directed at Harlan. "Hey, you old scoundrel, is that you?"

Harlan hoisted himself up and waddled off, greeting with surprising warmth an old colleague or adversary—Mara and Michael could not tell which. But as Mara watched him shuffle across the room, she saw the chubby young boy desperate for friends behind the self-protective adult heft. Lonely then by stigma, lonely now by choice, marrying work rather than a wife, and spawning cases and money rather than a family. For the first time, Mara felt sorry for him and understood why he was so closed off to any emotion.

Michael murmured, "May I invite you back to my place for dinner tonight? It's just a warm-up—I have a real celebration planned for tomorrow evening." He drew circles on her knee.

She couldn't suppress a little intake of breath, and she looked around to make sure Harlan had not seen the gesture. "I'd like that."

"Why don't you give me a few hours after we wrap this up? Do you want to meet at my place at eight?"

"Sure," she whispered, as Harlan returned to the table. After a few more drinks, Mara and Michael made their way to separate cabs, back to their own offices, keeping alive the subterfuge.

seventeen

HAARLEM, 1658

THE NEW PARTNERSHIP OF VAN MAES AND MIEREVELD CANNOT keep up with the blaze of commissions. The craze for their portraits has spread among the town's wealthy burghers, with the burgomaster's imprimatur fanning the flames.

The enterprise doubles its work as it serves two distinct clientele: those who ask for Master Van Maes and those who request Master Miereveld. This suits the master just fine; he continues to drown his grief in labor. For those subjects who seek a traditional likeness, with a simple composition and a few symbolic props conveying the message dictated by the customer, Master Van Maes is unparalleled. For those willing to surrender the conventional, Master Miereveld paints like no other. He uses a dramatic chiaroscuro, so Calvinist in its depiction of the irreconcilable nature of light and dark, heaven and earth, the likes of which few have attempted before. Johannes works without a set framework; he varies brushstroke and combines different composition types—a customary portrayal inside a genre painting, a still life containing a portrait, an architectural view surrounding a subject—to tell poignant stories about the essence of his sitters, and he never allows his subjects to script the outcome.

The master, having long ago fired Hendrick, lets Lukens and Leonaert go as well. Neither has learned to tolerate Johannes's new status. At Johannes's insistence, Pieter Steenwyck joins the partnership as an equal of sorts. More than a journeyman, though not yet an official master, he serves in all capacities: assistant, painter, manager, and comrade—to Johannes, at least.

The master tutors the friends in the business of art. The Guild of Saint Luke, he explains, must be appeased because it controls the art market. Membership and good standing are necessary to sell. Portraits should be the venture's focus because they publicize one's name in social milieus and promote careers. Genre paintings and architectural interiors are fine, and should be undertaken upon request, but they do not garner the same exposure as portraits. Religious paintings must be avoided at all costs, not just because the pictures themselves sin against God but also because they alienate clients of the true faith.

Free from his apprenticeship, Johannes finally has the liberty to travel to his parents, but the commissions are too many and the distance is too great. Instead, his few visits grow scant and then stop. Over the years, the master becomes father as well as partner, and Pieter becomes brother as well as colleague. A family and an enterprise grow together.

As the burgomaster's darlings, the Masters Van Maes and Miereveld, sometimes with Pieter in tow, attend banquets and balls, entertain visits by cultivated gentlemen on connoisseurs' tours of preeminent studios, and regale fellow guild members with insiders' tales of the courtly life in exchange for ribald marketplace gossip. Days are spent in the studio and evenings building business. Only in the late-night hours, when lips are loosened by wine, does the master lament the lost beauty of his young bride and the wasted promise of his infant son. Otherwise, the years pass by idyllically.

Then the master dies, and like orphans, Johannes and Pieter unravel in their sorrow. They leave commissions unfinished, supply accounts unpaid, and guild duties untended. The master's extensive holdings, his family home, its luxurious appointments, his inventory of paintings, even his library of engravings used by Johannes and Pieter for training, are auctioned off to pay wine merchant bills and gambling debts—part of the master's secret nightlife of mourning. Clients tending toward Master Van Maes's portraits go elsewhere, and even those favoring Johannes's innovative style chase other, less beleaguered artists. The studio fails.

The enterprise maintains precarious solvency thanks to the largesse of one wealthy patron, the linen merchant Carl Jantzen. He floats the venture, lending money and making advances for future commissions in exchange for preemptive rights over Johannes's output, though he dares not dictate the nature of all of Johannes's pieces. And so Johannes carries on, making painting after painting that are seen by no one but Jantzen and circulated nowhere but Jantzen's private *saal*. The patron is equal measures curse and blessing.

Johannes pores over the account books, drawing on the master's commercial tutelage in an effort to gather enough guilders together to purchase costly pigments and hairs for brushes. He trims all fat, letting journeymen and apprentices go, keeping only himself and Pieter to maintain the studio of Van Maes and Miereveld, a title Johannes continues to use in honor of the master.

As he balances the ledger again and again, hoping to see numbers overlooked and pathways to more projects, Pieter rushes into the studio, throwing open the door with a slam. "What say you to a commission?" he exclaims.

"Another Jantzen commission?" Johannes replies, without even lifting his eyes from the page. He will welcome the money but knows it will never garner more clients.

"No."

"Who, then?"

"A commission from a new client."

"Who?"

"The new burgomaster."

Johannes looks up in wonder, and Pieter greets him with a smirk.

"The new burgomaster? Come now, Pieter." Johannes grows impatient with his teasing.

"Yes, Johannes, the burgomaster Brecht."

The two men grin at each other in amazement and relief. As they wander off in search of an inn still open to share a *pasglas*, they speculate about how they were selected. A painting for the new burgomaster would have widespread exposure, and praise from the official would yield com-missions from his elite and monied circle. Jantzen would not dare exercise his preemptive rights to the painting; his linen venture depends on the burgomaster's support as well. Perhaps the purgatory of Masters Van Maes and Miereveld is ending.

eighteen
NEW YORK CITY, PRESENT DAY

THE NEXT DAY, MARA SNEAKED OUT OF WORK EARLY TO stroll through Central Park before meeting Michael for the evening he had planned in honor of the anticipated success. They were to have dinner at Daniel followed by the Metropolitan Opera's *Madame Butterfly*. Too apropos to pass up, Michael had said.

Mara floated through the park. For the past twenty-four hours, she had been walking on wispy clouds filled with dreams of a future with Michael and a successful career at Severin. Spring had arrived early this year and left in its wake a kaleidoscopic wash of green buds, blooming tulip tips, daffodils, hyacinths, and the scent of new chances. Throngs of cooped-up New Yorkers responded to the siren call and, despite the lingering chill, filled the park.

Mara made her way to Beazley's, where she registered in the lobby and hailed one of the security guards she'd grown to know. Larry was a former New York City cop, and he always regaled Mara with tidbits of local gossip and renditions of Sinatra tunes as he rode the elevator with her to the twenty-fourth floor. Mara loved it; he reminded her of her great-uncles, men whose brogues and unpolished ways had caused her father no end of embarrassment but whose warmth Mara had always adored.

Michael's assistant, Hannah, took over from Larry when the elevator opened and escorted Mara back to Michael's office. In her typically formal manner, Hannah explained that a meeting outside the office had detained Michael.

"He asked me to have you wait in his office. He plans on meeting you back here no later than seven thirty, in advance of your eight o'clock engagement." Hannah's voice carried no hint of innuendo. Mara wondered what Hannah really knew or suspected about her relationship with Michael. She was just too efficient to be oblivious but too professional to be suggestive.

Mara looked down at her watch; it was only 6:00. She and Michael wouldn't make dinner before the opera, so she'd just have to entertain herself in his office until he arrived. "That's fine, Hannah. I have plenty of calls to return and papers to review in the meantime."

"Can I get you a cup of tea while you're waiting? If I recall correctly, Earl Grey with lemon?"

"Thanks so much, Hannah. That'd be perfect."

Mara relaxed on Michael's couch with her steaming cup of tea. For an hour or so, she returned phone calls and reviewed some research a junior associate had prepared for her. But she grew restless and wandered over to Michael's desk.

She was a snoop at heart. Even as a child, Mara had carefully unwrapped, and then rewrapped, her Christmas gifts weeks before Santa's arrival just so she could begin dreaming about the treasures. Her father still joked that it was this instinct to unearth secrets that made her a successful lawyer. It was the same impulse that had propelled Mara to spend long evenings puzzling out whodunits with her grandmother and to devote long days in college to piecing together medieval mysteries. So when she started looking through Michael's papers and his calendar, she did so casually, almost unconsciously. Her fingers lifted and sifted, not looking for anything in particular but curious about what she could learn. Or at least that was what she told herself—though, if she were being very honest, she wanted to uncover more about Michael's life before and outside her, particularly since he divulged so much less than she in their late-night confessionals.

Sitting in his chair, she hit a button on his computer, and his e-mail screen popped up. Mara knew she should exit the screen, but she could not resist. After all, she rationalized to herself, it was just a list of e-mail headers. For the most part, the subject lines were clipped and official, and Mara's attention wandered as she mused on the differences between the businessman Michael and the Michael with whom she spent her nights. As she delved further and poked around in the e-mail texts, a very shrewd, methodical Michael emerged.

Suddenly, an e-mail folder with the subject "Baum SJ Briefs" snared her attention. She clicked it open and read the e-mails from the bottom of the chain to the top, her curiosity piqued particularly since it contained e-mails from Philip. Now her actions were much more deliberate and self-serving: She was consciously looking for compliments.

TO: Michael Roarke
FROM: Philip Robichaux
RE: FW: Baum Summary Judgment Briefs

I read the summary judgment briefs. It seems your pretty little friend can be quite the clever lawyer when she is persuaded to adopt the right frame of mind. Nice work—your uncle would be proud. I assume the actual papers are safe and sound?

TO: Philip Robichaux
FROM: Michael Roarke
RE: FW: Baum Summary Judgment Briefs

Under lock and key in St. Peter's own hands.

TO: Michael Roarke

FROM: Philip Robichaux

RE: FW: Baum Summary Judgment Briefs

Your dedication to the task has not gone unnoticed. I almost wish that I had kept the courting for myself, though. Why don't you arrange for one more of those romantic dinners? After all, we still have to wait for the judge to rule on the summary judgment motion. There may be more work for her to do if he doesn't issue the opinion we're hoping for.

TO: Philip Robichaux

FROM: Michael Roarke

RE: FW: Baum Summary Judgment Briefs

A good idea. I am thinking about a night at the opera.

TO: Michael Roarke

FROM: Philip Robichaux

RE: FW: Baum Summary Judgment Briefs

Keep me posted.

Mara froze. She read the e-mails over and over, and her mind raced through the possible interpretations. But only one seemed to fit.

The door behind her creaked open. Mara swiveled around in Michael's chair to find Hannah looming in the doorway. Mara blocked the computer screen, hoping that Hannah hadn't witnessed her prying, but Hannah seemed her usual imperturbable self.

"Michael just called. He's running extremely late and won't have time to meet you here. He wants me to apologize and to request that you meet him under the red Chagall at seven fifty. Does that make sense?"

"Yes, it does. Thanks, Hannah. I'll just pack up my things and head over there now." Mara prayed that Hannah couldn't hear her heart hammering.

Hannah shut Michael's office door. Mara pivoted back to the screen and hit Print.

nineteen

NEW YORK CITY, PRESENT DAY

MARA COULD NOT REMEMBER MAKING HER WAY TO LIN-coln Center, greeting Michael, locating their seats, watching the opera house's famous rock-candy crystal chandeliers rise, or listening to the melodic strains of Puccini. *Son venuta al richiamo d'amor.* She could see and feel and hear only the roar of questions in her own head.

A surge of emotions accompanied the roar. At first, she wanted to rage at Michael, confront him with her suspicions, and physically hurt him. But her fury faded away in place of shame, as she began to feel that every-one around her must know her secret. She must somehow bear the mark of her naïveté, her foolish, unknowing participation in Michael's decep-tion. She looked down at her hands. She saw that they clapped, just like everyone else's. She felt the fingers touch. But there was no sound.

As the crowd rose, she did, too. She could almost see herself through another's eyes, following Michael's lead and Michael's smile and touching Michael's hand as they exited through the throngs. Oh God, touching Michael's hand. Why were the people around her not staring? Worst of all, what would her grandmother think?

She must have allowed herself to be led into the cab. For, with a jolt, she came back into herself, just as Michael leaned toward her with a kiss and they approached her building. She recoiled, winding herself into the corner of the cab. His eyes anticipated the usual invitation upstairs, but Mara quickly muttered something about not feeling well and rushed inside.

Once upstairs, her door bolted shut, Mara reached into her fridge for a bottle of white wine. She knew that she really shouldn't, that she needed to remain clearheaded. But her confusion and pain were too much to bear. Hands shaking, she poured a second glass, and a third.

She awakened hours later on the couch, with a bone-dry bottle on the coffee table. For a moment, her consciousness was free of the specter of the e-mails, but when it rushed at her in a deluge, she returned to the fridge again and opened a new bottle, the pit in her stomach growing. Just one glass to take the edge off, she told herself. Then she could face it. Then she could decide what to do. But, of course, it wasn't the one glass.

It was still dark. She proceeded with her normal motions, washing her face, brushing her teeth and hair, changing into pajamas. She padded back to the family room, picked up the half-empty bottle, and poured the rest of it into a tall glass. She downed a good portion of the wine, crawled into bed, and, as she flicked through the channels, finished off the rest.

Early the next afternoon, she returned to herself. Foggy, but strong enough not to head back to the fridge, she checked into her impersonation of a life and reviewed her messages. At work, all seemed under control — just a few voice mails from legal assistants and junior associates, all excuses to let her know that they were working on Saturday.

At home, it was different. On Saturday morning, her father called on the return leg of a business trip, checking to see if she had reigned victorious on her summary judgment argument. Michael called three times to see how she was feeling. The pit in her stomach expanded. She had never once heard the phone ring.

Mara called Sophia and arranged to have an early dinner with her, even going so far as to suggest that she had an important issue to discuss. Sophia's curiosity would keep Mara focused and hopefully spark the anger that had diminished in favor of shame the night before. She needed to get herself into a more active mode. If what she was thinking were true, then she had been played for a fool, her professional authority taken advantage of, and her emotional vulnerability mocked. At the moment, she was still stunned and incredulous, but she needed Sophia to help her get her strength back so she could act.

Finally, she tried Michael. Thank God, she got his voice mail and could elaborate on her illness to explain her behavior. She told him she was heading back to bed for the day. He had plans to leave for Paris the next day, and she needed to buy herself as much time as she could.

Then Mara lined her stomach with a bagel and headed out for a punishing run. She showered, poured herself a cup of coffee, and removed the documents from her bag. Her hands trembled, but whether it was from the booze or the e-mails, she didn't know. She handled the papers with care and laid them out on the dining room table. Deliberately, she slowed her breath.

Maybe she'd misread them and jumped to conclusions. She carefully studied the printouts. But once again, it was clear that there was no other interpretation to make. The documents Michael had given her to prove the airtight nature of *The Chrysalis* provenance were false. "Actual papers" existed that told a different story. Although Mara did not know the exact details of this story, she knew that somehow her legal attacks on Hilda Baum's claim, her skillful, calculated undermining of the old woman's emotional appeal, had been based on lies. Most damning and humiliating of all, Michael had used Mara as his pawn and exploited her—blinded her vision with the pink clouds of their relationship—to ensure his victory. All of this duplicity and subterfuge to dupe a victim of the Holocaust. What game did Michael play? She assumed the Saint Peter of Michael's e-mails was the Saint Peter of Michael's office sketches, but what was Saint Peter holding "under lock and key"? She had to find out.

Mara sealed the e-mails in a bag and headed off to meet Sophia. She clenched her fist so tightly around the strap that welts formed on her palm. As she worked her way up Third Avenue, the doorways of numerous bars reminded her how she wanted to drown out the emotions starting to emerge from her night of anesthetization, the feelings of rage at Michael's abuse of her and devastation at the wound to her heart and her pride. She tried to focus her mind on uncovering Saint Peter's secret, on the practical steps she could take to rectify the damage done, but she kept coming back to the fact that whatever Michael had done, he had done with her oblivious help.

Mara arrived at the designated diner, sank deep into the worn crimson leather of her favorite booth, ordered a large coffee instead of the Greek wine she so desperately wanted, and waited for Sophia. She watched the clock tick with growing desperation. Of all the times for Sophia to be late.

After a seeming eternity, Mara saw Sophia round the corner toward the diner. She exhaled. Her friend walked in, and Mara rose to give her a hug and a kiss on the cheek. They faced each other in the booth, and Mara felt as if the past day had been a dream. Maybe she could slip back to her reality, no matter how ill-fitting it had become, and forget it all. After expunging Michael from her life, of course.

"So, what's going on? You sounded so mysterious on the phone."

Mara burst into tears.

She pushed aside Sophia's outstretched arms of consolation and dashed to the bathroom. There, in the corner of the coolly tiled room, she sank back on her haunches and let herself sob at the thought of Michael's deception, at her complicity, at the damage they had inflicted on Hilda Baum and all the others like her, at her own selfishness at even caring about Michael in light of the magnitude of their acts, at all of it.

When she recovered her breath, she ran her hands under the cold water and pressed them onto her eyes. She tucked her hair behind her ears and walked back to the booth with as much confidence as she could muster, even painting on a tiny smile. But Sophia was not to be deceived.

"Don't bullshit me, Mara, with that smile. What the hell has happened?" Sophia looked ready to fight, prepared to take on whatever, whoever had caused her stalwart friend such pain.

Mara reached into her purse and spread out the evidence for Sophia.

twenty

NEW YORK CITY, PRESENT DAY

THE NEXT DAY, MARA'S HEART QUICKENED WITH EACH AD-
vancing step as she strode to the front desk of Beazley's. She made a
point of giving Larry a little wave and a wide smile.

"Good evening. May I help you?" the receptionist cooed from her lair.
Though Mara had visited Beazley's more times than she could count, the
receptionist always behaved as though it were her first time.

"Yes, my name's Mara Coyne. I've an appointment to collect some
items from Michael Roarke's office."

"Certainly. Let me just ring his assistant."

An interminable pause followed, and a river of sweat poured down
Mara's back. She was never so thankful to be wearing black.

"Ms. Coyne, Mr. Roarke's assistant doesn't have you listed as an appointment in his calendar, and she says that he's traveling outside the

country at the moment." The receptionist held her hand over the phone's mouthpiece.

Mara prayed her voice would not quiver. "Oh, I'm aware of that," she answered in as haughty a tone as she could muster. "Michael actually left a box of documents for me to look through in his absence." She hoped that her use of the informal "Michael" would smooth the way.

"I see." The receptionist sounded skeptical. "Let me just check with Ms. McCordle." Another endless wait, with indecipherable whispering.

Gesturing to the elevators, the receptionist granted Mara a begrudging leave to enter. "Please go right up. Ms. McCordle will meet you at the elevator bank and escort you to Mr. Roarke's office."

Mara stopped a moment at Larry's desk for their routine exchange. His eyes twinkled. "Can I give a pretty girl a lift?"

"Sir, it would be my pleasure." Mara curtsied.

Mara maintained her composure and kept a lighthearted banter going with Larry on the ride up, but when the elevator doors opened onto Hannah's mirthless face, her fragile confidence faltered. Larry gave Mara a grandfatherly pat on the shoulder and handed her over.

Mara launched into her rehearsed speech, ignoring the shakiness of her voice. "Hannah, I'm sorry I've arrived unannounced. I just assumed Michael would've told you that I'd be over to look through the documents he left for me."

"Please, Ms. Coyne, it's no trouble at all. I just wanted to be sure you knew that Mr. Roarke wasn't here, that he'd be out for several days traveling in Paris. Of course, if he left some documents to look through, I'll lead you directly to his office." She was as unflappable as always.

With her key, Hannah opened Michael's office. "Shall I get you a cup of tea to sip on while you work?"

"How thoughtful of you. That'd be wonderful, Hannah. Thank you." As Hannah closed the door behind her, Mara unsealed the box she had asked Michael to leave for her when she called him in the evening after talking with Sophia and planning this exploratory visit to his office. She didn't mention she would be reviewing it right there in his office, but at least there was a box for her. As soon as the box was open and the papers spread out, Mara began scanning the wall that displayed Michael's sketches of Saint Peter, a study on a single subject, a muscular man draped in timeless robes with the outline of a key in his hand. The sketches had never drawn her in before; although exquisite, they were minute and monochromatic, not designed to lure the viewer. Even now, she was not inclined to admire the skill of their design, just what they were hiding.

Moments later, Hannah knocked. Mara, deep in the soft suede of Michael's couch, signaled for her to enter. As Hannah set up the tea tray, resplendent with a vase of roses and some miniature, exquisitely crafted cookies, she apologized. "Ms. Coyne, I have to leave within the half hour. Had I known you would be here, I would've made other arrangements. Will you be all right? Do you need anything further from me?"

Mara couldn't believe her luck. She had thought she would have to search under Hannah's watchful eye. To be allowed free rein of Michael's office was more than Mara had dreamed.

Mara contained her euphoria. "Thank you so much, Hannah. I'll be fine. I just need a bit of time to review these documents, then I'll be off. Do you need me to lock up or anything before I go?"

"Actually, if I could leave Mr. Roarke's keys with you to lock his door behind you, that would make me feel much more comfortable. I'd hate to think that his sketches would be accessible all evening."

Mara cast another, furtive look at the sketches. Regaining her composure, she said, "I'd be happy to. Will you show me how?"

Hannah instructed Mara on the wiles of Beazley's archaic lock system, then entrusted the keys to her possession. Hannah requested that Mara return the keys to their carefully hidden spot, a false drawer beneath her desk. Then she left Mara alone.

Mara spent the next half hour pretending to look busy, poring through meaningless documents, arranging them in equally useless piles, pushing from her mind the admonitory words her father would surely utter if he knew what she was up to. She eyed the sketches on the wall, knowing in her gut that somewhere, somehow they hid the treasure trove. She willed her heart to stop racing and the sweat to stop pouring in time to wish Hannah a respectable farewell.

Once Hannah left at 5:30, Mara thought it wise to wait an additional half hour to let the rest of the office depart, but the clock's hands dragged around its face. At 6:04 precisely, Mara made her rounds. Key tucked in her hand, she left Michael's office, closing but not shutting his door. She meandered, as if she were deep in thought, to the ladies' room, which was typically Beazley's: decorated with glowing pink cherubs and the most ornately bedecked chaise longues that Mara had ever seen.

Office by office, assistant's station by assistant's station, Mara checked to make sure that everyone was gone. Like clockwork, the employees all had vanished.

She hurried back to Michael's office. This time, she tightened the door behind her and dashed over to the five sketches. The four smallest sketches were arranged in a square, surrounding the largest like a frame. Mara feared that one of Beazley's famed security systems might protect the sketches, so she lowered the first of the four small sketches from its wall mounting very slowly. No alarm sounded—at least, none that she could hear. There was nothing behind the sketch but wallpaper. Mara breathed a sigh full of both relief and disappointment. Not sure exactly what she was looking for, she patted down the back of the sketch before she replaced it on the wall. It was clear to the touch that the framing was not hiding anything. Mara followed this same protocol for each of the four small sketches and found nothing.

Just as she sized up the fifth, larger central sketch, the door flung open. Mara squealed.

It was Larry. "Hey there, doll, sorry to scare you. What're you still doing here?"

"Larry, it's me who's sorry. For screaming like that."

"Don't worry, Miss Coyne. I was just doing my usual rounds when I heard some noises in here and, knowing that Mr. Roarke is away and all, had to pop in and check."

"My apologies. Should I have called down to security to let you know I'm still here working?"

"No, no. You're fine. You going to go home anytime soon, though? Shouldn't you be letting some nice young man take you out to dinner?"

"Larry, you're sweet. I do have dinner plans later, with one of my girl-friends. But I have something I have to finish up here first."

"You young lawyers. All work, no play these days. Well, I'll let you get to it. Give me a holler if you need anything."

"Thanks so much, Larry. I'll do that."

He closed the door behind himself. Mara sank into the couch, breathing as if she'd just run a marathon. She was unsure if she had the courage to go through with her search, so she looked for fortification from the e-mails in her briefcase.

After waiting a suitable amount of time, Mara made the sign of the cross and offered a silent prayer of intercession to Nana. Then she carefully lifted the fifth sketch off its hook. This time, instead of wallpaper, she found a safe built into the wall.

Now what should she do? Safecracking skills were hardly part of the typical law school curriculum. This one looked pretty straightforward, like those she had seen in movies, so she tried out a few combinations. Michael's birthday, her birthday, the date of Beazley's founding, but nothing happened.

Mara scoured the room looking for clues. She rummaged through Michael's drawers, his shelves, and his in-box. They yielded no secrets and only confirmed Michael's meticulous organization. His calendar proved more promising. She made a list of his family members' birthdays, including the date of a memorial service for Michael's uncle Edward—the one referred to by Philip—and tried them out on the safe. Still nothing happened.

Frustrated, Mara sat in Michael's chair and scrutinized the sketches from the vantage point of his desk. Maybe the code related to Saint Peter rather than something personal to Michael. She grabbed art history reference books off the shelves and recorded Saint Peter's celebrated dates to test them out. The safe refused to budge.

Stymied, Mara peered again at the sketches. Suddenly, she remembered a late-night conversation she and Michael once had about their Catholic upbringing with its attendant study of saints' lives and recalled that Michael's favorite was indeed Saint Peter, because he had formed the foundation upon which the Church was built. It triggered a memory from all the nights spent studying saints' lives with her grandmother: the biblical quote commonly associated with Saint Peter's keys and the formation of the Church. She grabbed an antique Bible off Michael's shelf and began poring through it. There it was: "You are Peter, and upon this Rock I will build my church, and the gates of the netherworld shall not prevail against it. I will give you the keys of the kingdom of Heaven. Whatever you bind on earth shall be bound in Heaven, and whatever you loose on earth will be loosed in Heaven." Matthew, 16:18–19.

She tried the numbers. Saint Peter had it "under lock and key" after all.

Mara reached into the safe, hands shaking. She slid out two large, unsealed manila envelopes. The first contained the will of Michael's uncle Edward Roarke—his great-uncle, as it turned out. The will named Michael as the sole beneficiary of Edward's rather substantial estate. It looked like traditional investments, the apartment in which Michael lived, and an impressive art collection, of which the sketches formed a part.

Mara examined the second envelope; it was directed to Michael, with Edward Roarke as the return addressee. It held a stack of aged documents, curling and frayed at the edges. The very first yellowed page looked almost identical to the copy of *The Chrysalis* purchase document Lillian had given her, even the same handwritten "September 20, 1944," in the upper right-hand corner. But one critical line was different: The name of the individual who had sold *The Chrysalis* to Beazley's was listed not as Albert Boettcher & Company but as Kurt Strasser.

Who was Kurt Strasser? Mara didn't recall his name from either her research or her sessions with Lillian. Whoever he was, his name instilled such fear, such worry, that someone—Michael, his great-uncle Edward, or Philip—wanted to eliminate it from the provenance. Perhaps keeping Strasser secret was an unspoken pact Michael had made with Edward in exchange for the inheritance. But why?

Mara continued to look through the yellowed pages as she thought, and there was more. It appeared that *The Chrysalis* was hardly alone. In 1943 and 1944, Kurt Strasser sold twenty-four paintings to Beazley's. Whatever the nature of the deception Mara had fallen victim to, it appeared that Beazley's had purchased and sold many paintings somehow tainted by Kurt Strasser's ownership—and that Michael was using Mara to cover it up.

twenty-one

NEW YORK CITY, PRESENT DAY

THE FRIENDS SAT IN SILENCE WITH A SECOND BOTTLE OF chardonnay between them. Sophia, known for her abstinence, joined Mara this time and chugged glass after glass. The evidence of their immoderation upset the equilibrium of Sophia's stark, nearly sterile apartment, where, unlike Mara's, even the concealed places were subject to merciless order. Tonight, however, Sophia ignored the empty bottle, crumpled napkins, and bowls of half-eaten pasta. Both women were focused on the purloined documents spread out before them.

Sophia shook her head. "Oh my God, I still can't believe you took these. This is not what we talked about, Mara. We specifically agreed that you'd go in there and look around—nothing more. What if you'd gotten caught?" The wine turned Sophia's wrath into mere terror. Just an hour before, she had raged at Mara for taking the documents from Michael's office. But Mara had known from the start that the strict, ambitious Sophia would never sanction the risk.

"Sophia, we've been through this before. I had no choice. Without these papers, I can't begin to understand what scheme Michael's involved in to hide this Strasser information and why he used me. I couldn't leave the documents there—I'd lose whatever leverage I have in Michael's game." Even saying the words aloud made Mara furious again, at the injury done to her pride and the damage done to the Baums and others like them.

"But, Mara, what are you going to do when Michael finds out you've stolen the papers from his safe? It's only a matter of time."

"I'll replace them before he discovers they're gone, I hope. He won't be back from Europe for a few days. In the meantime, I need them to investigate what he's really up to—and why he felt the need to use me like some kind of insurance policy." Mara wondered what had happened to the righteousness Sophia had felt on Mara's behalf on Sunday evening; it seemed to have disappeared. To be sure, it had been preceded by her anger over "the stupidity" of Mara's relationship with Michael, but Sophia had softened and even helped Mara plan her search of Michael's office. When Mara arrived unannounced at Sophia's apartment earlier in the evening, loot in hand, she harbored no illusions that Sophia would condone the extent of her search, but she was astonished that the damning documents did not make her friend more supportive.

"What do you mean by 'investigate' what Michael's up to?" Sophia asked, her tone sharp.

"I have to learn who Kurt Strasser is, or was, so I can appreciate what Michael's trying to hide. That means taking advantage of his absence and going back to Beazley's library to do some research."

"Mara, how do you know he doesn't have a perfectly good reason for keeping these papers tucked away?"

"I don't, and believe me, I hope he does. But I can't leave it to his word."

Sophia stood up, a little wobbly from the wine. She pleaded, "Mara, please forget about this nonsense. Return the documents before he notices they're gone and put this behind you. Please focus on what's important: yourself and your career." Mara silently added the words Sophia did not utter, the plea to consider Sophia's career, too; it was all too clear to her that Sophia was alarmed at how Mara's actions might reflect on her as well.

"Fee, I can't do that. I can't pretend this hasn't happened. Uncovering all this may be more important than winning the case and advancing my career." Curious, Mara thought, how comfortable she felt now that she had a clear line of principles to follow, how at peace she was with stepping off the path she had followed for so long. It was a thorny mantle, but it fit much better than the cloak of success. Her father would rankle, but her grandmother would be proud.

Sophia stared at Mara as if she had grown unrecognizable. "Then, Mara, I can't help you. I can't watch you destroy all that you've worked for. You're on your own."

Sophia retired to her bedroom. Without intending to, Mara fell asleep on the couch, utterly spent. She awakened in a sweat, remembering restless dreams.

===

THE NEXT EVENING, MARA EXITED THE ELEVATOR AT BEAZ-ley's. She did not feel at all nervous. She sensed the adrenaline pumping through her veins, but its speed was almost a relief after the endless day of feigning composure at the office. She advanced down the first hallway, already darkened for the evening, but so familiar that she could see without the light. Turning left, she spotted the guards in the distance. Coming closer, she forced herself to smile.

"Hey, guys, how're you doing tonight?" she greeted the men.

The guards looked up from their steaming cups of coffee and deeply layered pizza, astonished to see her, surprised to see anyone after 6:00 P.M. Her favorite, the jolly Santa-faced one with the long white beard whose name she could never remember, replied, "We're doing fine down here. What brings you to our neck of the woods so late at night?"

She attempted humor. "Late? You guys know that this isn't late for lawyers—I wish it were. Nope, some court ordered me to gather up more information. Sorry about that."

The jolly one retorted, "Nothin' to be sorry about. We're always glad to see your pretty face, Miss Coyne. We're just sorry you have to spend your nights poking around through some dusty old papers." She waited to see if they would let her in. "Come on, we'll get you in there."

Still chewing on a big bite of pizza, the other one—Tommy she thought his name was—hoisted himself out of his seat, wiped his greasy hand on his pants, and lumbered over to the door with the keys jingling in hand. Mara winced; Tommy was more of an adherent to the rules. She had been banking that Santa would unlock the door for her.

After he unbolted the door, she fluttered her eyelashes and asked, "Oh, I might need to have a few documents copied tonight. Would you mind unlocking the back door for me, too?" It was her entrée to the document room.

Tommy glanced back at his fellow guard. "You know, you're supposed to have a research staff person with you to do that."

"Oh, you're right. Shoot. I'm sure they're all gone by now."

Santa yelled over. "What the hell, Tommy, we know her by now. Let her in. Don't be a stickler." Waves of guilt engulfed Mara. She hadn't thought through the trouble these guys would get into if she were caught. But it was too late to go back.

She nodded at Santa. "Thanks." Then, at Tommy, "Thanks to both of you. I really appreciate it."

Mara trailed after the rotund guard into the library, trying her best to look nonchalant as he painstakingly opened the door to the document room. "We'll be right out here if you need anything."

Knowing her time was limited, and that the guards would keep the front door ajar the entire time, she proceeded to work. She ignored the beauty of the library and focused on PROVID.

Using Lillian's password, she logged onto PROVID, clicked the World War II icon, and combed category after category for references to Strasser: French archives, records from the Germans, Dutch files, and papers from the United States War Department. She tried permutation after permutation of searches. Nothing. Nothing. Nothing. Nothing. The hands raced around the face of the clock.

Before she quit PROVID, Mara hunted down whatever she could about Beazley's other purchases from Kurt Strasser. Having listened carefully to Lillian, Mara flew through the categories. She entered each painting's title into the myriad of categories: archival documents, sale catalogs, bills of sale, museum provenance files, indexes to public collections, governmental records, and collectors' files. When the title didn't yield any answers, she moved on to the artwork's other attributes: artist, subject matter, and time period. Results poured in, but she had to hurry, so she printed them without reading them.

Gathering up her papers, she crept to the document room, hoping not to draw attention to herself. She left the door open a crack and hurried to the climate-controlled inner sanctum of the room, to the direction Lillian had gestured when she made a veiled reference to classified documents. Opening the tightly sealed glass door, Mara noted that the air was very thin. She would have to work fast.

She hastened to the back wall, where several sturdy-looking wooden boxes were stored. She opened them up and sifted through their contents; they did indeed contain World War II papers. She scouted for documents from the United States Office of Strategic Services' Art Looting Investigation Unit in particular. The unit often prepared dossiers on various individuals; she trusted these would provide a quick answer. As she reviewed page after page, her rapid-fire reading skills came in handy and permitted her to scan for Strasser's name without getting bogged down in all the other information.

The stack of boxes containing no references to Strasser grew. There were only two unopened ones left, and Mara was disheartened. Even more, she worried how she'd explain her actions, her criminal acts really, if she got caught—especially without the damning evidence against Michael she had hoped to find. And what if she were wrong about Michael's actions? She played out different repercussions in her mind— firing, disbarment, and an indictment. What would her father say? Her grandmother? Michael? Harlan? With effort, she purged all their voices from her head and refocused her attention.

And then she found it: a transcript, from the United States Art Looting Investigation Unit, of the interrogation of Kurt Strasser.

Cross-legged on the floor, she scanned the transcript. At the start, the American soldiers from the Art Looting Investigation Unit asked Strasser seemingly routine questions about countless people, artists, paintings, and sculptures. Then the soldiers began asking Strasser about his work as a wartime art dealer.

Q: Where did you get the paintings we found in your shop? The Degas portrait, the two Corot drawings, the Sisley, and the Monet still life?

A: I told you, clients sold them to me.

Q: Clients? What clients? We found no records of the sales in your files.

A: You know, it was wartime. Sometimes clients didn't have time

for sales receipts. Sometimes clients had their own reasons for
not wanting them.

Q: You didn't get the paintings as part of a trade with any represen-
tative of the ERR?

A: No.

Q: You're certain of that?

A: Yes.

Q: Lieutenant Bernard, bring over the paintings. Strasser, are
these the paintings we found in your shop?

A: Yes, they appear to be.

Q: Turn them over. What do you see on the back of those paintings?

A: A stamp.

Q: Do you know what that stamp means?

A: No.

Q: I'm going to ask again. Did you get these paintings as part of a
trade with the ERR?

A: No.

Q: Really? You really don't know that when the ERR inventoried
looted artwork they placed stamps like these on the back of
those pieces?

A: I don't know what you mean.

(A *twenty-minute pause ensued.*)

Q: I will ask you one last time. Did you get these paintings from
the ERR?

A: Yes.

Mara understood the pauses in the interview to reflect the soldiers'
efforts—physical, she assumed—to get the recalcitrant Strasser to confess.
As the interview progressed and Strasser persisted in his obstinacy, the gaps
in the record grew longer. In the end, the soldiers succeeded. Strasser confessed to procuring artwork for and from the Nazis and selling it on the
black market. He also named names, including a reference that they did
not want to hear. His American art world launderer, he said, was a fellow
U.S. soldier whose name was blacked out from the transcripts.

"Mara, what on earth are you doing here?"

Lillian's voice unexpectedly broke through the voices from the past. Mara looked up, mouth agape.

"I asked you a question, Mara." Lillian enunciated each word with painful slowness. "What the hell are you doing here? You know you can't be back here without me or one of my staff. In any event, you told me you were done with your research."

Lillian's unprecedented coarseness stunned Mara even more. She had not planned for this.

Lillian pivoted. "I'm going to get the guards."

Jolted into action, Mara cried out, "Wait, Lillian, please. Wait. Give me a chance. I know I'm not supposed to be here. I know I'm breaking the rules. But I have a reason."

Lillian halted. Mara decided to take a gamble with the truth. She knew it was her only chance.

"Lillian, Beazley's didn't buy *The Chrysalis* from Boettcher."

"Of course we did," Lillian said, her back still to Mara.

"No, you didn't. Beazley's bought it from someone named Kurt Strasser." Mara waited for a reaction; she still needed to gauge Lillian's complicity.

"Who the hell is Kurt Strasser?" Lillian turned and glared at Mara. Mara usually found Lillian hard to read, but now she seemed sincere. Mara remained silent, hoping Lillian would grow uncomfortable and reveal something more. "I asked you, who is Kurt Strasser?" she insisted.

"He was a conspirator of the Nazis."

Lillian jeered. "Mara, stop acting like some kind of heroine. You saw the documents yourself. We purchased *The Chrysalis* from Boettcher." She shook her head. "You're speaking nonsense. I did that provenance myself. Many times over."

Mara was scared to go much further, but she could not turn back. Her safety depended on it. "You were given false documents to do the provenance all those years ago. And so was I, to put together our case."

"I don't believe it." Arms crossed, posture reassembled, Lillian assumed her usual unflappable façade.

"Don't believe me. Believe the documents." Mara reached down into her briefcase. She was loath to part with them, but she knew that she had no choice.

Lillian took the papers from Mara. She held them up to the light, turning them this way and that, and scrutinized them through her pince-nez for what seemed like hours. Mara stood by.

"Where did you get these?" Lillian finally asked, with what Mara thought was a bit less ire.

"Does it matter?"

"Haven't I taught you anything? Haven't I taught you the importance of the origin of things?" Now Mara was sure that Lillian's voice cracked.

Mara conceded, "Michael's safe. They came from his great-uncle Edward."

Lillian did not answer, just shuffled over to a chair and lowered herself down. She crumpled like an old tissue. Lines like fissures appeared on her brow and around her eyes, and for the first time, she looked all of her eighty-odd years. "I can't believe it," she said aloud, though not necessarily to Mara.

Mara didn't know what to say or do. Her instinct told her to try to comfort Lillian, to soothe the anguish that Mara guessed she was feeling, that Mara felt herself. But she was torn. She wasn't sure she wanted to elicit a shared indignation. Lillian could end Mara's plans if she chose a different pathway to retribution. If she even chose retribution at all.

So, kneeling next to Lillian's chair, hand on her hand, she settled on an empathetic statement of the truth. "I know. We've both been deceived."

"How could I have been so blind?" Lillian stared off into the distance, flicking away Mara's hand like an irritating fly.

"Lillian, don't be so hard on yourself. I mean, the forged bill of sale you were given to prepare that first provenance looked perfect; it looks exactly like the original except for the seller's name. Why would you have questioned it?" Mara hoped that, at the very least, she could help Lillian understand that she was not to blame.

Lillian disagreed. "Mara, you don't understand. It's not just that. I was having a relationship with Michael's great-uncle, Edward Roarke, at the time I first prepared the provenance. I was an easy mark."

Mara laughed at the similarity of their situations. Lillian shot Mara a shocked look at her seeming insensitivity, but Mara quickly explained. "Lillian, so was I. Having an affair with Michael, that is." She paused to let her revelation sink in.

When she caught Lillian's eye, they both exploded into laughter, irrepressible due to their nervous shock.

"Well, I guess we're quite a pair of fools, aren't we?" Lillian exclaimed, wiping away her tears. "They certainly pulled the wool over our doting eyes with no trouble." She sighed. "Although I'm a bigger ninny than you."

"Oh, I don't know, Lillian. I bet I can give you a run for that title."

"Well, if you knew the whole story, I don't think you would say so. I think you'd just cede victory to me."

"What 'whole story'?"

"I don't suppose there's any harm in telling you now. I mentioned to you that I was working at Beazley's in 1944, right?"

"Yes."

"Once I got here, they started me off doing provenance work, not that there was a provenance department per se at that time. It consisted of me and Mr. Weadock, who was in his sixties and crotchety, poring through moldy books in the basement."

Mara thought the grouchiness must come with the territory, but she didn't want to divert Lillian by sharing.

"Anyway, I'd been here about a month when I first met Edward. He approached me while I was working in the old Beazley's library, a pretty haphazard place. I don't know if you've seen any pictures of him, but he was quite handsome—dashing, really. And very charming."

"Actually, Lillian, I don't know anything about Edward."

"Michael never told you about him?"

Mara shook her head. "The few times I've asked Michael about his uncle, he's been cagey. Michael mentioned that Edward used to work at Beazley's but was vague about what exactly he did."

"Edward wasn't a founder of Beazley's—that was the British Beazley family—but he was one of the original, key employees here in America. He ultimately became a codirector for several years before his death."

"I never knew." Mara began to process that piece of the puzzle.

Lillian resumed. "Anyway, my relationship with Edward began slowly. There were coincidental meetings in the library or hallways. There was the odd lunch or cup of coffee. Then suddenly it accelerated into a full-blown romance, if such a thing were possible in wartime. He absolutely swept me off my feet with dinners, shows, and weekend trips. I had visions dancing in my head."

Mara had trouble imagining Lillian sailing along in the arms of love. "Why wasn't Edward at the war? He must have been the right age."

"The military wouldn't take him. He'd had polio as a child and had a noticeable limp. Plus, at thirty, he was a bit on the old side, although he seemed to have a number of friends in the war.

"In any event, going behind Mr. Weadock's back, he presented me with an opportunity to prepare my first provenance from start to finish. It was for *The Chrysalis*. Of course, I leaped at the prospect. With Mr. Weadock in charge, it might have taken years for such a chance. He really never saw me as anything more than a glorified secretary. Edward started me off with the bill of sale from Boettcher to Beazley's, but I had to fill in the rest, the older history.

"Sometime after this, our affair tailed off, almost imperceptibly at first, then with resounding, painful clarity. I begged to understand and pleaded with him to change his mind. Edward declined, offering up the excuse of a stern talking-to by his boss at the time, one of the British Beazley heirs apparent. Something was said about not dipping your quill in the company inkwell or some such nonsense. I believed him, even stood by his decision, but I was crushed."

"Did you stop speaking to him?"

"No. We remained very close, after some time had passed. Because of, rather than in spite of, our affair, I think. The fact that neither of us married made it easier. I continued doing provenances for him, of course, and he became my biggest supporter at Beazley's, really the driving force behind the decision to create a truly substantial provenance department with me at the helm. I was indebted to him, particularly at a time when women had few such chances and when no other museum or auction house had yet set up a provenance department. So I toiled to build the department that he envisioned, trying all the while to live up to his expectations, keeping our past relationship and my lingering feelings for him secret." Tears forced Lillian to stop.

Mara didn't know what else to say, but she was unable to bear the quiet. "And you succeeded," she blurted out.

Though Lillian sat stock-still, her voice reverberated throughout the room. "Yes. I succeeded. By forgoing other things: marriage, children. Beazley's became my family, and the Provenance Department turned into my home." Mara thought how her track at Severin had paralleled Lillian's path, at least before *The Chrysalis* forced her to swerve off course.

Lillian sank back into her memories. "Now I see I've been a pawn in Edward's game all along. I wonder how many provenances he laundered through me. How many of these Strasser paintings I wrongly verified. How many other auction houses have sold these Strasser paintings, too." Mara guessed at the number Beazley's had palmed off based on the Strasser bills of sale she had found in Michael's safe but didn't dare tally it for her just yet.

"How does Philip factor into this?"

"Well, he and Edward were very chummy. In fact, Edward groomed Philip to be his successor. From those e-mails, it's obvious that he knows all about *The Chrysalis* con, but to what extent he's involved I don't know." Lillian shook her head in disgust. "And to think of how Michael befriended me on the strength of his uncle's name, with all those lunches and afternoon teas. He's no better than Edward."

Mara began to toy with the idea of enlisting Lillian in her cause. Lillian would be an invaluable ally, but Mara wasn't sure if she would abandon Beazley's, her home. There was nothing left to lose, though, Mara told herself. "Then would you consider helping me?"

"Helping you with what?" Lillian peered out through the cloud of her musings.

"To find out all we can about Kurt Strasser, so we can understand what Edward and Michael were up to and discover what happened to the other paintings."

Lillian was silent for a long moment. She rose from her chair and ran her fingers along the cabinets and rows of books, almost as if she were saying a long goodbye. "How could I do that? After I gave up so much and worked so hard to build all this." She motioned around the room. "I'd be sacrificing it all, maybe even Beazley's itself. Please don't ask me to do that."

The delicate threads holding Mara together unraveled. "Don't ask you to help! Lillian, do you think you're the only one at risk? I've trespassed into your library without authorization, broken into Michael's safe and stolen papers out of it. I've violated countless codes of ethical conduct for lawyers and innumerable criminal statutes. I've put myself at risk of disbarment, indictment, and God only knows what else. And, when all this is over with, I've probably ruined my career. I've done it all for the sake of righting the wrong that your precious Beazley's committed, that Michael and Edward perpetrated, through you. So don't you dare tell me not to ask for your help."

The women stared at each other, for a split second that felt more like an eternity to Mara. Lillian broke the impasse first. "Shhh, Mara. Lower your voice. I don't want those guards in here."

Mara dropped down into the chair Lillian had vacated, with the same defeated slump, and felt every bit as ancient and weathered as Lillian had looked. She could not hold back the tears any longer. "I'm sorry, Lillian. I'm way out of line. This situation is not your fault, and I'm not angry with you. I'm angry with Michael. And at Edward."

"I know, Mara. I know. I'm the one who's sorry."

"What for? I'm in way over my head here, and I'm asking you to jump into the deep end with me. What the hell am I doing?" Mara shook her head, surprised at her outburst. But she was steadfast in her conviction that she must right the wrong, even if she had to do it alone, even if she risked everything.

Lillian whispered, "I'll help you."

"What?"

Lillian repeated herself, her voice growing louder and stronger. "I said I'll help you."

"Really?" Mara was astonished.

"Really. But I have a few conditions."

"Anything." Mara meant it—anything not to be in this quagmire by herself.

"I don't want my name associated with this should it come out. For obvious reasons, I don't want it known that I prepared the provenances using the false bills of sale, particularly the first provenance. But that's not all. You can never mention my help in resolving this."

"Why?" Mara understood why Lillian didn't want her part in the initial provenance fraud to be known, but why didn't she want her name associated with the rectification?

"If the scandal doesn't devastate Beazley's altogether, if it doesn't utterly decimate my department's reputation, somebody's going to have to put the pieces back together again. I want to be that person. And I can't do that if my name's embroiled in this debacle."

Mara was wary. She craved Lillian's help but couldn't see how to keep her assistance under such tight wraps. "So, if we go public with this, I'll have to present it as the results of my research, my investigation? All illegal, of course."

Lillian responded quickly. "Yes and no. If asked, I'll explain you had open access to Beazley's files for the *Baum* case, so your perusal and usage of that information was authorized to that extent. But I can't help you with Michael's safe. Or with any breaches of your ethical duties. Or with Severin's reaction, obviously."

"I didn't think you'd be able to help me out with those last ones. So, if we go this route, your reputation will be as intact as possible. You'd be Beazley's white knight?"

"Yes."

"I agree."

twenty-two

HAARLEM, 1661

JOHANNES CLEANS HIS BRUSHES ONE BY ONE. HE TENDS TO them every day, each time with the same attention and care. He tests the sharpness of his metalpoint. He arranges his palette again, the circle of lead white, topaz, cerise, sapphire, fir, slate, and ebony. All the while, he keeps his eye on the door, waiting for Burgomaster Brecht.

He surveys the studio, then checks the setting again and again. He adjusts the drapery of the tapestry covering the table. He repositions the globe, the porcelain bowl of ripe fruit, and the urn of tulips, all motifs of the burgomaster's wealth, power, and fecundity.

His eyes register the lines of perspective defining the room: in the rays of sunlight, in the right angles of the furniture, in the black-and-white, geometric design of the floor tiles. They guide the destiny of the as yet unbegun painting.

From the soft rumblings in the front entryway and the low murmur of

Pieter's voice, Johannes guesses that the burgomaster has made his entrance. Johannes raises himself up to his full height as Pieter leads the official into the studio and prepares to greet his town's austere leader.

A hawkish nose rounds the corner in advance of its prim owner. The burgomaster does not bow but offers his bony hand to Johannes in the royal custom. He has changed the commission from a pendant to a family portrait and now beckons his family to enter the studio. They form a somber sea of black and white: a wife, two sons, and a daughter. The decision to do a family portrait is a boon for Johannes, a rare chance to display his varied talent on each subject and to earn much-needed guilders.

Johannes gives silent thanks that protocol demands he bow low. For this protocol prohibits him from looking directly at the burgomaster's daughter, except as she poses for the portrait. He cannot trust that he will not stare. Her lucency pierces through the black clouds of the family that swirl round her.

The burgomaster permits Johannes to lead his family to their appointed seats and to begin arranging them like flowers in a vase. There is no discussion about the group's composition; the burgomaster seems in accord with Johannes's unconventional approach and surrenders himself as a sitter. The burgomaster need not fear for his portrayal, though, for Johannes has made a promise to Pieter to find the most flattering likeness, to utilize the most conventional arrangement, and to disregard the dark realms of the soul that his brush might find. The studio cannot afford to highlight them.

Johannes settles the burgomaster in the location that accords with his societal position—a central wooden armchair so high of back and so intricately carved that it resembles a throne. His wife takes her place at his side in a lesser version of his seat. He guides the two sons to spots flanking their parents, the elder at his father's side and the younger at his mother's. So alike despite the divergence of years, the brothers favor nothing so much as bookends, necessary bolsters for the family, and assurances that the Brecht tree will grow. Johannes gestures for the daughter to take her traditional place behind her mother.

The burgomaster clears his throat. "Do you know why I chose you for this commission, Master Miereveld?" he asks.

Johannes is unsure how the burgomaster wants him to respond. "No, my lord."

"My dear friend Jacob Van Dinter knew your Master Van Maes very well. He tells me that, having been raised in the home and studio of the late master, you must be the most Calvinist of painters. That is why I chose you."

Having shared the nature and breadth of his charity, the burgomaster's conversation is complete. Johannes, cognizant of his place, steps back to assess his handiwork. The composition is somehow unbalanced, wrong. It is the daughter. She is too substantial, too vital to be relegated to the back row. Yet where shall he place her? He assesses her peripherally, afraid to look at her face directly, fearful he will reveal himself. Through a sideways glance, he spies a lock escaping from her scalloped lace cap, the gentle curve of her neck against her stiff ivory collar, the glint of a golden earring, and an impression of her face muted by shadow.

Johannes requests the burgomaster's permission to approach. Afraid to touch the daughter, he nevertheless reaches out to square her shoulders and move her forward, closer to her mother's side. He feels her warm skin through the heavy brocade of her somber dress.

He returns to the safe haven of his easel. Hidden behind his work, Johannes allows himself to take full account of the incandescent Amalia.

Johannes sits in the darkening studio, re-creating the day in his mind. Imagining Amalia's face, he rises and walks to the space she inhabited during the long afternoon. He runs his fingers along the chairback where she rested her elegant virginal-player's fingers.

"Did you see her, Pieter?" Johannes asks the footsteps at the back of the studio.

"See who?" Pieter's tone makes clear that he knows the answer.

"The daughter."

"For a moment only. What of it?"

"Wasn't she luminous?"

"I suppose, for a burgomaster's daughter." Pieter shakes his head. "To even think of it is folly."

Pieter scurries off to answer the knock at the front door. He bears a letter upon his return. "For you, Johannes."

Johannes uses the sharp edge of his palette knife to loosen the sealing wax. He holds the rough material up to the lamplight, poring over it with care. He stops, his hands release, and the creased letter flutters to the floor, covering the carpet of fallen tulip petals.

He stumbles to the door.

"Johannes, what is it? Where are you going?" Pieter cries. But the door slams. Pieter grabs the letter from the floor and recognizes the script of Johannes's father from long ago. Johannes's mother has passed on.

Pieter chases after him, but Johannes manages to wander alone down the inky-black streets. He turns down an alleyway; it seems familiar, and yet he cannot place it. Running his hands along its rough, narrowing walls, he discovers that the path ends. He peers through a gateway into a tiny slit of a window, dimly lit with candles. Pushing the gate aside and passing under a gentle arch to the interior, he recognizes the place, from rumor, from others like it: a Catholic church, its identity as concealed as the allegories in his paintings.

The congregation looks up, startled at his interruption of the Mass. They ready themselves for repercussions for their forbidden worship. But Johannes only stands in the shadows, inhaling the familiar aroma of the incense, a tonic for his heart. He wanders toward the farthest, darkest corner and lowers himself into a pew.

On the altar, the priest raises his arms, offering the bread to God. He pours wine into the chalice, then lifts it high to the Lord. The remembered rituals wash over Johannes.

The priest imparts a farewell blessing: "*Benedicat vos omnipotens Deus Pater, et Filius, et Spiritus sanctus.*" The congregants file out of the little church, staring at the trespasser. The place of worship empty, the priest returns to the altar, replacing the precious chalice and its linen purificator in the sacristy.

"Father, I seek confession," Johannes whispers.

The priest, a Jesuit by his garb, turns from his sacred task toward Johannes, wary after so much persecution. "Do I know you, my son?"

"No, Father. I am a stranger to you, but not to the Church. It's been many years since my last Mass, but I seek to return."

"The apostle John tells us that Jesus is a shepherd; he always welcomes lost sheep back to the flock. Where did you worship, my son?"

Johannes describes the house of his furtive childhood worship. From the set of the priest's shoulders, he senses that a test has been passed.

"I would be pleased to hear your confession."

He leads Johannes to the confessional and notices that Johannes hesitates before the two doors—one for the priest, one for the penitent. "Are you unfamiliar with the sacrament?"

"Yes, Father."

"But I thought you were a member of the Church."

"I know the Mass, Father, but I have never taken the sacraments."

"I see. Well, the sacrament of penance is not one that requires initiation." He gestures toward the sinner's door.

Closing it tight behind him, Johannes genuflects onto the hard kneeler. The priest lifts the screen separating cleric and repenter, God and man. "Father, I ask forgiveness for breaking the fourth commandment: I have not honored my mother." Johannes cries.

twenty-three

NEW YORK CITY, PRESENT DAY

MARA AND LILLIAN NEEDED TIME AND SECRECY. FIRST, THEY placed a near-exact copy of the Strasser documents in Michael's safe but kept the original set as well as another working copy. Then Lillian scattered her researchers to the wind in a variety of remote, purportedly urgent activities so that she was left essentially alone.

For Mara, time and seclusion were more difficult to secure. She navigated the minefields of the office, where her every minute was measured and invoiced, and of Michael.

Harlan didn't care a whit for the excuse Mara offered of lengthy depositions on other litigations; he expected her to be as responsive as ever to his needs. Nor were the other partners she served appeased by the pretext of Harlan's demands; they were tired of his tyrannical domination of the associate pool, even if his client load justified it.

So she tore into the office first thing, answering e-mails and calls, drafting briefs, and conducting meetings with furious abandon. Then she darted off to Beazley's under the ruse of a conference or court appearance. She sprinted back to Severin as night fell and Beazley's closed up, to fulfill her shirked duties. In between, she prayed that no Severin partner or client worked too hard to find her.

She worried about running into Sophia. Once Sophia had revealed that there was a limit to her support, she became a threat. Sophia could endanger Mara's progress on *The Chrysalis* either by playing on her feelings of loyalty or by revealing her secret to someone who could stop her. Each time the two passed in the halls, the library, or the elevators, the coldness that had developed between them seemed to keep Sophia at bay. Mara marveled at the drastic change in their relationship since their first day at Severin, when they had come to the orientation knowing no one. After standing alone, like stiff wallflowers at the prom in their new navy suits, they gravitated toward each other and instantly felt such a strong sense of familiarity. Now they were like two ships in the night.

One time, Sophia attempted to thaw the ice. Alone in an empty hall in the chilly midnight hours, she asked Mara if she was continuing with her expedition. She begged Mara to end it, reiterating how far off course Mara had veered. But Mara remained resolute.

Still, despite the difficulties, work presented the least explosive of her challenges. More troubling, she had to disarm Michael upon his return from Europe.

Mara crossed her fingers that she would not run into him in Beazley's hallways or that he would not make an uncharacteristic visit to the library, where she and Lillian camped out. She prayed that the pretext she offered him for her absence—lengthy depositions for another client—would go over better than it had with Harlan.

At night, she created more inventive excuses, and despite her best efforts, they succeeded only for a bit. Besides, while Mara needed time to work with Lillian, the women also needed Michael to believe that his relationship with Mara thrived, or he might start to feel suspicious. So on Saturday, Mara had no choice but to meet Michael in a favorite local French bistro. Despite her promises to herself to remain clearheaded, Mara bolstered herself for the meeting with a few glasses of wine.

As she approached the bar, she forced herself to smile in his direction. He beamed back, and she saw him as if for the first time. Though he was still disarmingly handsome, his grin now seemed the bared teeth of a dog on the heels of his prey.

"God, Mara, I've missed you." He breathed into her neck. For a moment, she felt herself warm to his touch and sensed her body surrender.

She held on to that sensation throughout the dinner, to keep her façade intact. They chatted about the past days' activities, real and imagined, and she giggled over his jokes and even stroked his hand. All the while, she moved her steak frites round and round on her plate, unable to ignore the leaden feeling in her gut. Her sense of sinking increased as the hour grew late, and she faced her biggest challenge, an act for which she numbed herself with more wine. The only way left to buy the time she and Lillian needed was to let go of her body.

When she awakened, it was still night. She peeled Michael's arm off her and stumbled naked to the bathroom. Looking in the mirror, she saw a stranger, a mercenary, someone who had so cut herself off with drink that she had had sex with a man she despised. A man who had betrayed her. A man who felt no compunction about continuing to deceive countless others, people already victimized, all for his own benefit.

She smelled Michael on her. She had to wash him off. Turning the shower on hot, she stepped in and scrubbed her skin until it was red and raw. As tears streamed down her face, she prayed he would not hear her sobs.

IN THE SHELTER OF BEAZLEY'S LIBRARY, MARA AND LILLIAN made proficient use of the time they procured: Lillian with the remaining twenty-three provenances and Mara with *The Chrysalis* and Strasser himself.

Black-and-white photographs were propped up on Lillian's library desk like tombstones; among them were a pensive Morisot woman in white before her vanity, a disturbing van Gogh still life of creeping flowers and jagged greenery, and a bleak Sisley winterscape with smoke billowing over the fields as a reminder of the encroaching industrial revolution. Their heartbreaking stories cried out from the provenances Lillian prepared with archaeological patience.

The sound of a chair scraping over the library floor broke the silence.

Mara looked up to see Lillian standing by the French doors, shaking her head as she stared out at the park. "What is it?" Mara asked.

"This poor painting. Worse, its poor owners."

"Which painting are you talking about?"

"The Rembrandt. "

"You mean the *The Portrait of the Elderly Jew with a Fur Hat*?"

"Do we have any other Rembrandts?"

Mara knew the answer to Lillian's snide rhetorical question. Of course they didn't have any other Rembrandts; the Nazis coveted Rembrandt's work and normally would never have parted with one of his treasures to a dealer like Strasser. Some high Nazi official would have made it the centerpiece of his Berlin office. The subject of this particular Rembrandt, however, made it repugnant to the Nazis.

"No, of course not."

"It turns out that the Rembrandt was part of the Schultze family collection," Lillian said, and Mara understood the reference. By the 1940s, the Schultze family, French-Jewish industrialists, had amassed a renowned collection of more than 300 paintings, modern and Impressionist pieces mixed with seventeenth-century Flemish and Dutch masters. The Nazis were eager to get their hands on the collection, particularly since it contained the northern European pieces preferred by Hitler and Göring. When they eventually unearthed it from hiding, the Nazis took the loot and the Schultzes' lives. The surviving Schultze relatives had managed to recover 140 of the pieces and were still hunting for the rest.

"Well, the bill of sale that Edward gave me stated that Beazley's bought the Rembrandt from a Belgian art dealer, Alain Wolff, another dealer whose documents were conveniently destroyed in the war. Edward also provided me with a bill of sale demonstrating that Wolff purchased it from Lucien Schultze in the early 1940s. Since the title appeared clear, we sold it to Chad Rosenbluth, who was an important collector of Dutch and Flemish art in the forties, fifties, and sixties. In the seventies, he bequeathed the work to the Reeve Museum of Art, where it hangs on the walls today."

"What do the Strasser documents show?"

"Well, the bill of sale you found in the safe shows that Beazley's bought the Rembrandt from Strasser. When the Nazis took the Schultze collection, they must've tossed the *Elderly Jew* Rembrandt to Strasser, and Edward must have forged the Wolff-Schultze bill of sale from scratch."

"Would that explain why the Rembrandt doesn't appear in any of the Nazi art records?"

"Yes, it would." Lillian's eyes began to well with tears, so she turned away to face the park. "I can't believe Edward made me an accomplice in all of this duplicity."

"I'm so sorry, Lillian. I know exactly how you feel." Mara rose and stretched her hand out to Lillian's shoulder in a gesture of consolation.

But her emotion was too raw for Lillian, who shook off Mara's touch and changed the subject by pointing to Mara's table, with its tangle of boxes and papers. "So, what have you learned about *The Chrysalis* or Strasser from that mess?"

Mara walked over to the boxes of still-classified World War II documents and picked up a particularly dog-eared report. "Listen to this. It's from the Compendium of the Art Looting Investigative Unit's Detailed Interrogation Reports: 24 November 1946. 'With respect to the history of the complex web of art looting and acquisition spun by the Nazis, Kurt Strasser was one of the most important German figures based in a neutral country, Switzerland. He does not seem to be a leading force in the art-looting activities, but he was willing to profit from them. His level of culpability in the events is difficult to ascertain. It may be said, however, that during World War II, Strasser actually made financial gains from the misfortune of others."

"That sounds like our man."

"It then goes on to describe just how he perpetrated his schemes." Mara grew quiet as she reread the report to herself.

"Well?" Lillian faced Mara, her face dry and her curiosity piqued.

"It seems that old Kurt, having been a German soldier in World War I, was something of a German nationalist and Nazi supporter. He even contributed to the Nazi Party from time to time, although he never joined. The report says that he described himself as 'consultant and expert' to dealers rather than a dealer himself."

"That's all well and good. But what about his trafficking in stolen art?" Lillian was impatient with Mara's meandering.

"I'm getting to that, but this background is critical. He seems to have had a whole network of German art cronies who were linked to the Nazi Party, connections that stemmed from his own military days. Like his pal Walter Andreas Hofer, who was the 'director of the art collection of the reichsmarschall.' And he also had a whole network of art dealers in France, Switzerland, and Germany who were known Nazi sympathizers."

"Come on, Mara." Lillian was antsy.

"Okay, okay. Strasser's system worked like this. Somehow, he would land upon an old master or a Germanic painting preferred by the Nazis, then go to one of his usual cast of characters, a fellow collaborationist dealer or a Nazi contact like Hofer, and exchange the painting for a number of 'degenerate' pieces, valuable paintings that the Nazis loathed. Strasser would then transport these paintings to the United States for sale via an American army officer, who could spirit away the paintings courtesy of the military mail."

"Is that what happened with *The Chrysalis*?"

"I can't say for sure, but it makes sense. *The Chrysalis*'s subject must not have been to the Nazis' liking for some reason, despite its lauded Germanic origin—much like *Elderly Jew*—so once they stole it in Nice, they must have palmed it off on Strasser along with some of the 'degenerate' pieces he really wanted, such as all of those Impressionist paintings you've got propped up on your desk. Strasser then got the paintings to the United States, most likely through that mysterious American officer. And Edward somehow got the paintings from that connection."

Lillian grew silent. Mara said, "Lillian? I think we should follow up on that."

"Follow up on what?"

"On this American officer. This report never says anything more about him, not even his name; it just cites another interrogation report. The referenced report isn't here, and I'd really like to track that down."

"What are you suggesting?"

"Well, you got these classified World War II documents from someone, somehow. Is there any way you could go back to that source again and ask who the American officer was?" Mara implored. She knew that Lillian was growing impatient with the rate of their progress and nervous about the outcome. And every time Mara had to ask for more, she felt how tenuous their alliance really was. More and more, she missed Sophia and the solidity of their old connection.

"I can try, Mara, but I don't even know how well my contact is these days. He's quite old."

"Please, Lillian. It's the only way to close the loop on all this, to really understand Edward's scheme."

"All right. I'll see what I can do."

The women returned to their work in silence. The daylight waned, and darkness settled in. When Lillian rose to switch on the brass desk lights, Mara dared to ask, "Can we go look at *The Chrysalis?*" Mara had begged Lillian to take her to the warehouse where *The Chrysalis* was stored before. Like a junkie in need of a fix, she hungered for a glimpse of the painting, craved its tranquillity as a salve for the treacherous times. Lillian complied without protest, as if she understood, maybe even shared, Mara's need.

Lillian smiled at her. "Why not?"

They wandered the long, dark hallways to the storage area. Lillian unsealed its various locks with methodical care and entered. Mara followed. Whenever she stood before the painting, Mara felt a kinship with the offering in the woman's hand, the yellow butterfly bursting forth from the ruptured cocoon.

They stood in reverential quiet, as they did most visits, but Mara heard Lillian whisper a fragment of an Emily Dickinson poem:

> *From Cocoon forth a Butterfly*
> *As Lady from her Door*

Mara understood the meaning of Lillian's eerie words and comprehended why Lillian felt such an affinity toward the poet, who had dedicated much of her life's work, her poems, to a secret male lover referred to only as "Master."

Without breaking the silence, she reached out her hand to rest on Lillian's shoulder. This time, Lillian allowed it.

twenty-four

NEW YORK CITY, PRESENT DAY

MARA'S CAB RACED UP FIFTH AVENUE, LONG BEFORE THE streets came alive with the sounds of the workday. Having decided to start the day at Beazley's, she arrived at the designated meeting spot, the side entrance to the mansion. Lillian was waiting for her with the key in hand. They slipped down the empty hallways and passages. Lillian gave the royal wave to the sleepy night-shift security guards, and she and Mara gained access to the library, closing the door tightly behind them.

"We're going to London." Lillian handed her a first-class ticket on British Airways. Mara understood that Lillian, with her own personal wealth, always traveled well.

"London?"

"Yes, for the army officer's interrogation report. Be careful what you ask for, Mara, you just might get it."

"Wow. When?"

"Tonight. So you'll have to go get your passport at some point today."

Mara and Lillian did not speak for the remainder of the day as they wrapped up the loose ends of their research and Mara made sure her other Severin work would be tended to during her short absence. Mara circled back to all her open questions on Kurt Strasser and his schemes, while Lillian plugged away at holes in the provenances of the other paintings Beazley's had purchased from Strasser. As the departure hour neared, they packed up their material, including the original Strasser papers and the copy set. There was no time left before the flight to lock them away in a safe hiding place, and neither of the women felt comfortable leaving any of the papers behind.

They exited Beazley's in the same surreptitious manner as they had entered, emerging from the dark labyrinth of the library and squinting into the waning light of day. Just as Lillian's limousine pulled up, Mara heard her name being called. She reeled, afraid to turn round.

"Hi there, Miss Coyne! Long time, no see!" Larry waved at her.

Mara half leaned into the car, which already held Lillian. "What should I do?"

"Go over and speak to him as normally as possible."

"And if he asks what I'm doing here?"

"Just explain you're picking up the last batch of documents for the case."

Mara strolled over to Larry. She gave him a little hug in greeting. "Larry, it's so good to see you. I looked for you when I got here today, but you weren't in." A lie and a gamble, but she needed to divert him, if possible.

"Yeah, I switched shifts with Sammy today, as a favor. We've missed you around these parts. What brings you here?"

Slowing her breath in an attempt to calm her palpitating heart, she explained, "Oh, just rounding up a bunch of papers for that case I'm working on."

"Has that case kept you workin' here over the past few weeks?"

Mara wasn't sure how to answer but thought it best to stick as close to the truth as possible in case others had spotted her. "Just the past few days."

He paused. "I'm surprised I didn't see you come in or leave. I don't miss much."

His comment took Mara aback for a moment, as she thought about her use of Beazley's back entrance. She attempted diversion with a laugh and a teasing pat. "We must have just passed each other."

"Well, I'm sorry I missed you. I hope you'll be back soon."

"Oh, I'll be back from time to time. How could I not?" Mara eked out a flirtatious grin. "Probably not as frequently as before, sorry to say."

"Well, I'm sure glad I got to see you, then. I better run—Sammy'll be chomping at the bit to leave." He squeezed her forearm. "Bye, Miss Coyne."

"Bye, Larry."

She climbed into the car, with her heart pounding. Lillian had a scotch at the ready. Mara, who didn't even like scotch, downed it. Lillian commanded her driver, "George, we're going to JFK, British Airways. Please hurry."

A couple more stiff drinks were had, but no words passed between them on the ride to the airport. There was no need for speech; each knew how the other was feeling. Not until they settled into the British Airways lounge did they relax into conversation; even then, they began with rather desultory exchanges. Then Lillian asked about Michael.

"You did let him know you'd be unavailable tonight?"

"Dammit, I completely forgot to call him." Given the way Michael plagued her mind, Mara couldn't believe her oversight.

"It's not too late. You told him you'd be at depositions all day, so you really wouldn't have been available until now anyway, would you?"

"That's true. I guess I could tell him I have to travel for business, but I usually give him the hotel information when I do. Or he calls me on my cell phone. Neither of which will be possible in London."

"I'm sure you can fabricate some Severin 'emergency' that will require you to be out of reach for an evening, can't you?" Lillian quaffed her scotch.

"Yes. But pray he doesn't pick up or that a departure announcement doesn't sound throughout the club just as I'm talking." After several long, painful rings, Mara got Michael's voice mail and closed her eyes in thanksgiving.

Between the drinks in the car and the British Airways lounge, the pre-liftoff Moet & Chandon, and the luxurious fully reclining seats on the subdued upper deck of the 747, Mara slept for nearly five hours. The rest allowed her to waken refreshed, if a bit hungover. The women zipped through passport control and customs and were quickly outside in the drizzly, gray London dawn, where a Mercedes and driver awaited them.

"So, how did you manage to get the army officer's interrogation report?"

"We're meeting with an old friend of mine, Julian Entwistle. He used to be the provenance director at Beazley's in London, before he retired some twenty-odd years ago—at the ripe old age of sixty-five." Lillian chuckled to herself, Mara assumed at the thought of her own "ripe old age."

Lillian continued, "You and I have talked about the fact that, during the war, the Office of Strategic Services requested the formation of a special intelligence unit of military men with a fine arts background to deal with looted art, called the Art Looting Investigation Unit, whose goal was to trace and prevent the flow of art assets used to finance the Nazi war machine, right?"

"Of course. I'm very familiar with them now." Mara was irritated with Lillian's habit of repeating long-trodden ground as if she still thought Mara was a simpleton.

"Well, Julian was the British liaison to the unit. Through his work with it, he gained access to the classified documents to which you've been privy."

"Why did he give you a set?"

"Because he thought it was critical that I have them for my work. And because he knew he could count upon my discretion."

"Why didn't he give you the full set? One that included the U.S. Army officer's interrogation report."

"Even he didn't have easy access to all the classified papers. He collected what he could without arousing suspicion."

"So how's he going to get us the report on the army officer now?"

"I didn't ask. I assume he called in some favors."

As they drove the rest of the way in silence, Mara reveled in the unfamiliar sights: the Thames, Covent Garden, and the Embankment. When the car veered off the Embankment, Mara caught sight of The Savoy hotel's sign. A formally dressed attendant, adorned with a top hat that reminded her of a cherry on a sundae, assisted them out of the car. Mara and Lillian entered the lobby of the London landmark, opened in the late 1800s and destined to become an institution unto itself, the home away from home for royalty, the rich, and the renowned. Mara wondered what Sophia would think of it all.

In the hotel boutique, Mara bought a new blouse and a fresh pair of undergarments—or knickers, as the sales clerk called them—then checked into her room. The room was far too fussy for Mara's taste, and she felt stifled by all the cornflower blue and gold, but its windows offered marvelous vistas of the Thames and Big Ben. She stood for a minute looking out over the cityscape, then collapsed into the downy bed.

Precisely two hours later, as instructed, Mara entered the hotel lobby and found the Thames Foyer. She admired the room, awash in bucolic murals, bordered by rosy-hued marble columns that soared high into whimsically carved ceilings, before she spotted Lillian settled in a pale green banquette at a table in the cozily lit far back corner.

For an instant, Mara watched her from afar, captivated by Lillian's unguarded smile and girlish looks, all directed at the mysterious Julian, whose back was toward Mara. For a fleeting second, Mara saw the beautiful young woman Lillian must once have been.

Lillian looked up as Mara approached. "Ah, Jennifer, you're here. I'd like to introduce you to my dear friend Julian Entwistle." Lillian gestured in the gentleman's direction. "Jennifer Cartwright, Julian Entwistle."

Mara reviewed the biography of her assumed identity, Jennifer Cartwright, a new provenance research assistant in Lillian's department. Lillian wanted Julian to know nothing about the nature of their investigation.

Julian got up to greet Mara. Though an elderly gentleman with thin white hair, he towered over her. He was elegantly dressed in a custommade navy suit, a blue-and-white gingham shirt, and handmade black oxford shoes. A cane against the wall served as the only concession to his advanced years, although Mara supposed it could just as well be the final accessory of a properly outfitted Englishman. Given his august appearance, Mara braced herself for an intimidating greeting worthy of Lillian, but instead, she received an engaging, wide grin.

Mara extended her hand, and much to her surprise, Julian kissed it. "Miss Cartwright, it's my pleasure."

"Julian, would you mind terribly if we ordered a proper tea? Even though it's nowhere close to the proper time?" Lillian asked.

"Time. What's 'proper time' to an old man like me? We shall have the works! Lillian, if I recall correctly, the cucumber sandwiches were always your favorites. Oh, and the smoked salmon with tomato. And scones with lots and lots of clotted cream and strawberry preserves."

"Oh, Julian, I've missed you." Lillian actually giggled. Another flash of youth crossed her face, but this time, it was followed closely by a look of regret, a feeling Mara only guessed had been worsened by the recent revelations about Edward. Lillian reached out and clasped Julian's hand. Mara leaned back in her chair to give the old friends a moment of their own.

Over sips of steeped Savoy house tea and bitefuls of buttery scones heaped with cream and jam, the threesome chatted about Beazley's, old times and new; about Lillian and Julian's decades-long collaboration over the creation of their respective provenance departments; about the Wild West of the art world in the days of their youth; and about the bureaucracy and lack of romance of the current times. They talked about everything but what they'd come for.

But then, as if on cue, Julian rose as soon as they finished their last sip of tea.

He reached into the inner pocket of his suit jacket and withdrew an envelope. "Well, ladies, I believe I'll leave you to it," he said as he laid the packet on the table. "Let's not discuss how I came by it. Only know that I must return it shortly, with a promise that no copies will be made. I'll see you back here in about an hour." The gentle, repetitive thud of his cane accompanied his departure.

Mara moved over to Lillian's side of the table. Lillian unsealed the envelope with a clean butter knife and flattened the contents out on the table. The aged pages contained such small mimeographed words that Lillian pulled out her pince-nez, and Mara leaned close to decipher them.

```
CONFIDENTIAL


WAR DEPARTMENT
OFFICE OF THE ASSISTANT SECRETARY OF WAR
STRATEGIC SERVICES UNIT


ART LOOTING INVESTIGATION UNIT
WASHINGTON
```

And

OFFICE OF MILITARY GOVERNMENT (U.S.)

ECONOMICS DIVISION, RESTITUTION BRANCH

MONUMENTS, FINE ARTS AND ARCHIVES SECTION

Detailed Interrogation Report

18 September 1946

Subject: Frank Shaughnessy

SSU

CONFIDENTIAL

"Frank Shaughnessy. I know that name," Lillian murmured.

"You do? From your research?"

Lillian spoke as if the words themselves were unpalatable. "No. From Edward. Frank Shaughnessy was his best friend."

The women looked at each other, neither one daring to break their gaze. The scheme Edward and Frank had hatched together passed unspoken but completely understood between them. Lillian averted her eyes first and refocused on the report. She turned the pages one at a time, and Mara scribbled down the words. They were so engrossed that they jumped when Julian silently reappeared.

"Sorry to startle you, ladies. It's just that your hour's up. Unfortunately, I must get the document back as promised. And I believe you have an appointment with an airplane."

In a daze, they gathered their few belongings. "Julian, how can I thank you for this?" Lillian asked as they walked through the lobby to their waiting car.

"Lillian, you know I'd do anything for you."

Julian and Lillian embraced, and Mara saw the deep affection and lost opportunities pass between them. "At my age, this may be a true goodbye," Julian said in a hushed tone.

Lillian's eyes brimmed with tears. "Oh, Julian, please don't say that."

"It's the truth, my dear. I'm just thankful for the opportunity to say it, to let you know how blessed I've been to know you."

They pulled each other closer. "Julian, it's I who've been blessed with you all of these years."

Mara slipped unnoticed into the car and left the two a last quiet moment together. When she joined her, Lillian's eyes glistened, and she spent the ride back to Heathrow facing the window.

twenty-five

AMSTERDAM, 1943

ERICH HEARS THE CRUNCH OF THE GRAVEL AS THE CAR AP-
proaches the house. The rare sound rouses him from his early-
morning slumber. He looks over at Cornelia, who has not stirred, silently
throws on his robe to ward off the dawn chill, and rushes to the window.

An enormous black Daimler-Benz rounds the drive. The driver's door
opens, and a uniformed officer steps out. With military precision, the soldier opens the rear door and bows to a bedecked S.S. officer exiting from
the backseat. Erich knows he should wake Cornelia, and they should rush
to dress, but he is frozen with fear. What do the Nazis want from them
now? Since they received the reichskommissar's letter of protection, the
Dienststelle Mühlmann officers have stopped harassing him for the location of the paintings not turned over to Lippman, Rosenthal and Co.
Bank, paintings that the officers hear once hung on Erich's walls.

The ringing of the front bell rouses him. By the time Willem knocks on the bedroom door, the couple has donned their somber finest. Hand in hand, they descend the front stairs.

The decorated officer greets them with a smile. After they make their introductions, he says, in heavily accented Dutch, "I come with good news. We've got your visas to Milan and your train tickets."

"Our visas to Milan?" Erich asks. After receiving his daughter's recent communication, he is surprised that she is able to secure the visas but is, of course, overjoyed.

"Yes, here they are." The officer hands the couple a packet. "Go and pack your luggage. Your train leaves in two hours. You can take anything you can carry with you."

Before returning upstairs to pack, Erich opens the packet and looks over the visas and first-class train tickets. One of the items on the train itinerary makes him pause. He dares to ask the officer, "Why does this train stop in Berlin?"

The officer is quick to assure him, "All international trains departing from the Netherlands must go through Berlin."

Erich is still wary but mollified by the explanation. The newspapers had reported the development, the upshot of another of the reichskommissar's many regulations.

He and Cornelia scurry from room to room, adjudicating the fate of their few remaining worldly goods in the one hour allotted before their departure. Was an heirloom silver Cartier humidor worthy of the journey, or should they assign it the uncertain destiny sure to accompany its abandonment? Might a cherished desktop clock given as an anniversary gift merit inclusion, or should they take only Cornelia's jewels and other portable, salable items that they have squirreled away? Erich's pronouncements are harsh but necessary, and Cornelia holds back tears over leaving behind a collection of photographs and keepsakes amassed over a lifetime.

At the end of the permitted hour, the couple makes their way down the front stairs again, this time weighted down by suitcases and parcels. Willem follows them with a trunk.

The smile so carefully arranged on the officer's face freezes. "I thought I said you can bring what you alone can carry. Your manservant will not be going with you."

Erich answers, his voice tremulous. "My wife and I can manage the trunk along with our other belongings. Willem is only helping us carry it to the station."

The officer's smile reanimates. "It will not be necessary for Willem to come to the station. We will be accompanying you to the train. My man here can help you get on board with the trunk, as long as you can handle it on the train."

"We can."

The officers are solicitous, helping pack the Daimler-Benz with the couple's possessions. They describe with enthusiasm the private railway car reserved for their journey instead of the hardships of recent wartime travel. The senior official settles into the front of the Daimler-Benz, as the junior officer opens the rear door and gestures for the couple to get into the crowded backseat. Cornelia slides in as best she can, and they all wait for Erich.

Before he gets into the car, Erich turns to embrace Willem, the very first time he has done so. Tears glint in the corners of both men's eyes, as each understands that the embrace will certainly be their last as well as their first. He then hastens into the car, not wanting to leave Cornelia alone in the company of the officers for too long.

As they pull away and round the drive, Erich turns back. He is just in time to see Willem, Cornelia's maid, Maria, and his home grow small and blurry in the distance, in the low blue light of the dawn.

twenty-six

LONDON, PRESENT DAY

IN THE BRITISH AIRWAYS LOUNGE, LILLIAN'S OFFICIOUS DE-meanor returned, perhaps even more pronounced. She practically ordered Mara: "It's time for you to make a move on this."

"There's not more research to do?" Mara asked.

"No. I've completed enough of the provenances for all the other paintings Beazley's bought from that bastard Strasser. And we now know very well what happened. Edward and his friend Frank hatched a scheme whereby Frank, acting on behalf of Beazley's, bought looted artwork from Strasser at cut-rate prices. He then sent it to his wife by military post, thereby avoiding any chance that it would be examined en route. Finally, Edward picked up the artwork on one of his many trips to Boston." She stopped. "Oh God, come to think of it, I believe I met Frank's wife on one of our visits to the Cape. Our first one."

She drained her glass of scotch. "At some later, safer time, Edward would create new bills of sale for the paintings, using the real ones as a model but changing the names of the sellers. Instead of some tainted dealer like Strasser, he'd substitute an immaculate one like Boettcher for *The Chrysalis* or Wolff for the Rembrandt. He picked dealers with spotless reputations, particularly those whose files he knew were destroyed or compromised in the war. That way, there was no reason to challenge them and no way to cross-reference the sales with the dealers' files should any questions arise. And then he'd give them to me—his patsy—to launder with an unblemished pedigree. Edward would sell his flawlessly provenanced painting and share the proceeds with Frank. Or at least, I assume that was the deal, since Frank never gave up Edward's name to the Art Looting Investigation Unit despite what I can only assume was a brutal interrogation." She shook her head. "I can't believe I gave my approval to all those Strasser paintings."

A singsong announcement called out over the speaker. "We now invite our first-class passengers to board the plane departing for New York."

The women made their way to the gate and then onto the Jetway. As Mara advanced, she felt Lillian poke her in the back. She turned around to see Lillian gesture toward the back of a man's head with silvery hair, a few passengers ahead of them. There was something familiar about him to Mara, but she couldn't place it until Lillian whispered, "Philip Robichaux."

Mara froze, but the line of passengers boarding the plane pressed forward, so Lillian nudged her. "Mara, you can move ahead."

"Sorry." Like an automaton, she walked onto the plane, took her seat next to Lillian, and stored her bag, all the while following the man with her eyes.

Once he settled into his seat a few rows ahead of them, she whispered back to Lillian, "What should we do?"

"We need to be certain first—absolutely certain—that it is him. See if you can get a look at him."

"Me?"

"Surely you are not suggesting that *I* try to steal a glance at him? He would know me in an instant. He has seen you only once."

Mara knew Lillian was right, but she needed to find a way to identify him without putting herself in his line of vision. Just then, he stood up to stow his suit jacket and bag in the overhead compartment, and an idea came to Mara.

She walked to the back of the aisle, surreptitiously grabbed a pink *Financial Times* off the cart, and approached an air hostess. "Miss? That gentleman over there dropped this. Would you mind returning it to him?"

"Certainly."

The air hostess approached the man with the *Times* in hand, while Mara waited and watched from the back. "Sir? Did you drop this?"

The man turned. Instead of Philip's tan, chiseled face, one with near-translucent skin and a weak chin welcomed her. The hair was the only commonality. Mara's whole body relaxed. "No, miss. That's not mine," she heard him answer.

Mara walked back toward her seat, her heart still pounding.

"So?" Lillian asked.

"It wasn't him."

Lillian fell back into her seat. "Thank God. What would we have done?"

"I don't know. But I do know that you're right—I need to act. It's time." Mara's breathing returned to normal.

With a big sigh, Lillian reached into her purse, pulled out a prescription bottle, unscrewed it, and popped a pill in her mouth.

"What's that?" Mara asked.

"Is that really any of your business?" Lillian responded, with an arched eyebrow.

"No, of course not. But are you all right?"

"As 'all right' as one can be at my age. Let's stick to the topic, Mara."

The women reviewed their options. Mara wanted to do justice, return *The Chrysalis* and the other paintings to their rightful owners, even if it meant she would pay a price; after all, why else was she taking all these risks? Lillian, too, wanted to see the stolen art returned but also wanted to shelter Beazley's and safeguard her life's work. Neither was sure how to join their visions until Lillian suggested a compromise.

"What if you confront Michael with all that we've found and give him the chance to restitute privately? He could even protect himself by claiming he'd just found the documents. That way, we'd be able to keep the whole matter under wraps."

Mara was skeptical. "Do you really think he'd be willing?"

"I don't know. Maybe. I think it's worth a shot."

"But, Lillian, if he doesn't agree, then we've tipped our hand. Who knows what he might be capable of at that point?" Mara did not really believe that the Michael she knew, the Michael she had loved, could inflict harm upon her or Lillian, but her legal training compelled her to consider and plan for all possibilities.

"If he won't agree, then I suppose *you* must proceed with an alternate plan. As you know, I've come this far. Once you cross the breach, I have to drop out."

Mara needed no more reminders about the impending change in Lillian's role. It had loomed over her head like a guillotine from the start. "I know. I understand our deal."

Lillian posited another possibility. "If Michael won't agree to restitution, what about approaching the partner on the case? Maybe he could reach out to his contacts at Beazley's to see what can be done quietly."

"Maybe . . ." Mara's stomach flipped over at the thought of divulging her possibly criminal, or at the very least unethical, handiwork to Harlan.

"All I ask is that you do your best to preserve Beazley's. That you bring the matter to court or go public only as a last resort. Resuscitating Beazley's will be very difficult once the truth is known."

"I promise you that, Lillian," Mara said. "I agreed to that from the beginning."

Lillian rummaged through her bag for her address book and pulled out a business card. "If all else fails and you need to go public, here is the contact information for a reporter at the *New York Times*, Elizabeth Kelly. She's a straight shooter." She handed Mara the card.

Mara tried to sleep but could not. The various paths she had to choose among bedeviled her. There was one remaining thing, though, that she needed to know.

"Lillian," she whispered. "Lillian, are you asleep?"

"I was," she replied, eyes still closed.

"Before you drop out of this and into your Beazley's savior role, I need you to tell me something."

"What's that?" Lillian muttered, half asleep.

"Who owns *The Chrysalis* now?"

"Oh, I thought I told you that already." She stretched out felinelike in her reclined first-class seat, then rolled over so her back faced Mara. "Back in the 1940s, Beazley's sold *The Chrysalis* to the Catholic Church's largest religious order, the Jesuits. If you want to get technical, the New York Province of the Jesuits." In the quiet roar of the plane engine, Mara almost heard her grandmother groan.

twenty-seven

HAARLEM, 1661

JOHANNES RETURNS TO WORK, AND THE BURGOMASTER'S FAMILY portrait evolves. With characteristic ability but uncharacteristic flattery, Johannes depicts father, mother, and sons in perfect accord with each of their stations. He saves Amalia for last.

Johannes paints the burgomaster's daughter with deliberation. He savors each stroke and moment of observation. He uses the burgomaster's desire for perfection as a way to prolong his private veneration of Amalia. Unconsciously first, then with conscious surreption, she becomes the subject of another commission: a clandestine painting for the Jesuits of the Catholic meetinghouse, an unusual penance for dishonoring his late mother.

Johannes's secret painting becomes an allegory of Catholic faith. Specifically, it reminds the viewer of faith's gift of salvation. While Johannes paints Amalia as the burgomaster's daughter in black, standing next to her mother, he also paints her in white as the Virgin Mary, the emblem of the Church. He swaths her in ivory robes and decorates her in lapis lazuli and ruby. He crowns her in ivy, the evergreen signifier of eternal life, the conquest of death by resurrection. He surrounds her with the Virgin's objects of devotion: the lily, flower of purity; and the single-flamed candle, which personifies faith. He pierces her virginity with a single beam of God's light that streams through the unbroken oval window to her right and enters her heart. The light transforms her from girl to mother, from mortal to eternal, from faith to resurrection. Finally, Johannes places the goldfinch, symbol of Christ, in her open left hand, poised for flight.

The symbols in the painting signify the Virgin Mary, but the visage and light are fully Amalia. Johannes infuses the painting with the burgomaster's daughter's luminosity, a joyous white-yellow glow that pours from and around her, radiating from her hair, dancing off her skin, sparkling from her eyes. Her light reaches into the painting's shadiest corners, bringing the promise of illumination to even the blackest nooks. It is a harmonious, Catholic light with no hint of discordant Protestant chiaroscuro.

Long days pass, each day longer than the next as spring turns into early summer. Each night grows ripe with the smell of the unplucked berries that climb the wall outside Johannes's studio. His world revolves around Amalia and the canvases. He paints by lamps long after the midnight hour in order to keep his work a secret from Pieter, who would disapprove of a commission for the Jesuits. This religious order seeks to counteract the spread of Protestantism, and any association with them could ruin Pieter and Johannes's chances for other clients. Johannes is not capable of heeding these concerns; he can only answer to his ardor for Amalia.

Amalia returns his gaze. It is not the stare of a curious subject trying to discern the painter's particular alchemy. She is looking directly at him, Johannes the man, not the painter. Her gaze lingers, and Johannes sees a barely repressed smile.

Enchantment descends upon Johannes. He is feverish to capture that moment, that smile, in the Jesuits' painting. He works through the night. He wakes at his easel to the morning sun penetrating his lids and to the sound of light footfalls. He recognizes Amalia's footsteps; she is early for their appointment to work further on the Brecht family portrait. She crosses into the painter's sphere, coming behind the easel.

She stands for a long time in front of it. He knows the interwoven symbols have only one interpretation. The image demands a response: Do you accept her, do you accept Him, do you accept the Catholic faith?

He awaits. She turns her turquoise gaze on him. She reaches out to him. Closing his eyes, he braces himself for the deserved slap for his audacity, his sacrilege, in featuring her in this blatantly Catholic work. Instead, he feels the soft pads of her fingers on his cheek, on his eyelids, on his hands. He hears her voice for the first time. "You have captured me, Master Miereveld."

Their connection strengthens with a walk. They step out to the medieval ramparts that enclose the town. It is a safe, empty promenade in the early morn. Their first steps are tentative and their glances sideways; they talk innocuously about the celebrated views from the walls, agreeing that the market square formed by the rising towers must be the finest in the land. As they note the way the canal reflects the bridges that connect the city gates, she interrupts the formal dance and asks how his brush understands her so well. He cups her cheek in his hand and explains.

Gradually, they extend their furtive walks farther and farther away from the town walls, through the city gates into deserted country meadows. Here, Amalia shines to her full luminosity under Johannes's passion.

Their bond intensifies with a lesson. She wants to understand his magic, how he renders her interior so exactly. She arranges herself at the paint table, mortar and pestle in hand, gleaming pigments surrounding her. He stands behind her, leans against her back, arms on her arms, and guides her efforts to mix the oil and colors in a gentle rhythm.

Their intimacy deepens with a stolen kiss. Tentative caresses turn into breathless, impatient envelopings. The envelopings grow closer, become flesh on flesh as he unlaces her corset. He brings her closer still, pulling her to him, entering her, transfiguring them both.

With Amalia's consent, the Jesuits' painting begins to change. Johannes imbues it with a second, private meaning for him and Amalia alone. The Virgin's crown of ivy becomes a crown of myrtle: the crown of brides, an emblem of marital union and fidelity. The Virgin's belly swells as a sign of her fertility. Over the Virgin's head, in perfect parallel with the pierced window, a silver mirror appears, capturing the blurred image of Johannes, as he in turn captures his subject: Amalia the Virgin, and Amalia his lover. He moves the vanishing point from the Virgin's hand to Amalia's face. Underfoot, the Virgin crushes a serpent; she vanquishes the heretical Reformation and the secrecy of their relationship. The lovers crave revelation, purification.

In the Virgin's hand, the goldfinch of Christ becomes a rupturing chrysalis. Its growth from pupa to butterfly symbolizes a transformation of the spirit but also a transition to a new life. The lovers lay claim to the painting; *The Chrysalis* is no longer the Jesuits' alone.

Johannes and Amalia lie naked, wrapped in the fabric depicted in the burgomaster's painting. They plan for the time when they will walk freely along the canals, for the time when her father will give his leave to their union, for the time when Amalia will become helpmate and partner to Johannes, for the time when the world shall see the wished-for swollen belly of Amalia the subject become the real swollen belly of Amalia the lover and wife.

Johannes cannot bear their twilight partings, and he takes to spending nights with her image. He holds a lamp close to the canvas and imagines the silken feel of her real flesh. He hears a rustling in the eaves and hurries to cover the painting.

"Don't do this, Johannes." Pieter's voice reaches him.

"What do you mean?" Johannes is not sure what Pieter has seen, what he knows.

"This painting, this relationship with the burgomaster's daughter."

"Her name is Amalia."

"Johannes, she will always be the burgomaster's daughter, and you will always be a tradesman. Skilled, yes, but a tradesman always."

"We will make her family understand."

"Make them understand? Make them understand that their precious daughter, their priceless commodity, has given herself to a struggling tradesman? And a Catholic one by the looks of it? That's rich, Johannes."

"We are only for each other, Pieter, even if they do not support her choice."

"What about me, Johannes? What about the studio? Who will be for us? Don't you see you are destroying all that we have built, all that the master gave us? The relationship, the paintings, they will take all of it away."

Johannes pushes past Pieter's outstretched hand and disappears into the night.

twenty-eight
NEW YORK CITY, PRESENT DAY

AT THE FORMIDABLE WROUGHT-IRON GATES TO HER FIFTH Avenue apartment building, Lillian turned and waved to Mara. Two uniformed concierges and doormen fluttered to her aid and ushered her inside while the limousine taking Mara home proceeded. Mara watched the privileged Upper East Side street scene through the car's darkened window. Moneyed matrons set out for dusky promenades, nannies strolled with their infant charges, and Vuitton-bangled young celebutantes dashed off to exclusive benefits. In that moment, the trip to London—capped off with the furtive stashing away of the Strasser documents in an airport locker—seemed like a dream, and she was able to forget the task that lay before her, the weighty responsibility that was hers alone now.

As they made their way down Fifth Avenue, Mara glimpsed the enormous blue Dutch art exhibit banner flapping over the entrance to the

Metropolitan Museum of Art. "Stop," she called out, but the car kept moving. Mara struggled for a minute to remember the name of Lillian's driver, and then it came to her. "George, please stop here."

"But, miss, my clear instructions from Miss Joyce are to leave you at your apartment building."

"Don't worry, George, I'll find my own way home."

Although he shook his head at her impertinence, George pulled up where Mara had indicated. He turned back toward her and eyed her suspiciously over the glass partition; he was reluctant to defy Lillian's orders quite so easily. "Are you certain?"

"Yes, I'm certain." So he sighed and heaved himself off his seat to open her door.

As soon as George pulled away, Mara started up the grand exterior staircase to the Met. Her boots clicked up the mercifully unpopulated expanse, and she breezed past security and the admissions desk with uncharacteristic ease. For once, there were no tourist throngs to bar her way. It was the museum's one late evening of the week, but it was nearly empty.

Mara walked through the Great Hall and up the vast staircase leading to the second floor. Signs heralding the Dutch art exhibit marked the route through the maze of rooms. She entered the exhibit by passing over the heavy kilim rug, evocative of so many Dutch paintings, that delineated its space. Guide in hand, she took in the breathtaking array of landscapes, still lifes, portraits, and genre paintings, borrowed from public institutions and private collections from all over Europe and North America. The collection, unprecedented in its breadth and immensity, dwarfed the offerings at the Beazley's auction and reminded her of the importance of the risks she was taking for *The Chrysalis*.

She exited the exhibit via a back staircase that passed by the Sackler Wing. She couldn't resist a quick visit to the Temple of Dendur, hoping that its tranquillity would somehow seep into her head to clear away the stain left by *The Chrysalis*'s sordid past and illuminate the steps she knew she had to take to rectify its history.

The ancient Egyptian temple, set high on a marble platform overlooking black reflecting pools, was housed in its very own wing of the museum. It was created in 15 B.C. to honor the goddess Isis. When ever-rising lake waters from the Aswân Dam threatened to destroy it, the enormous sandstone temple was transported block by block from the banks of the Nile to New York City. Egypt gifted the temple to the United States in 1965 in recognition of America's contribution to the UNESCO campaign to save Egyptian monuments.

Mara passed by the two marble statues guarding the temple entrance and stepped onto the pinkish-hued platform. For a moment, she stood at the barred entrance to the interior, noting the etched papyrus and lotus flowers that grew from the temple's base, the two pillars that rose to the sky like bundles of papyrus stock, and the image over the temple gate: a sun disk sporting great wings, a symbol of the sun god Re and the sky god Horus.

After a while, Mara stepped back and settled onto a marble bench facing the temple. She reveled in the stillness and the momentary escape, until the setting brought an old conversation with Michael to mind. One day, after their Byzantine art class, they had had a heated discussion about where a country's prized artifacts should reside, with Michael strongly advocating their display only in the home country and Mara taking a more moderate view that they should be housed where they would be best studied and valued. Mara shook her head thinking just how far Michael had drifted from his youthful idealism.

Then the thought of the next day came at her in a rush, and her stomach churned. Mara fashioned proposals for Michael and speeches for Harlan, if her appeal to Michael proved fruitless. She tried to steel herself for every possible ramification, but nothing calmed her inner turmoil.

It was almost a relief when the guard interrupted her and announced that the museum was about to close. Mara wound her way through the empty exhibit halls to the heavy exit doors. Like eager daffodils in early spring, a line of yellow cabs waited at the curb.

But Mara didn't hail one. Instead, she walked down Eighty-fourth Street to a little French bistro she had passed many times before and had been told had exquisite mussels and a long mirrored bar with an extensive wine list. She opened the door to find the bar crowded with couples waiting for tables, so she grabbed one of the only empty stools. Mara caught the bartender's eye and asked what chardonnay he recommended. While she waited for her wine to be poured, she noticed a familiar Hermès scarf on the shoulders of the woman sitting on the next bar stool; it was just like one that Lillian often wore.

The wine arrived. As Mara reached for it, the woman turned toward her. At first glance, the woman looked like a well-appointed Upper East Side matron, complete with a Ferragamo handbag and coordinating shoes, and the two exchanged cordial smiles. But, as Mara drew deeply from her glass, she noticed the boozy bob of the woman's head, the uneven red smear of lipstick applied with a tremulous hand, and the glassy, unfocused eyes and recognized the woman for what she was: a heavy drinker barely hanging on to the threads of her façade. Mara saw a flash of a possible future. The wine, which had begun its journey down Mara's throat in a welcome burn, transformed to a bilious liquid and rose up in her gorge. She put the wineglass down, tossed a ten on the bar, and rushed out. She flagged down the first cab she saw and headed home.

By the time she reached her street, Mara was exhausted. She rolled out of the cab and into her lobby, then stumbled into her apartment without even turning on the lights. She dropped her bag in the front hall and headed to the bathroom to wash off the residue of her long day—days, really.

As she dried her face and hands with a towel, she flicked on the switch in her living area, and there sat Michael, quiet as a mouse, waiting for her.

Mara screamed.

Michael didn't flinch. "Oh, I'm sorry. Did I scare you?" His voice was a curious blend of sarcasm and arid concern.

"Of course you did. What're you doing here?"

He stood up and walked toward her. "What do you mean 'What am I doing here?' Can't I surprise my girlfriend with a visit?"

Mara couldn't tell how to read him. She rapidly reviewed the roles she could assume and settled on the safety of girlfriend. "Oh, of course you can. That's sweet of you to surprise me. You just startled me, that's all."

"Just like you startled me," he responded, moving in her direction as if to embrace her.

Mara had no overt reason to second-guess him, but his movement toward her felt calculated. She backed away with slow steps, trying to keep at a safe distance without alarming him. "What do you mean I startled you?" She smiled and hoped her voice sounded light.

"What do you think I mean?"

Mara faltered in the face of his challenge. "I don't know," she whispered. She wanted to know what he knew before she revealed anything herself.

He continued toward her, speaking so softly she could not read his voice. "Where shall I begin, Mara? Let's see. I was 'startled' to learn from

Larry that he'd seen you outside Beazley's yesterday—with Lillian, at that. He found it very strange that, though you said you had been working at Beazley's for several days, he never saw you come in or leave. And I thought you were off at depositions."

Taking another step closer to her, he said, "Let's see, let's see. How else did you 'startle' me? Well, after checking with Lillian's secretary to find out where you and Lillian were headed, I was 'startled' to learn that you and Lillian had left for London."

He advanced. "Hmmm. So, that got me wondering, just what were you two up to? Why were you heading off to London together without telling me? So I did some investigating, checked with some of the security logs and guards. And there you 'startled' me again, by holing up with Lillian down in Beazley's library, day after day. I'm sure you can imagine that I was confused by all this 'startling' news. I asked myself, what were you two doing down there? What were you undertaking that would necessitate a trip to London? So I had to keep digging."

He took a further step toward her, then leaned her up against the kitchen doorway off the living room as though to kiss her. He continued, "And that's where you 'startled' me the most. Do you know how you did that, Mara?"

She knew, of course, but couldn't bring herself to answer.

His face was so close to her that she felt the heat of his breath. "You don't know? Really?" He feigned surprise. "Well, I'll tell you, then. You 'startled' me the most by breaking into my office safe and stealing my uncle Edward's papers out of it. Sure, you—or perhaps you and Lillian, for all I know— replaced the documents with copies that looked pretty close to the originals. But I could tell the difference. . . ."

Mara was speechless. He knew everything.

"So, I guess you've discovered the dirty Roarke family secret." He brought his face even closer, almost resting it in the arch of her neck. If on-lookers saw them through a window, they would have assumed that they were lovers.

When he spoke next, his voice was gentle, disarming. "Why didn't you come to me? Ask me about what you had found? Mara, I can only imag-ine that you think I have been playing a game with you, that all of this be-tween us is just one big deception. But I do care about you. I'm not going to pretend that my motivations were entirely pure in the beginning, but that's all changed. However this began, I have grown to care about you very deeply. Let's put the past and its secrets behind us. We have something more important to focus on." He pulled back to look at her and caressed the curve of her jaw, a place he knew was particularly vulnerable to his touch.

For a moment, he seemed like the Michael she thought she knew. But Mara couldn't be sure that his appeal to her emotions wasn't just another of his ploys. She didn't know what to believe, and his touch on her skin burned. The moment had come to make her proposal, so she danced along with him. "Michael, I'm sorry for lying and for not coming to you with this. But maybe we can make it right, together. What if we said that we found your uncle's documents when we were doing discovery? Then we could return *The Chrysalis* to Hilda Baum and the other paintings to their rightful owners without any stigma attaching to you. We could even restitute privately, so the court and the public need never know about the deceptions."

He shook his head, casting his eyes downward as if repenting. "I'm sorry, Mara, I can't do that. No matter how hard we might try to keep my uncle's documents secret, eventually they'd come to light as we went through the process of returning the paintings. Someone would be bound to leak the story."

"Please, Michael," she implored him. If only he agreed to her proposal, then Mara could serve all her masters—Lillian, Nana, her own conscience—with the least jeopardy to herself and to the career she was hanging on to by a very thin thread.

"You saw my uncle's will when you were in my safe, didn't you?"

"Yes." There was no sense in feigning innocence now.

"So you saw, then, that I am the sole beneficiary of his entire estate."

"Yes."

"Well, where do you think he got all that money? Certainly not from his Beazley's salary. Certainly not from family money, like yours."

Finally understanding, Mara whispered, "If all this came out, even if you were entirely innocent, the law wouldn't permit you to keep the fruits of his crime."

"Exactly. And, even if we managed to keep it secret, where do you think all the money for your private restitutions would come from? So I have no intention of letting all this come out. I have no intention of giving up my inheritance. Mara, you don't know what it's like to come from nothing. That's what I grew up with, Mara, nothing—no trust fund, no security blanket, only debts—and I will not return to it." His hand moved from her face to her hand, lacing his fingers into hers. "Please give me the documents, Mara. I'm going to destroy them, and we're going to pretend that this never happened. And so is Lillian."

"I don't have them," Mara answered truthfully; they were in a temporary storage locker at the airport.

Michael pulled his fingers from hers and clutched her wrist instead. "What do you mean you don't have them?" The sudden sharpness in his voice revealed how much of an act it had been for him to play the caring, decent Michael.

"They're in a safe-deposit box." She tried to wrench her arm free, but his grip tightened.

"Then let's go get them." He dragged her toward the door. Her arm began to bruise under the pressure of his fingers.

"Just let me get my bag. It has the key in it."

"All right," he conceded.

As Mara bent down to pick up her bag, Michael let go of her arm for a moment. Seizing the opportunity, she ran out the door. She sprinted toward the elevator, pressing the Down button over and over in an attempt to speed its arrival. A door slammed. Without turning around to confirm what she already knew, she ran to the stairwell. Flying down the ten flights, Mara reached the lobby just seconds before Michael got off the elevator. She bolted through the lobby, nearly running over several of her neighbors, and heard Michael yell her name.

She hurled herself in front of the first available cab, opened the car door, and was climbing in when Michael grabbed her. With one leg already in the cab, she struggled to escape from him and get into the cab fully. "Start driving!" she ordered the cabbie.

Without even turning around, he answered in a thick accent, "I can't get involved in this, miss. Sorry. Please get out of the cab."

"Please," she begged, as she fought to pry Michael's hand off her arm. "Please. He's my ex-husband, and he's trying to hurt me."

The cabbie turned around to witness Michael trying to drag her out of the car. "Okay, miss, okay. We'll go."

With the door open and Michael grasping on to her arm, the cab started to peel away. Michael ran alongside the cab, still gripping her, until it picked up speed. Once his clutch slackened and he dropped off, Mara slammed the door shut. She did not even dare to turn back.

"Where are we going, miss?" the cabbie asked, after Mara thanked him over and over.

Mara started to give him Sophia's address but then stopped herself. Not only would Michael think to look for her there, but Sophia was also unlikely to welcome her. And she could not run to Lillian, as she felt certain that was where Michael would turn next. So she directed the cabbie to the first hiding place that came to mind, the anonymous business hotel across the street from Severin.

Alone in a tiny hotel room, Mara paced back and forth. She had dialed every number she had for Lillian but never got an answer. Mara was afraid to leave any messages.

Finally, on Mara's second time through the list of numbers, Lillian picked up the phone. By now, Mara was in a feverish state. "Lillian, where have you been? I've been out of my mind with worry," she exclaimed.

Lillian was perplexed. "Whatever for, Mara? Can't a woman get some sleep after a twenty-four-hour transatlantic turnaround?"

Mara's voice hardened. "Lillian, Michael knows. He was waiting for me at my apartment when I got back."

"What do you mean 'he knows'?" Lillian's voice rang with alarm.

"He knows that I've found Edward's documents and that I've been on the trail of *The Chrysalis*'s real provenance as well as those of the other paintings. I discussed our proposal with him, but he has no intention of restituting the paintings. In fact, he wants to destroy Edward's documents."

"Well, then, our plan isn't going quite as we hoped." Lillian's calm struck Mara as cavalier given the circumstances. "I guess you'll have to resort to the alternative. Approach Harlan; see if he'll reach out and use his contact at Beazley's to resolve this privately. Perhaps his contact can deal with Michael. Then, with Beazley's, make use of the history we've re-created. Ensure that the paintings get returned, at least *The Chrysalis*. Do you think you can still do that and keep my name out of it?"

Mara was loath to answer but knew she must tell Lillian all of it. Lillian did not seem to appreciate the gravity of her situation—specifically, the threat Michael posed. In fact, she seemed almost callously concerned only about her reputation and perhaps Beazley's. "I'll try, Lillian, but Michael realizes that you've been helping me."

The line was silent. When Lillian's voice came back on, it seethed and crackled. "You didn't tell him, did you? You promised you wouldn't."

"No, of course not." Mara was hurt by the accusation. She had put herself on the line in ways she couldn't even believe to rectify wrongs she didn't perpetrate, and Lillian—who, despite her help, risked very little—dared to accuse Mara of betrayal. Exhausted and defensive, she shared with Lillian the details of Michael's angry visit. "So you see why I'm concerned? If he can't find me, I think he's going to come to you, hoping that you'll give him the documents."

"I'll be fine," Lillian assured Mara. "My apartment building is like Fort Knox. I'll leave explicit instructions with my doormen not to let anyone up. Will that suffice?"

"Yeah. But I don't want you to be accessible to Michael at work tomorrow. Maybe you think I'm overreacting, Lillian, but please stay away from him. At least until I work this out."

"I won't go in. How's that? Not until this is all resolved."

Mara relaxed. "Thank you. I'd never forgive myself if anything happened to you."

To Mara's relief, Lillian's usual haughty tone resurfaced. "Mara, don't overestimate yourself. I chose to be part of this. You didn't drag me into it."

Mara smiled at Lillian's insult. "Then I stand corrected."

"Please call me only after you've made your decision about proceeding and you've executed it. Then I'll do my part at Beazley's." The women agreed and exchanged curt goodbyes.

Mara fell back onto the bed, her posture slack for the first time since the flight. For a moment, she almost imagined that it was all a bad dream.

Mara awakened in the dawn, before her wake-up call. She paced the room, reviewing her strategy over and over again, practicing her speech for Harlan, even allowing herself to think about the ramifications to her. She felt the butterflies begin their dance, looping and fluttering against the walls of her stomach. She had come too far to turn back, and even if she could, for the first time, she truly knew that she no longer wanted to sacrifice her sense of justice, or her right to devise her own goals, on the altar of success—or her father's expectations. She was ready.

twenty-nine

AMSTERDAM, 1943

THE GROUP WALKS THE LENGTH OF THE TRAIN TO REACH the private railway car, with the senior official at the helm and the heavily laden Baums and junior officer in tow. The Amsterdam station teems with travelers, but the jumpy crowd parts at the presence of the decorated officer.

The distance, which Erich had walked so often, so easily before the occupation, seems interminable to him now. There are no other yellow stars at the station, and he knows that the other travelers stare at the sight of the Nazi occupiers helping Jews onto a train. Especially when Jews no longer ride on regular passenger trains but on trains of a very different sort.

Erich looks back at the trailing Cornelia, who had insisted on changing into a fussy silk dress and an ermine-trimmed jacket. She wants their daughter to see them looking well when they disembark in Milan, but her ensemble slows their pace through the station. He chose to dress more solemnly—more shrewdly, to his way of thinking—in an unobtrusive gray suit, plain black coat, and fedora. He did not want the extra attention beyond that garnered by their yellow stars.

Erich heaves a sigh of relief when the officers usher them out of sight and into their private car. It is indeed as luxurious as the men had touted. Heavy damask fabric covers the tufted banquettes, a marble-tiled private lavatory is at their disposal, and sumptuous ruby curtains frame the window.

After stowing the couple's suitcases, parcels, and trunk on the racks above and the seats beside them, the officers bid them a safe journey, tap their heels, and salute them with a "Heil Hitler" before exiting the compartment. The whistle cries out, and the train begins its slow departure, click by click down the track. Though their car begins to lurch and sway, the couple remains standing, still frozen with incredulity at the blessing of their situation. Only when the train pulls away from the Amsterdam station do they lower themselves down into the banquettes on either side of the car.

Cornelia asks with hesitation, "Should we keep our coats on?"

Erich knows why she inquires. The reichskommissar's rules mandate the display of the Star of David, and removal of their coats will hide the stars. Not familiar with the laws of the occupied countries they will pass through, he says, "I think it's the wisest course, dearest." He pats the inner pocket of his coat, the one holding their precious Seyss-Inquart letter of protection. "Plus, I want to keep this close by. . . ."

She nods in understanding.

The whistle announces their arrival in Berlin after a journey quiet with nerves and expectations. As the train pulls into the otherwise silent, dark station, Erich and Cornelia sit stock-still, facing each other, waiting wordlessly to pass through the dreaded city. He can hear the low rumble of passengers boarding, but the process seems to take longer than at the other stops. As he takes the envelope out of his inner coat pocket, he looks out the window, straining to see the source of the delay between the billows of steam.

In the dim light of a station lamppost, Erich makes out a sweeper standing on the platform. The man is alone in the now-desolate station.

The two men make eye contact for a brief moment before the sweeper hastily retreats into the shadows.

    With a sudden slam, the door to the compartment opens. The couple springs to their feet to greet the soldiers as Erich readies his letter of protection.

thirty

NEW YORK CITY, PRESENT DAY

A SHORT HOUR LATER, MARA SLIPPED INTO THE BACK EN-
trance of Severin, passing her identity card through the screening
device and waving to the security guards still on duty from the night shift.
She slid into a waiting elevator and hit the top button on the panel for
Harlan's floor.

Mara steadied her flapping and wafting nerves as the elevator completed
its ride. She exited into the vacant reception area for the partners, distin-
guished by its mahogany paneling and beige leather furniture, decadent
sprays of freshly cut exotic flowers, and understated modern paintings.
Mara had spent so much of her career aiming for these rich heights, but
now she was repulsed by their display of life-sapping greed.

Mara worked her way down the maze of hallways to Harlan's corner office. She found herself at his door without his secretary present.

Mara steeled herself, knocked, and waited for the grunt of admission, but nothing emerged.

Harlan always beat the other partners in to work; he should be in his office. So Mara tapped again. This time, she received a guttural utterance of surprise. "Huh? Who is it?"

"Mara Coyne," she announced through the closed door.

A long pause ensued, and then, much to her astonishment, she heard a greeting. "Well, come on in."

Pushing open the door, she found Harlan in his usual position. Mara began to apologize. "I'm so sorry to disturb you—" But he interrupted before she could finish. "Mara, you're just the person I wanted to see."

She was too shocked to do more than stammer "R-really?"

"Really. Do I have some good news for you!" he exclaimed, in the closest thing to a giddy voice she had ever heard from him.

Mara had no idea how to react, but Harlan's disposition was so unprecedented that she felt more than just a twinge of fear. "What is it?" she asked. His joviality had to be a trap of some sort.

"I just heard from my man at Beazley's. It seems as though your *Chrysalis* case has resolved itself to our client's satisfaction."

"What?" Mara was flabbergasted. How could the scenario have resolved to Beazley's satisfaction? If the judge had issued an opinion, Harlan would have heard about it first, not Beazley's. So it could not yet be that Beazley's had won on summary judgment, for which Mara said a silent prayer of thanks. Knowing all that she did, Mara could never forgive herself if Justice Weir adopted *DeClerck* based on her *Baum* arguments and made it nearly impossible for Holocaust survivors to recoup property.

"Yes. *The Chrysalis* was stolen from the Beazley's warehouse early last evening." He grinned like a fat cat, as if this statement explained everything.

"Stolen?" Mara was altogether mystified.

"Yes, stolen." Harlan closed his eyes and inhaled deeply in an attempt to control his irritation. "Mara, the insurance money will allow our client to settle this matter between the contenders. Presumably, the current owner and Hilda Baum will each get a piece. Beazley's discussed it with the current owner last night as well as with Hilda Baum. It seems as though they'll be able to reach some amicable agreement to dismiss the case. The client didn't offer details, and I didn't ask. It's enough that they're thrilled with the outcome. And with us."

She was still confused. "Beazley's worked all this out with Hilda Baum last night?"

"Yes, late last night. They can communicate without us as long as no outside lawyers are present."

Mara tried to make sense of this and wondered whether Lillian had heard the news through her Beazley's grapevine. All the while, Harlan stared at her, waiting for her jubilation. She stammered, "O-our client told you this?"

"Not in so many words, but Philip didn't need to. I understood how it would play out."

Mara's heart leaped to her throat. She was afraid to ask but knew she had to. "Philip?"

"Yes, Philip Robichaux. He's my contact at Beazley's as well as an old friend. Have you met him?"

Time stopped for Mara. Harlan continued talking, but she couldn't hear a word. She considered Philip's ties to her boss. Did Harlan know the truth? Did he already understand that the Nazis had stolen *The Chrysalis* and that Beazley's had purchased it from the Nazi henchman Kurt Strasser? Was he aware that Philip and Michael knew this and were complicit in hiding the truth? And that there were many more paintings like *The Chrysalis*? She couldn't reveal her findings to him. She knew he would not come to her aid. But she wished she knew for certain the extent of his involvement.

Somewhere in the distance, she heard him continue. "And as I said, Mara, I wasn't one hundred percent sure you'd rise to the test, but you took a dog and turned it into a winner. Ruthlessly, too." He laughed, a macabre cackle.

Then he bestowed the golden ring upon her. "So, I'll be backing you next month during the partnership review." Was this a bribe for her silence? His face seemed devoid of artifice.

The moment had come for Mara to acknowledge Harlan's gift, to convince him of her ignorance and loyalty. She should have felt honored, but the most she could muster were a few listless words of gratitude before she left his office.

Mara headed back down toward her office. It would be pretty easy to slip back into line, to let go of everything she'd uncovered. She could assume the mantle of partner, finally feel rewarded and successful. Perhaps she could get a bigger apartment or take a vacation. There would be other men. Mara knew that she could play along with whatever game she was tricked into and that no one would ever question her integrity or legal skill. But something had happened during her covert work with Lillian. A long-suppressed desire for moral strength had finally emerged, and Mara would no longer ignore its importance.

Just as the elevator doors were about to close behind her, a hand slipped into the crack, and the doors bounced back open. It was Sophia. The women stared at each other, and then, as the doors began to slide closed, Sophia stepped in.

Sophia broke the silence first. "How've you been?" she asked with genuine concern.

Mara stared at the floor numbers above the door; she couldn't afford to connect with Sophia right now. So when she answered, her tone was cooler than she felt. "I've been better."

Sophia scanned the elevator panel. "You're heading back from Harlan's office awfully early. I thought he didn't see people before Marianne got in at nine."

"He doesn't." Mara didn't see the point in explaining the scene that had just transpired. It was easier to pretend her visit hadn't happened.

"Oh, Mara, please don't tell me you were heading up there to see him privately on this *Baum* case."

"I was."

Sophia reached forward and hit all the buttons on the way to the associates' floor. "Mara, what're you doing? You're trashing years of hard work. I don't understand what has happened to your sense of priorities. Thank God he wouldn't see you yet. You still have a chance to walk away from all this and to resume your own work."

"Sophia, what do you care?" Mara answered angrily. "You made it very clear that you want nothing to do with all this."

Over the ring of the elevator door opening to an empty floor, Sophia shouted, "Mara, I care about you, even though you're right—I don't want to jeopardize the hard work and the time and money I've invested in realizing my dreams. Neither do I want to stand by and watch you hurt yourself. But it seems as though I'm witnessing that anyway." An irrepressible question rose in her throat. "Are you going to go up there again later to tell him about the documents you took?"

Mara took a deep breath. The goals and passions that drove Sophia hadn't entirely lost their shine. Nor had any of her feelings for Sophia and their friendship diminished. But she needed to detach from her friend in order to finish the task at hand. And she had to trust that there was a way, when this was all over, to forge a new relationship. "Yes, about the documents and all the other schemes I've uncovered since you and I last spoke."

Sophia crossed her arms and moved to the front corner of the elevator. "I suppose there's nothing I can do to stop you."

"No, there isn't."

The elevator doors opened again, and Sophia stepped out. "Then, I guess I'll leave you to it." She began to walk away, then turned back. "I'm really sorry, Mara."

thirty-one

NEW YORK CITY, PRESENT DAY

I T WAS STILL TOO EARLY FOR THE FIRM TO FEEL ALIVE, AND Mara wound her way deeper and deeper into the associate rabbit warren unheeded. Finally reaching her door, she grasped for its handle like a life preserver.

She stood against the closed wooden door for a long spell, trying to calm her mind and form a fresh plan. What should she do next? Both of the paths she had discussed with Lillian—offering Michael a proposition to absolve himself by privately restituting the paintings or enlisting Harlan in the cause as a safe entrée with Beazley's—were impossible. Now the decision was whether to contact the reporter or the authorities. She needed the documents in either case. Mara considered calling Lillian for advice but remembered her promise to make contact only after executing the plan.

The door shuddered from a strong knock. She jumped back.

"Who is it?"

"It's Sophia. Can I come in?"

"I guess so."

With a tentative step and an abject expression, Sophia walked in. "I've come wearing ivy wreaths and bearing olive branches."

"What do you mean?" Mara replied curtly. She had neither time nor patience for Sophia's southern aphorisms.

"I mean, I've come to apologize. I'm sorry for second-guessing your decisions and for giving you so much grief. I can't pretend that I'm gonna jump in and help you—I'm still too protective of our dreams for that—but I can at least make amends."

"If it's forgiveness you're looking for, I don't think I can give it just now."

"I'm just looking for a chance to reconnect with you. I miss you."

Though still hurt by Sophia's earlier reaction, Mara felt herself soften, particularly if Sophia wasn't going to try to lure her away from her chosen path. She felt more isolated than ever, and she was eager for contact. "Okay, then."

"Can I buy you a cup of coffee at the diner?" Sophia asked.

Maybe a brisk walk and some fresh air would help settle her spinning thoughts and provide some clarity. "All right, just a quick cup. And only if you promise not to ask me about *The Chrysalis*."

"That's a promise I'm happy to make."

As the women took the elevator to the lobby and then walked down the long city block, Sophia chattered on about the indecisive female partner with whom she was working, a woman who advised heads of major corporations on the most intricate deals with seeming confidence but behind the scenes made Sophia run circles with her indecisiveness. Mara enjoyed the distracting banter, but she held herself in reserve. When they pushed open the door to the empty diner and the hostess, Bev, greeted them with a familiar hello, Mara felt momentarily transported back to safer times, before *The Chrysalis* and all the wounds she had sustained.

Mara and Sophia sat at the counter for a moment to place their coffee orders—black for Sophia, lots of milk and sugar for Mara—and chatted while the waiter headed to the kitchen for their drinks. As Sophia divulged office gossip, Mara heard the bell over the diner door clang. She turned and saw Michael.

Mara sprang up from her seat, warning Sophia, "We need to get out of here. Fast."

Sophia reached out for Mara's arm, pulling her back down on the stool, while Michael took a position blocking the door. "Mara, you have every right to be furious with me, but please listen. I know you find it hard to believe, but I want to help you get back on track. I understand that nothing *I* can say will stop you from sabotaging yourself in Harlan's office or in whatever way you might think of next. When Michael called this morning looking for you, well, I thought maybe he could convince you to keep your findings private. It's in both of your best interests, after all. So I agreed that we'd meet here."

Mara froze for a moment, in shock at Sophia's actions. At her betrayal. "Sophia, how could you do this to me? You have no idea what's going on"— she gestured to Michael, who still stood in the shadows of the doorway— "no concept what he's up to . . ."

"You're right, I don't know any details. But Michael's told me that he knows you took those documents from his safe and that he's not angry. He has good reasons for keeping them there. When you hear them, I'm sure you'll be glad that we stopped you from tossing your career down the drain." She nodded to Michael. "I'll leave you two alone to work it out." Michael stepped to the side to let Sophia pass. The diner door slammed behind her.

Mara rushed to the door, the only exit in sight. She darted around Michael, lunging for the handle. But he was quick. "You're not going anywhere without me." A small smile appeared on his face even as his nails dug into her flesh.

"Isn't it enough that you arranged to have *The Chrysalis* disappear so that the *Baum* suit would magically vanish?" she asked as she tried to wrest her arm free.

"How do you know that?" His eyes and fingers bore into her more deeply.

"Harlan told me."

"You lied to Sophia about not being able to see him?" He seemed astonished.

"Yes, I lied to her. How could *you* possibly be surprised at that?"

"What did you tell him? Did you give him the documents?"

"I gave him nothing, and I told him nothing." From the fear on

Michael's face, Mara realized that Harlan was not involved in the provenance cover-up. Why else would Michael be scared that Mara might have divulged the dirty family secret to him?

"I don't believe you."

"Believe what you like. His announcement of *The Chrysalis*'s disappearance threw me for a loop. I thought he might be caught up in all of this with you and Philip. So I was hardly going to tout my findings to him."

"Well, he's not involved. Come on, let's go." He pulled her toward the door.

She resisted. "Please, Michael. Why doesn't the painting's disappearance put an end to all this?"

Michael's curious smirk returned. "Of course *The Chrysalis*'s disappearance doesn't put an end to all this, Mara. The 'theft' may be a tourniquet on the public bloodletting you had hoped for, but I'm sure you could still wreak havoc with the documents if you set your mind to it. Anyway, there's much more at stake than just *The Chrysalis*, and you know that. Surely you haven't forgotten about all those other paintings? Mara, I want the documents back."

Mara's breath labored shallow and fast. She felt as if she was going to faint. "I can't do that, Michael."

He drew closer to her face, the sneer mutating to something more wicked. "Really? Funny. Lillian said the same thing. But I don't think you want to go the way of Lillian."

Mara's breathing stopped altogether. "What do you mean?"

"Have you spoken to her today?"

"No."

Michael pulled out his cell phone and dialed. He spoke in hushed tones, then handed her the phone. "Why don't you have a word with her?"

Mara grabbed for the phone. "Lillian? Lillian, are you there?"

The phone was silent.

"Lillian!"

"I'm here." Her voice was weak.

"Are you all right?"

"Well, I'm here with Philip, if that tells you anything."

"Have they hurt you?"

"No. Not yet, anyway. Mara, is Michael asking you for the documents?"

"Yes."

Lillian's voice quavered. "Remember what you promised? About the paintings?"

"Yes." Mara understood Lillian to mean her promise to restitute them.

"Then, you know what to do. Make sure you—" Mara heard a man's voice, and the line went dead.

Mara handed Michael the phone. "You bastard. You better not hurt her."

"We won't, Mara. As long as you get me the documents."

"How did you guys get into her apartment?"

"Oh, that was easy enough. She buzzed us right up when I described what I would do to you if she didn't."

"How could you do this, Michael?" She twisted herself away from his grip and lurched for the door, but the entryway was too small, and he was too fast. Pinning her arms behind her, he backed her into a corner. But he was careful; from a distance, his move looked like an embrace. His hot breath scalded her cheek. "Don't fight me, Mara. Don't forget that you broke into my safe. You broke into Beazley's. You stole our documents. I could easily turn this into a matter of your lawbreaking. Not mine." He bent her arm into a position she didn't think possible. "Mara, I don't want to hurt you. And I know you don't want me to hurt Lillian or Sophia or your family."

"My family?"

"Don't you remember all our bedroom confidences? How much you told me about your father's political dealings, his sordid partners?"

His words wrapped like a noose around her neck, strangling out any retort.

"I'll leave it to your imagination." His grimace returned. "Come on, let's go."

Mara started to resist, but an image of a weakened Lillian flashed through her mind, and she thought better of her actions. Mara turned back toward the exit, with Michael's hand pressing down hard on the small of her back.

Just as they were about to walk out onto the street, Mara heard Bev call her name. "Mara. Oh, Mara, hon." For a moment, Mara thought that Bev suspected. Instead, she looked back to see Bev waving a white bag in the air. "You forgot something."

It was the coffees. Mara retrieved them with a gracious thanks.

Michael hailed his waiting limo and pushed her down onto the seat. Inside, behind the darkened windows, he slapped Mara full across the face. She fell to the floor, too shocked even to scream at the pain. She had expected retribution, but not this.

Pushing her down farther onto the floor with both hands, he snarled into her ear, enunciating each word with terrifying clarity. "Where are we going?"

Blood streamed from her nose. She tilted her head back to stop its flow but refused to look in his direction. She hesitated, unsure what to tell him. He snapped her neck back by the hair. "I asked you a question, Mara. You'd better answer me."

A strategy dawned on her as she thought of her museum visit. "The Met."

"The Metropolitan Museum? I thought you put them in a safe-deposit box?"

"When we reached the city yesterday, the banks were closed. I picked someplace with guarded lockers."

"You really expect me to believe that you left them at the museum?"

She sneered at him. "I left them someplace I thought you'd never look for them."

"You'd better not be bullshitting me, Mara. For your sake and for Lillian's."

She picked herself up from the floor and slid back onto the black leather of the seat, in the farthest possible corner from him. Mara stared out the window at Korean delis unfurling their awnings and the investment bankers hustling through throngs of deliverymen. As the city awakened on such a delightful, crisp morning, she sopped up the blood trickling from her nose and felt hopelessness descend upon her.

But Mara was a fighter, and so despite her bleak prospects, she used the few blocks of travel to plan. As the limo pulled up in front of the long line of cabs outside the Met, Michael shoved her out the door. "Come on. Get out."

Mara stumbled from the car into the intense morning sun, made stronger by its reflection off the Met's granite steps. For a moment, she was blind. When her vision returned, the tourist hordes bombarded her. She thanked God for their presence; they would provide much-needed cover.

Arm in arm, like any other couple, Michael and Mara strode up the museum's immense steps. They pushed through the revolving door together, of course, since he would not let her leave his sight or his touch, and entered the Great Hall. Even now, threatened and afraid, Mara was moved by the soaring ceiling and weightless cupola. Somewhere, beyond her nightmare, there was a solid, enduring world.

The museum teemed with security guards. With Michael at her side, Mara wove through their inspections without incident. She headed toward the long line at the ticket counter. "We have to buy tickets," she told him.

Michael saw the enormous coat checks that flanked the entryway to the Great Hall and gripped her arm tighter. "What kind of bullshit are you trying to pull?" he whispered, and pointed. "That's the storage."

She murmured, "The papers you want aren't there. They're in the storage facility on the lower level, inside the museum."

He looked blank. She explained. "We need tickets to get into the museum, to get to the storage space."

He dragged her to the information desk and thrust a museum map in her hand. "I'm not going anywhere until you show me on this map the exact location of this storage."

Hands shaking, Mara unfolded the map. She zeroed in on the lower level of the museum. She found the symbol designating storage—through the Greek and Roman galleries—and pointed it out on the map. What the map did not reveal was that, in fact, the museum didn't have any storeroom that allowed visitors to leave their belongings overnight. Or that this particular storage facility in no way contained the Strasser documents.

Mollified, Michael moved to the long queue for tickets, his hand on Mara's wrist. He sweated as he was forced to wait out the line with patience and a pleasant expression, and Mara nearly smiled. But the quarter grin disappeared from her face as soon as the tickets hit their hands. Now she needed unfailing precision and a good measure of luck.

Michael allowed Mara to lead him into the Greek and Roman galleries. But Michael and Mara did not linger. They passed by the tour groups that encircled their guides like flower petals. A particularly dense pack crowded around the legendary first-century A.D. Roman *Statue of an Old Market Woman* halted traffic. Mara and Michael navigated their way through the still throng. Despite the crowds, the hall was hushed, and Mara felt scared about her plan.

Michael's cell phone rang, shattering the quiet. He checked the number and picked up. As he murmured into the receiver, his expression grew troubled. He slowed their pace, and Mara strained to discern his words. From the snippets she made out, she gathered that he was speaking to Philip and that something serious had happened to Lillian. Michael seemed shocked by the news.

A security guard approached. "Sir, you cannot use your cell phone in here."

Michael ignored the warning.

The guard got closer. "Sir, I will have to confiscate your cell phone if you do not turn it off right now."

Michael waved him away with his free hand, saying, "I'll only be a minute." For an instant, he lost his grip on Mara's arm, and she slid back into the crowds, allowing them to envelop her as Michael and the man exchanged words. Moving within her protective camouflage, Mara darted off to the right, into one of the small galleries off the central hall. She knew that these galleries connected, one to the next, ultimately emptying out into a hallway with a little-used elevator.

Every muscle in her body longed to sprint down the corridor linking the galleries in the direction of the pulsing red Exit sign. But she knew that speed would draw attention to her. Over and over again, she repeated an old phrase of Nana's: "Slow and steady wins the race, child." She almost felt her grandmother's hand restraining her, steadying her gait.

Mara spotted the elevator leading down to the parking garage. She pushed the Down button. The door opened, and before she entered, she looked back. She spied Michael turning down the hallway in the opposite direction, toward the coat check she had designated. As he rounded the corner, she saw him in profile, his eyes narrow, his gait fast, like a dog in a foxhunt.

By the time she reached the garage, tears streamed down her face. She would have loved nothing more than to collapse in a corner and give in to her fear, but it was an emotional indulgence she couldn't afford. She ran through the garage and exited onto Fifth Avenue and, from there, into Central Park.

When a lit cab passed by, she jumped in front of it. She grabbed the door handle and slid into the backseat. The cabbie hurled incomprehensible epithets at her, but she pushed several rumpled twenties through the divider. "JFK, please. I have to make a connection. There's more money for you if you get me there fast." Mara was worried about Lillian but knew she had to get the documents first for their mutual protection.

"Okay, miss." The cab driver's wrath disappeared, and he sped away.

When she got to the British Airways terminal at JFK, Mara selected the next flight scheduled to depart and proceeded to the first-class British Airways desk. She needed to get through security and into the boarding gate area fast; the storage area was designed only for short-term use. Oozing a feigned sense of entitlement, she purchased the last remaining first-class seat to Brussels and asked for an escort to expedite her way through security. Once through the line, she parted with the escort and broke into a sprint, this time toward a neglected hall containing the storeroom.

Instinct, not memory, propelled her toward the storage area, a lingering remnant from the days of leisurely, elegant travel. Full speed ahead, she thanked her lucky stars that an attendant was manning the storage area. The first time around, when she had stashed the documents, she had had to search high and low for an airport employee to unlock its dusty gates. She could not afford that time today. She slowed down and fumbled in her bag for the ticket stub. She saw the ticket, but her hands shook so violently, she could not grasp it.

"I have it!" She finally, desperately thrust it toward him. She needed those documents—for the authorities, for the victims, for herself, for Lillian.

He took the ticket. "Okay, miss. Okay. Hold your horses. Let me see what I can do." The elderly man put down his *New York Post* and shuffled off toward the grimy corners of the storage room.

"Hurry, hurry. Please hurry."

"Got a plane to catch, miss?"

Tears of futility welled up in her eyes as she heard him continue to shamble. "Yes."

"Let me see, let me see . . . This might be it back here. Is it black, with a leather handle?"

"Yes, yes. That's it!" He handed her the bag. She tossed down another twenty, much more than the storage fee, and dashed off.

Up the stairs to the terminal, down the endless corridor, past the gates, down the stairs to the Baggage Claim sign once again, Mara ran. She veered off at the first sign of an exit and blended into the stream of incoming travelers, hoping to find the arrival area and a taxi driver willing to break the no-pickup rules for a price. It took another fistful of bills, but the first cab quickly jumped forward as she shouted, "Just go as fast as you can into Manhattan."

With the documents in hand, Mara could refrain no longer from contacting Lillian, so she negotiated for the use of the cabbie's cell phone with more money. She dialed Lillian's home phone first, nervous that Philip might pick up but confident that the cabbie's cell phone rendered her untraceable. No one answered either at Lillian's home or on her cell, so Mara called information and connected to the concierge in Lillian's building. After explaining her concerns as innocuously as possible, Mara asked if he'd check on her.

Mara waited a full fifteen minutes, passing an additional bill to the anxious cabbie, before the concierge came back on the line. "Miss, are you still there?"

"Yes." Her heart beat so loudly she was certain he could hear it.

"I'm afraid I have to call you back. I found Miss Joyce lying on the floor of her apartment, and I've just called an ambulance. I need to escort them to her."

"Go, go! I'll call you back later."

Mara sat frozen, cell phone in hand, watching the clock. After another twenty-five minutes had passed, time enough for the concierge to conduct the EMTs to Lillian, she contacted him again. "Sir, it's Mara Coyne calling back. How's Miss Joyce?"

"Well, the ambulance has taken her to Mount Sinai, but I'm sorry to tell you that it doesn't look good. They said it looked like her heart gave out."

"Her heart?" Mara was puzzled; Lillian had never mentioned a heart condition—not that she would. Suddenly she remembered seeing Lillian take that pill on the plane. Had Philip done something to precipitate an attack?

"Yeah, she's given us some scares in the past. But nothing like this."

Mara thanked him and hung up the phone. Too shocked even to cry, she was trying to process the concierge's words when the driver asked, "Where to, miss? We're getting close to the city."

Mara didn't know how to answer his question. She felt unmoored by the possibility of Lillian's death, uncertain of what course to take, where to land. She thought back on her conversation with Lillian on the plane ride home, one of their last, and suddenly the right path appeared to her. Reaching down into her purse, she pulled out the business card Lillian had given her.

She read aloud to the cabbie the address inscribed on the card, and they headed toward the offices of the *New York Times*.

thirty-two

HAARLEM, 1662

ALONE, JOHANNES AND AMALIA DISCUSS THE POWER OF painting and the force of the image. To deny the potency of the symbols, to assent to the Calvinist belief of faith based on the Word alone and not the icon as an intermediary, would be to disavow what they embrace, to renounce the very spirit that has drawn them together. They decide upon a union with the Catholic Church as the final step toward their own union.

Johannes strides down the aisle first, with a candlestick in hand to light the way. Meeting the priest at the altar of their little hidden church, he waits for Amalia. The deacon opens the door, and she enters, as he closes it behind her. A nimbus of light outlines her form and the intricate lace headdress over her loosened hair; as she walks down the aisle, her steps are a little shaky. Johannes longs to rush to her side, to help stabilize her gait, but knows she must make the journey down the aisle alone. When

Johannes and Amalia join hands at the altar, her hand is steady, and the couple beams at each other.

As the priest readies the water, a door slams in the back of the church. The couple jumps. The priest reassures them. "It is only Brother Witte, helping prepare for tonight's Mass."

They give a nervous smile to the priest, who asks, "Shall we proceed?"

"Yes, Father," Johannes answers for them both.

"Have you undertaken a course of study of the Catholic faith?"

"We have."

"Have you reached the conclusion that the Catholic Church is the true Church?"

"We have."

"Do you believe the Catholic Church's teachings because God has revealed their truths to you?"

"We do."

"Wilt thou be baptized?"

"We will."

The priest first extends his arms to Johannes and Amalia in welcome, then he sweeps his hands to the heavens in thanksgiving. He smiles at the couple and gestures toward the baptismal font: "Come and be christened in the name of the one true Church."

Amalia leans back first, then Johannes. The priest pours the water over them.

thirty-three

NEW YORK CITY, PRESENT DAY

R AINWATER STREAMED FROM MARA'S HAIR, JACKET, AND SKIN. It pooled at her feet while she waited. The wetness washed clean the reporter's clinging cigarette smoke, and tears sprang up in Mara's eyes again at the thought of her conversation with Elizabeth Kelly.

She had met the reporter at a coffee shop just outside the Times building. As Mara shared with Elizabeth *The Chrysalis*'s tortured history, highlighting Beazley's involvement in its abuse, and turned over a set of *The Chrysalis* documents to her, the magnitude of Lillian's loss began to impact Mara. Mara started to experience intense guilt, no matter Lillian's earlier protestations that Mara did not "drag" her into anything, and sensed her strength start to crumble. But she knew she had to stave off those feelings until she completed her final task: meeting with Hilda Baum.

Mara rang the doorbell again, then reached for the heavy door knocker.

A familiar cloud of white hair and a pair of milky blue eyes appeared over the chain.

"Ms. Baum, I'm not sure you remember me, but I'm—"

"I know exactly who you are. You're that lawyer for Beazley's." The soft eyes hardened into steel.

"Yes, I'm Mara Coyne. There's something I need to tell you. May I speak to you for a moment?"

"You want to speak to me? Oh, that's rich. All those hours you spent questioning me in that deposition, lecturing me, muffling me every time I opened my mouth to speak. Strangling the words right out of me. And you come here expecting me to sit silently again when you want to speak? I don't think so." She slammed the door shut and turned the dead bolt.

Mara rested her forehead against the door. "Please, Ms. Baum. Just hear me out. It's important."

After a long moment, the dead bolt clicked again. The face reappeared over the chain. "What is it, then? Tell me your important news. But if you're here to inform me that *The Chrysalis* has been stolen, I already know."

"No, Ms. Baum, it's not about that. I understand that you've been told about the theft and that you've reached an accord with Beazley's. I'm here to talk to you about something different, which I'm afraid will take more than a moment. May I buy you a cup of coffee?"

Hilda scanned Mara up and down, then hesitantly unfastened the chain and opened the door. "Come in, then. But before I'll sit mute again, listening to you rail on, Ms. Coyne, you're going to let me finish my story."

Mara waited in the vestibule for a sign of where to follow. The apartment had the hallmarks of wealth, solid bones, and a good Upper East Side address but was distinctly down at heel. There were packing boxes and luggage everywhere. Hilda motioned for Mara to step over them toward the kitchen, to a chair across from a steaming cup of tea and a copy of *La Stampa*, a daily Italian newspaper. She tossed Mara a tea towel with which to dry off.

Settling in the chair across from Mara, Hilda began. "You know, of course, that my father owned and ran an insurance company. But what you don't know is that the business was merely his work, not his passion. Art was his passion.

"My earliest memory is walking with Father down the long hallways of our creaky seventeenth-century family home just outside of Amsterdam.

Every wall, every corner, every tabletop, every nook and cranny of our home, every one of the three floors, was alive with art. I couldn't have been much more than three, but I vividly recall being carried in my father's arms as he pointed out each of the paintings on the walls. I listened to him tell their stories with such love, such regard, that I remember feeling jealous. I was particularly envious of his little Degas ballerina sculpture. I felt sure that she could steal my father's love for me. . . . Children's imaginations.

"Of course, at that time, many of the paintings on the walls, Dutch old masters and early German portraits by Cranach and Holbein, were very dark, very serious, even a bit scary to a child. In time, though, they became interspersed with color as my father became a connoisseur of Impressionist paintings. I loved the vibrancy of these more modern works, the bold swaths of brushstroke, the pictures of families.

"But the most treasured item in Father's collection was not the dazzling Impressionist paintings or the old masters or even the Degas ballerina. It was a private, intimate painting, one that hung alone in his study. One that radiated a light that illuminated my father's study more than any window ever could. It served as an altar of sorts for him, a place for meditation. I am referring to *The Chrysalis*, of course. This painting I recall above all others—not for its value or its aesthetics but for the place it held in my father's heart.

"As I grew older, war came again to Europe. Hitler hung about the periphery of my teenage years, always looming in my parents' conversations and in movie reels, but he never quite threatened my little world. Classes at the convent school, music lessons, language instructions—these were my daily fare. I had all the training necessary to be presented as the proper daughter from one of Europe's leading families. We all moved as if the world around us were perfectly normal.

"You know from my deposition that I was an only child, but what you don't know is that mine was not a lonely childhood. Father was one of four, and Mother was one of five. So my world overflowed with cousins of all ages. They were the brothers and sisters I never had. Madeline, in particular." Hilda's voice cracked, revealing a chink in her carefully constructed reminiscence. "She and I were born exactly nine days apart. She never let me forget that she came first. Maddie was my constant companion. We were infant playmates, tomboys dangling from tree limbs, adolescent partners in crime, and dreamy, inseparable teenagers in love with the same movie idols. I have very few memories of childhood *without* Maddie."

As Hilda rambled on, it occurred to Mara that Hilda wasn't sharing such intimate recollections for her benefit. Hilda seemed to be reliving her history for a greater audience that Mara could not discern—or for herself.

"But then my world began moving so very quickly, so very differently. It seems as though I left the protected, guileless days of my girlhood behind in an instant—the night I met my husband. I remember the rain of that night so well. The late-fall storms, which bring the kind of wetness you cannot shake off. A wetness that clings to you. I do not think you have so many types of rain here as we Dutch have. The downpour of the early-spring showers, the light drizzle at the start of winter that wants so much to turn to snow, the damp night air that is always present." She stopped, steeped in her memories. Her story was growing long, like so many Mara's own grandmother had told her, so Mara coughed, hoping to bring her back to the point of her tale.

"The umbrellas made such a colorful patchwork of the narrow streets that night. Maddie and I did the best we could to stay dry, bobbing and weaving through them. We arrived late to the party. Oh, and the club was lit so low we almost did not see them." She chuckled. "Imagine not having seen them." She sighed.

"My dear friend Katya had arranged a little party at a jazz club in Amsterdam. Maddie and I, of course, had never been allowed to go to such a place. So we left our houses in secret, each telling our parents we were at the other's home. Then we dashed off to meet Katya. Do you know the word *rendezvous*?"

"Of course."

"Well, that is what we did. Had a rendezvous." Amusement welled up in her voice. "We were so scared, so innocent. Neither of us had ever disobeyed our parents before—but what an adventure! We could hear the chanteuse from the street. Her voice held a promise of the exotic, and we worked our way inside, finally finding Katya's table. Making our excuses, we sat down. And there he was, with his coal-black hair and eyes and easy smile, so different from the men I knew."

"Who?"

"Giuseppi Benedetti, my husband. Not that he was my husband then.

Oh, but the moment I looked at him, I knew he would be. Later, he told me he knew at that instant, too.

"Things moved quickly back in those days. Girls didn't date for years, live together as man and wife as you girls do today, only to find the man to be unsuitable as a husband. No, no. Within a few dates, mostly chaperoned by Maddie and held in secret, we orchestrated a meeting with Mother and Father, and Giuseppe asked for my hand. You see, he was an officer in the Italian army, Mussolini's army, and had to return. I was determined to go with him, but Mother and Father would hear none of it. Mother sobbed that I was only nineteen, and what did I know of the world? Father was devastated—that I could see—but he knew my will. So he did what he could to assure himself and Mother about this man, this Italian stranger whom I wanted to marry. Father telegrammed his sister in Rome, who years before had married an Italian man. Thankfully, through quite a bit of poking around, my aunt was able to vouch for Giuseppe and his family. Giuseppe and I exchanged our vows under the trellis in the courtyard of my family home. I had all of my family around me, and Maddie was my maid of honor.

"How I loved Italy. Everything was baked golden by the sun, a sun that burned bright even after my eyes closed. I loved the smell of sunbaked tomatoes and cypresses in the air, and the impossible warmth after all that Dutch rain. Our first days in Italy were a dream."

Hilda's eyes closed as if experiencing the warm rays one last time. Mara hungered to hear more, wanting to know that her sacrifices, to say nothing of Lillian's, were not in vain.

Hilda's voice grew thick and low. "But I awoke. With Giuseppe's return to duty came knowledge of Europe's disastrous economic situation, of the worldwide depression, of the Nazis' tyrannical march back and forth across the Continent, and of the Final Solution.

"At this time, the family insurance business was in dire straits. Father could maintain the family home only by going deeply into debt and selling assets. The house was mortgaged, the family trust heavily borrowed against, certain precious paintings sent off to dealers on consignment—all as a way to generate some money.

"But I knew none of this until much later. Father was of the old school. He thought that his daughter, his only child, should know nothing about money. So Father's letters were full of chitchat about this cousin, that party. Even when I traveled home for Christmas in 1939, Father presented a perfect picture of normalcy. I do remember that some paintings had been changed. For example, a Degas had moved to a premier position where a Holbein once reigned, and the Holbein was missing altogether. Silver serving pieces that we always used at meals had been replaced with porcelain. I asked Father about these absent pieces. He laughed and said that he had gotten tired of certain paintings and so had rearranged them. As for the silver, well, it had been sent out for polishing. I wanted to believe the fiction that nothing was changing, so I did not ask more.

"But I would not be allowed the luxury of denial much longer. In May 1940, Germany invaded the Netherlands. We had heard rumors, but we were stunned. After all, the Netherlands had stayed neutral throughout World War I, and the world assumed that it would be permitted to remain so again.

"I was so worried for Father and Mother, and for the rest of my family, and of course, for Maddie. From my husband, I knew all too well what became of the citizens of Hitler's conquered countries. I also knew what became of the Jews. At first, I thought this had nothing to do with my family and Father's family: After all, we were Catholics. Then we learned that my parents were being classified as Jews because of Father's grandfather. Mother could have fought the label, but she understood that doing so would part her from Father, which she could never do. I knew then that my parents were in grave danger, no matter how agreeable my father's letters were. I knew that the occupied Dutch government would replace Father as the head of his own business with a German administrator. I knew that, as a Jew, Father would not be permitted to conduct even the most rudimentary form of business, including withdrawing money from his own bank accounts. I knew that Father and Mother would be required to wear yellow stars outside the house. I knew that, without the yellow stars, they would be more or less prisoners in their own Amsterdam home. And I knew that they could face the camps.

"You know, of course, about the letter of protection from Reichskommissar Seyss-Inquart that Giuseppe and I procured for my parents. And you also know that, as the situation worsened and we knew the letter would not keep them safe, Giuseppe and I tried to get my parents passage to Italy. Certainly it was war-torn, but we thought it more secure for them, with my husband's connections and the connections of my aunt. I relentlessly lobbied the Italian government for such permission, without success. Then, curiously, one day, glorious news arrived through the Italian embassy from my parents. They were given leave to come to Italy. They had managed to obtain travel visas, although I could not fathom a way in the absence of our help."

Hilda's voice dropped to a whisper. Mara tried to catch every word. "So I rushed to Milan. In those days, all international trains came to Milan via Berlin, and I went to the station immediately. I remember so well that cool winter day. I had dressed in my wartime finest, my highest heels with a matching bag, a fur stole around my thin shoulders, and some black-market lipstick to warm my wan face. I wanted to look my best to greet them. I did not want them to see the hardships I had been enduring, so small in face of their own. I stood in the very spot where their train would disembark, under the enormous ticking station clock. The Berlin train announced its arrival with a deafening horn blast and a bellow of steam. I could not wait to see them, touch them, and embrace them—to make them real again. A stream of soldiers and important-looking officials passed by. But not my parents.

"Surely they would be on the next train, I thought to myself. So the next day, I repeated my vigil. And the next day. And the next. And the next. And the next. A whole week of waiting and watching. I grew intimately familiar with the soaring metal skeleton of the station; with the routines of the station workers, who had grown so un-Italian in their punctual attention to schedule; with the endless flights of refugees looking for a safe place to land. At the end of the week, I had to acknowledge that something had happened to them and that they would not be on the next train.

"I tracked down my husband, desperate with worry. We tried to find out where they were. At last, after an endless fortnight, we got the information that my parents had been taken to a concentration camp, to Dachau. We knew what that meant. I cannot even explain to you the depths of my devastation, but I was forced to deny it for the time being. My husband and I went to Rome and were received by one of Mussolini's own ministers. We told him of the terrible mistake, of the letter from Seyss-Inquart, of the promised safe passage. He pledged to try to help save my parents. But the war was turning against Germany. By 1943, the Italian army was losing to the Allied invasion force, which meant the end of any influence on the Nazis through my Italian connections. Then Mussolini fell, and blackness descended upon me."

Hilda stopped. Not wanting to interrupt, Mara sat without making a sound.

Hilda shook herself from her deep reverie. Her voice grew strong and businesslike. "As you know, on that first day of peace, I undertook the search for my parents and learned what had happened to them at the Berlin train station, at Dachau." The mask did not hold; Hilda began to weep. She got up from her chair and went through the motions of putting on more tea. Mara felt tears stream down her own face, overwhelmed with the horror of it all and the role she had played, however unwittingly.

"I had to wait until 1946 to go back to Amsterdam. Because I was traveling on an Italian passport at that time, I was regarded as an enemy of the Netherlands. Imagine that." Mara saw Hilda shaking her head from the back. "I remember well approaching my parents' house. From the outside, it looked exactly the same. The gardens were in full bloom, and Mother's prize tulips were flowering. I kept expecting Mother and Father to rush out in greeting. On the inside, however, the Nazi ravages were evident. Walls stripped bare of paintings, tapestries, and mirrors; floors left naked of carpets; rooms fully exposed, without so much as a stick of furniture for cover. The Nazis left only the bare bones of a house.

"I scoured the neighborhood, looking for anyone who'd been with my parents in their last days. Searching for a keepsake, any kind of remembrance of them. I found Maria, Mother's lady's maid, drunk in a nearby pub. She'd been with my mother in the final days, and inebriated ever since.

"Maria told me what had happened. On that last morning, an S.S. officer arrived at the house, pulling up in a black Daimler-Benz. My parents were terrified at first, but the officer greeted them with an enormous grin and first-class train tickets to Italy. My parents were thrilled, thinking I had arranged them. While my parents scampered about packing their worldly goods like rats in a trap, the officer and his aide went slowly from room to room looking at the few remaining paintings, touching the furniture. The smiles returned as the officers helped load the Daimler-Benz to escort my parents personally to the station, to their own private compartment in first class, a rarity in those days. Maria bade my mother farewell as the car pulled away from my parents' home. Along with Willem, my father's servant, she watched my graying parents, mother bedecked in her finest, both sealed in by crates and trunks, grow smaller in the distance."

Hilda turned from the stove, drawing close to Mara. "I wanted something of my parents, Ms. Coyne. Something tangible that I could touch, feel, caress in those dark moments when I could hear them crying out from Dachau. I wanted *The Chrysalis* most of all.

"If only I could have found it in Europe after the war. Any civilized country would have returned the painting to me. But *The Chrysalis* was long gone. Gone to the United States where your laws are so very different and so very unjust."

Mara spoke, her voice raspy and dry from sitting so long in silence. "That's why I'm here, Ms. Baum, though it may seem an empty gesture now that *The Chrysalis* is gone. I hope perhaps to make up, in some small way, for the injustice that has been done to you and to your family."

Hilda's eyes narrowed. "What do you mean?"

Mara cleared her throat, more nervous than before any judge or tribunal. "I came to tell you of a deception perpetrated by Beazley's upon me, upon you, and upon countless others like you."

Mara longed for absolution, but the remnants of her old, self-protective persona stepped in with justifications. "You must understand that, from the beginning, Beazley's assured me they had obtained *The Chrysalis* legitimately, that they'd purchased it from Albert Boettcher & Company, an impeccable dealer. They even showed me the documents to prove it.

"Ms. Baum, it was all a lie. After the summary judgment motion, I learned that Beazley's bought *The Chrysalis* from Kurt Strasser, a man who's been described as an eager profiteer of plundered Nazi art loot. So I did some investigation. Beazley's—I should say my client, Michael Roarke's, great-uncle Edward, who was a chair of Beazley's—forged a bill of sale showing instead that it'd been bought from squeaky-clean Boettcher. They hoped to bury forever the fact that the Nazis must have stolen the painting from your father's aunt in Nice, where your father sent it for safekeeping, and laundered it through Strasser, like so many others. Even worse, the person through whom Strasser laundered it in turn was an American soldier working in league with Edward Roarke."

Hilda's face was blank; she said nothing. "Ms. Baum, I'm so sorry. I wanted to share this with you before you read about it in the papers. To protect us all, to shield us from what Michael Roarke and Philip Robichaux might do to prevent all this from becoming known, I told the story to a *New York Times* reporter and gave her copies of the documents about *The Chrysalis*. The truth about *The Chrysalis* will become public tomorrow. I know it's not much of a consolation for you, now that *The Chrysalis* has been stolen, even though I hope the settlement money is something of a comfort. Regardless of the fate of the painting, I wanted the truth to be known. I'm sorry."

Hilda's voice escalated into rage. "You're sorry? Do you think your little investigation into the truth offers justice? Before you found out that Beazley's had forged the bill of sale, you were ready to hand *The Chrysalis* to them. Ms. Coyne, it doesn't matter if my father sent *The Chrysalis* to storage for the Nazis' ripe picking or sold it to the Nazis himself. Either way, the Nazis stole *The Chrysalis* from him. They forced Father to wear the Jewish star. Forced him out of his business. Forced him deep into debt. So deep that maybe he tried to sell some of his precious art to purchase freedom for himself and Mother, or maybe just to buy food to survive. If I'd been able to bring the suit in the European courts, I could have argued that even a voluntary sale in such circumstances is forced and tantamount to Nazi wartime theft. The European courts might have returned *The Chrysalis* to its rightful owner: me. But no. The battle for *The Chrysalis* took place here in the unsympathetic American courts—with you and all your crafty little arguments."

"Ms. Baum—"

"You've heard my story. Now leave and take your apologies with you."

Sick to her stomach, her head spinning with the possible futility of her efforts, Mara staggered to the door. Briefly she turned back, and as she did so, a wooden crate, tucked into the far corner of the packaging-strewn living room, came into her vision. She had missed it during her hurried entrance, but the crate now looked familiar. Mara pinpointed it in her memory: the storage room at Beazley's. It was the crate that had housed *The Chrysalis*.

So this was how Michael and Philip had laid the *Baum* case to rest, how they had planned on keeping *The Chrysalis* bomb from a public detonation. They had arranged for the painting to be conveniently "stolen." The insurance money would go to the empty coffers of the current owners, the Jesuits, and the painting landed in Hilda Baum's eager hands. The controversy mooted and settlement achieved, the case of *Baum v. Beazley's* would be dismissed, with prejudice, of course. Everyone was happy, except perhaps the insurance company, but it had premiums to placate it. The scheme would work as long as Michael silenced the truth and got back the documents from Mara—which he had failed to do.

Mara stared at Hilda, who stood tall and firm, defiant in the face of her accusatory gaze. "Ms. Coyne, I'm sure you now understand that I couldn't leave it to the courts. Your arguments—about the possibility that Father willingly sold *The Chrysalis* to the Nazis, about the delay in filing suit, about my search, about that damned release—were too clever to take the chance. You and your courts were all too ready to give the painting to Beazley's. So, when I was offered *The Chrysalis* last night, well, you left me no choice but to accept."

"Of course you had a choice."

"Ms. Coyne, I would do a deal with the devil himself to get back *The Chrysalis.*"

The right words came to Mara. "Ms. Baum, I think you did."

thirty-four

NORTH OF MUNICH, 1943

T HE SOLDIERS DRAG ERICH OUT OF THE DARK INTERROGA-
tion cell into the light of morning. Though slate-gray clouds blanket
the sky, the sun somehow penetrates the cloud cover and blinds him.

His eyes stream through his swollen lids; the outside world seems
unimaginably vivid after so many days of blackness. He does not want
the soldiers to mistake it for weeping, so he reaches up to wipe them. His
pale blue tattered shirtsleeve returns red, stained with fresh blood. The
wetness is not tears.

After his battered eyes adjust, Erich realizes that the soldiers have de-
posited him in the middle of the camp courtyard. To his right, he recognizes the gate he passed through when the soldiers brought him and
Cornelia here. There, Dachau's incongruous motto is scripted in wrought
iron: *Arbeit Macht Frei*, or Work Will Set You Free.

As he looks around the courtyard, he begins to appreciate that he stands alone at the center of a large circle of inmates. He scans the crowd, desperate to catch a glimpse of his wife, from whom he's been separated since their arrival, too many excruciating days before to count. The shorn, skeletal women, distinguishable from the men only because of the differences in their camp uniforms, bear no resemblance to Cornelia. Her absence terrifies him.

The prisoners encircle him, and heavily armed soldiers ring them in turn. He notes that the prisoners' eyes are averted from him, though their bodies face toward him. It is as if they have been ordered to look at him but cannot endure it.

An officer breaks through the masses surrounding him. The officer, whom he recognizes from the interrogation chamber, calls out to him in German, "Prisoner Baum, I will ask you one last time. Will you divulge the location of your art collection and sign it over to its rightful owner, the Third Reich?"

Erich knows what is about to happen, what will transpire regardless of his signature. The Nazis want it only for slavish adherence to their own complicated laws on confiscation of property, and perhaps the appeasement of Seyss-Inquart. He is scared, but he will not allow his last words to be those of a victim; he will not sanction the Nazis' sins. "No, I will not."

"Then you know what I must do." A firing squad materializes from the crowd, and the officer gives a signal.

As they ready their guns, he closes his eyes and sees the turquoise eyes of the woman in *The Chrysalis* before him; he feels her outstretched arms wrap around him as if welcoming him home. In his mind, an epitaph forms in defiance of Dachau's own motto: "Faith will set you free." He smiles.

The guns fire.

thirty-five
NEW YORK CITY, PRESENT DAY

T HE MARBLE BENCH FELT COLD AGAINST MARA'S SKIN. THE air around her was still and frigid, even though the day outside burned bright and warm. The long room was a haze of gray-and-white granite honoring Lillian's ancestors, indistinct through the blur of Mara's tears. Lillian's memorial plaque alone appeared clear.

Silence engulfed the mausoleum now that the mourners had departed. Mara was relieved. She wanted to be alone with her pain, her loss, her guilt, and not to feel the old impulse to put up a good front for others.

The loud clack of approaching steps echoed through the chamber. At first, Mara started to flee. As she rushed about looking for an exit, she wondered how the intruder got past the guard she had engaged for protection from Michael, from Philip, from those they might hire to stop her from revealing the other purloined Strasser documents. They didn't know she planned on keeping those documents secret, for proper restitution and private amends; she no longer counted on the courts as an equitable recourse.

Mara was almost at the heavy wrought-iron gates when she collided with the intruder: Sophia.

Sophia reached out to stop her old friend from running, hurried in her speech, and stumbled over her words. "Mara, I've come to apologize. I know there is nothing I can say or do . . . I don't know how I can make it up. . . ." Eyes brimming with contrition, she began to weep. "I can't believe I didn't help you. Worse, I can't believe I brought you to Michael in the diner, after all I've read about him in the papers. I should've trusted you."

"Yes, you should have. Sophia, I didn't think that you'd help me, but I didn't expect you to betray me."

"Mara, please believe me that I didn't think I was betraying you. I thought I was rescuing you, stopping you from destroying your career." The words were barely intelligible through the sobs. "It's just that my moral compass was so off course. I was righteous about all the wrong things."

This was really the first time Mara had seen Sophia cry, and it weakened Mara's resolve. She knew that Sophia hadn't acted out of malice, but full mercy still eluded her. "I believe you, Sophia. But I may never get to forgiveness."

"Oh, Mara, I don't expect forgiveness. How could I after I threw you in the lion's den? Or should I say, brought you to the lion? I'm just thankful you're willing to talk to me." She wiped the tears from her face and, out of long habit, patted her hair back into place. "Well, I guess I'll leave you alone now. Mara, if there's anything I can do . . ."

Mara paused. "You could tell me about the fallout from the *New York Times* article three days ago."

"You really don't know?"

"No, I've kind of been in hiding, ignoring reporters' messages and too many calls from my father to count. Today's the first day that I've been back in public since the article ran."

"The authorities dove right in; in fact, the federal and state agencies fought a little turf war as to who should lead the charge. They contacted that reporter you talked to and got the documents from her. Then they made Michael and Philip targets of their investigation. They haven't filed any charges just yet, but the rumor is that they'll bring Michael and Philip before a grand jury on criminal fraud for their *Chrysalis* scheme."

"Are they being blamed equally for it?"

"Philip tried to distance himself and pin it all on Michael, but Michael dragged him right back into it. They're hardly a unified front right now."

"What about Lillian's death? Has that been associated with all this?"

"Should it be?" Sophia's mouth dropped open.

Mara paused for a moment, struggling with whether to answer the question. She had made a vow to shield Lillian's involvement, and she knew if she revealed the connection between Lillian's death and Michael and Philip's actions, she would be revealing Lillian's connection with *The Chrysalis*'s flawed provenance. Yet Mara did not believe that Lillian would want Michael and Philip to escape punishment for their involvement in her death.

"Yes, it should be."

Sophia's mouth widened. "Oh my God."

"I know," Mara uttered softly. "I need to go to the police. I'm just a little overwhelmed by the prospect of reliving the past few days for them."

The women sat in the oppressive quiet of the mausoleum, each lost in her own thoughts.

Sophia broke the silence. "Let me go to the police for you, Mara."

"You? Why should *you* go?"

"You've been through too much, and it will buy you some time. It's the very least I can do . . . after I betrayed you to Michael." Sophia turned to Mara, her eyes red from crying. "Please."

Moved by Sophia's plea, Mara softened and decided to let Sophia pay her uncommon penance. She shared with Sophia the information she would have to impart to the police and then, emotionally drained, changed the subject to less charged matters. "Has any of this impacted Harlan?"

"Not really. There's been some gossip about his suspicious ties to Philip; maybe that scuttlebutt will shrink his stature one day. But right now, he's still as big as ever, literally and figuratively."

"And what about me?"

"What do you mean?"

"How does the firm judge my actions?"

"Oh." Sophia broke the eye contact she had been so desperate to make minutes before. "Certain partners sympathize with your actions, but they're in the minority. Most don't condone your behavior, even though the authorities seem willing. The naysayers worry about the impact on the clients' confidence."

"That's what I figured. I didn't think there'd be a job waiting for me. I accepted that the minute I contacted the *Times*." As the women sat in silence, Mara thought about what she had kept hidden, beyond the other Strasser documents: the new domicile of the "stolen" *Chrysalis*. Had she taken the right route by not heading back to the reporter? Mara thought so. Hilda had endured enough loss; if *The Chrysalis* helped ease her suffering, then let it stay with her, however deceitfully she had obtained it. The Jesuits would receive the money they sought anyway. All Mara still wanted was to see Michael punished and to have a clear pathway for a private return of the rest of the Strasser paintings.

Just then, a finger tapped her shoulder. Mara jumped. A gentle, non-threatening face, with graying brown hair and soft eyes magnified by thick glasses, stared back at her. Sloping shoulders and a nondescript charcoal-gray suit completed the man's unassuming appearance.

His voice matched his countenance and put her at ease. "Ms. Coyne, please forgive me for bothering you during this difficult time, particularly today, but I've been trying to reach you for days. I understood from mutual acquaintances that you were lying low, after all the news articles about *The Chrysalis* and the investigation at Beazley's. I thought this might be our only chance to speak."

On guard, Mara demanded, "Who are you?"

"Again, my apologies. My name is Timothy Edwards. I'm the late Miss Joyce's attorney."

"Oh . . . I guess it's my turn to apologize."

"Not at all, Ms. Coyne. Not at all." He glanced over at Sophia, uncomfortable with her presence.

His unease registered with Sophia, who stood. "I guess I'll take my leave. Mara, if you need anything, anything in the world, please call me." Sophia's eyes welled up again. "Again, I'm so sorry."

Timothy, as he insisted she call him, asked if they could sit together.

"Of course." Mara listened as Timothy shared with her his firm's long-standing representation of Lillian. The relationship stemmed back to his father's time and Lillian's father's time, and included the handling of Lillian's father's will as well as Lillian's own.

Mara grew confused. "Timothy, while I appreciate all this history, I really don't see what it has to do with me."

"Ms. Coyne, it has everything to do with you. You're a beneficiary of Miss Joyce's estate. She has left to you a painting of particular importance to her, and she has made you the beneficiary of a substantial trust."

Mara, who had believed she now possessed a certain immunity from shock, was dumbfounded. She explained to the hapless Timothy her deep feelings for Lillian and her enormous gratitude, but weren't there others who might prove more worthy recipients?

Timothy placed his hand on hers. "Ms. Coyne, it's not for me to understand, or to judge, my client's wishes. It's my job to carry out those desires. Miss Joyce came to me ten days ago and asked me to change her will in accordance with her directions. She explained her warm affection for you and the fact that she wanted to leave you the trust and the painting on the stipulation that you would carry out certain work you two had begun." He cast his eyes down.

"What kind of work?" Mara thought she knew but needed to hear him say it aloud.

"I'd prefer to let her explain it to you. She left you a letter, which is back in my office."

"Can you at least give me a hint?"

He coughed, a nervous tic. He obviously knew but was reluctant to say. "I believe it has to do with the restitution of the Strasser paintings. It's all highly confidential, of course."

As they drove back into the city in Timothy's car, he explained that Lillian had, in fact, no family to speak of. An only child of only-child parents, their legacy was hers exclusively, hers to pass on as she wished. Lillian had earmarked her birthright—not enormous but not inconsequential, Timothy assured Mara—for a number of charities. But, with the entry of Mara into Lillian's life, that had changed in part.

Entering his office, Timothy fended off Mara's relentless questions. "Really, Ms. Coyne, I would prefer Miss Joyce to explain it for herself. Here is her letter."

Timothy left Mara to her privacy. She settled into one of his high-backed leather wing chairs and opened the envelope. Tears streamed down her face at the first sight of Lillian's perfect penmanship. Brushing them away, she savored Lillian's parting words.

Dear Mara,

It feels unbelievably maudlin and trite to be saying—as if we were in some stormy mystery novel—that if you are reading this letter, then my time has come. But it must be so, and rather than wallow in the inevitable, I prefer to discuss the terms of my bequest, which I expect that my steadfast Timothy has now shared with you.

I am certain that my bequest will come as a shock to you. Oh, I know, you think that I tolerated you at best, but the truth is that I admire you. You alone rose to defend right when no one else would do so—including myself, very nearly. Thus, I have every confidence that you will embrace the conditions for the trust of which you are now the beneficiary: the restitution of the Strasser paintings, as I am loath but forced to dub them, to their rightful owners. I cannot allow my legacy to be besmirched by Edward's maltreatment of me, even if no one but you and I ever discover it. The return of the Strasser paintings is a necessary tonic for the easing of my tormented conscience and, quite possibly, my wandering soul.

The bequest of the Miereveld painting above my mantel, however, has no such provisos, no conditions whatsoever. Of all my possessions, it is my most cherished one. I acquired the painting some years ago in commemoration not only of the very first provenance I completed— the now-tainted *Chrysalis* provenance that launched my career— but also in honor of my distant ancestral relationship to its creator, Johannes Miereveld. Yes, I know, I should have told you of this genealogical tie, but, until very recently, with some private research I undertook as part of our *Chrysalis* crusade, the connection was only anecdotal, and I felt a bit foolish in flaunting it. In any event, the painting is for you and you alone, and I believe you will appreciate it as no other.

AS THE CAB DROVE TO FIFTH AVENUE, MARA RAN HER FINGERS along the undulations of Lillian's apartment key. She got out of the car, and the doormen greeted her with solemn warmth that conveyed their lingering grief. Lillian was a longtime and much-beloved resident, one of the building's first. Mara consoled herself with the image of police cars pulling up to Michael's own lavish apartment, with the thought of the punishment she would ensure was exacted.

As she crossed over the apartment's threshold, a wave of loss engulfed Mara, a keen sense that she would never know all the sides of Lillian. Yet in Lillian's private space, Mara hoped to capture more of her lost friend than the tiny sliver she had revealed, to bring her close, even now. Stepping into the foyer, she was surrounded by unembellished, stark white walls and an austere, formal black-and-white marble parquet floor, arranged in the familiar diamond pattern seen in long-ago Dutch paintings. The only decoration was a gleaming round table in the center of the small entryway, with wilted flowers in a vase at its center. Mara recognized Lillian here immediately: the severe Lillian of their first meeting, ever formal, even thorny, on the outside.

Moving into the next room, Mara felt a softening, a hint of a different, warmhearted Lillian, one she had only begun to know. The room was ivory, of varying textures and hues. Mara touched the damask couch, the marble bookshelves with their varied worn leather spines, including many first editions of Emily Dickinson's works, the nubby silk drapes that framed the panoramic views of the budding park. Here, too, the ornamentation was sparse. The room's sole adornment was a portrait over the granite mantelpiece, a seventeenth-century Miereveld portrait. In minute detail, it depicted a middle-aged woman, bedecked in the finery of the day and lustery pearls, challenging the viewer from her black-and-white parquet vantage point. The softly curling map on the table behind her signified her sphere of influence and authority, her unusual empowerment for a woman of her day. Looking closer, Mara made out Miereveld's distinctive spiky signature. She shook her head in astonishment and wonder that this was Lillian's unconditional legacy to her.

Lifting away the final layer, Mara stepped into Lillian's inner sanctum, her bedroom. Here was the youthful, almost girlish Lillian whom Mara had glimpsed with Julian but would never know firsthand. The walls were apple green; cosmetics jars festooned a vanity table; rosy-cheeked cherubs danced around a country French headboard; and black-and-white photos framed in silver dotted the room. It was clearly and distinctly a woman's bedroom.

Mara returned to the living room. She lingered over the chaise longue.

With an antique portable writing tray perched on top and an empty teacup nearby, it seemed the space Lillian had inhabited the most, the space she had inhabited last. Wanting to slip into Lillian's skin, even for a moment, Mara lowered herself into it, settling the tray over her, as Lillian must have done.

Running her hands over the tray's peeling edges, Mara felt the outline of a surprisingly deep drawer. She slid it open, finding a cache of documents. From the dates of the faxes and memos within, it appeared that Lillian had kept herself quite busy working away in the evenings on the private project she referenced in her letter; Mara surmised that Lillian must have wanted to learn all she could about *The Chrysalis* once she discovered how her very first provenance—which had birthed her life's work—had emanated from such deception.

Two X-radiographs, special photographs revealing the different, earlier versions of paintings that lay beneath current canvas surfaces, spilled out. The first was of *The Chrysalis*. Looking closely with Lillian's monocle, she saw Miereveld's original handiwork: the standard Virgin's crown of ivy underlying the bridal crown of myrtle, the addition of a swelling belly where a flat stomach was previously portrayed, the late insertion of the silver mirror capturing Miereveld and his subject, and the transformation of the goldfinch cupped in the Virgin's hand to the chrysalis. And, in the upper right-hand corner, a dedication to the Jesuits appeared. Mara wondered what Miereveld's alterations meant. The second X-radiograph depicted the last painting attributed to Miereveld, the *Portrait of the Family Brecht*. Squinting at the portrait of parents and their two sons, Mara made out a subject painted over roughly in the final portrait, a subject converted into background fabric by an unskilled hand. She recognized the face; it was the same woman depicted in *The Chrysalis*.

Mara sifted through the rest of the papers, hoping to make sense of the X-radiographs. Amid a stack, she found a copy of a Guild of Saint Luke document listing the members of the studio Van Maes and Miereveld, including the name Pieter Steenwyck. Behind it were two official forms with the names of Johannes Miereveld and Amalia Brecht; the translations identified the documents as a baptismal registry and marital banns. Beneath these documents were a stack of birth records, including one dated 1662 for a child born of Amalia also named Johannes, and a roughly outlined family tree ending with Lillian and stemming back centuries to Amalia Brecht and Johannes Miereveld.

But what did it all mean? Bells were ringing in Mara's head, and the possible *Chrysalis* story, as unearthed by Lillian, began to take shape in Mara's imagination.

It seemed to Mara that Lillian had discovered the true tale behind *The Chrysalis*'s creation. She had revealed the love between an unlikely pair—a Catholic, tradesman painter, Johannes Miereveld, and his inaccessibly patrician subject, Amalia Brecht—and the hopes that they shared for their joint future. And she had uncovered the enduring fruit of that union: a child, Johannes, Lillian's distant ancestor.

Mara speculated that Lillian's discovery of *The Chrysalis*'s dual iconography—the overt symbolism of Catholic redemption and the concealed imagery of the lovers—laid bare much more than the truth behind the painting's formation. She guessed that Lillian had exposed the intertwined nature of the painting's symbolism and its ownership history. Mara imagined that Amalia's father, Burgomaster Brecht, somehow learned of *The Chrysalis* with its double message and banished the painting to the home of his fellow Calvinist townsman Jacob Van Dinter, robbing the painting's initial patron, the Jesuits, of their commissioned masterwork for centuries. And possibly banishing Johannes Miereveld to obscurity along with it. She hypothesized that Miereveld—and *The Chrysalis*—had reemerged into the public consciousness due only to the Steenwyck auction, when the Miereveld paintings so painstakingly gathered and stored by Pieter Steenwyck after Johannes's death, perhaps as an homage to his master, came to light. And she conjectured that *The Chrysalis*'s ultimate destiny was dictated by its religious iconography—to be purchased by Erich Baum as a source for private veneration; to be rejected by the Nazis because of its Catholic theology; to be embraced by the Jesuits as a lost treasure, once again found; and, finally, to be reclaimed by Hilda Baum as a memorial to her late father.

Mara lay for a long time in the chair's embrace, turning the players' surmised stories over and over in her thoughts. She could barely wrap her mind around the impact Lillian's discoveries had on the legal ownership of the painting but decided that it didn't matter. Lillian, the descendant of the ill-fated lovers—and, in some ways, the painting's rightful owner—would approve of the final fate of *The Chrysalis*. Rousing herself from her rumination, Mara reached down into her bag for Lillian's letter. Her eyes raced to the last lines of the letter, which she read and reread:

Mara, I leave you not with my words but with the words of Emily Dickinson, my most beloved poet. I can think of no better way to call you to rise to the legacy which I bequeath to you.

> *We never know how high we are*
> *Till we are called to rise;*
> *And then, if we are true to plan,*
> *Our statures touch the skies.*
>
> *The heroism we recite*
> *Would be a daily thing,*
> *Did not ourselves the cubits warp*
> *For fear to be a king.*

Mara understood now what she would do. She would rise. She would let *The Chrysalis* glide with unfettered wings toward its own uncertain destiny, but she would not yet let the other Strasser paintings go. Each of the paintings told a story more layered and complex than its provenance alone could ever reveal—a story of the passions, hopes, and dreams of the artist, subject, patron, and owners. Mara would set out to uncover these paintings' deeper lineages and tie the paintings to their past so they could achieve the full destinies that had been stolen from them. Like the Saint Peter of Michael's etchings, who had been exhorted that "whatever you bind on earth shall be bound in Heaven, and whatever you loose on earth will be loosed in Heaven," she would tether their future to their past.

thirty-six

HAARLEM, 1662

THE BURGOMASTER SEES THEIR LONG GAZES. HE NOTES THE absences and daydreams of his only daughter, his prized chattel. Yet he cannot believe her capable of treachery.

He does not want to receive the unwelcome visitor but knows he must. His duty toward his daughter's soul mandates it; he must be certain of her innocence, and if he cannot, he must protect her from further sin. He signals for his footman to grant the caller admittance.

"Did you bring the evidence?" He engages in no conversational niceties. There is no need.

"I have. Have we reached an accord?"

"We have."

The man hands him a sealed envelope.

The burgomaster uses his bejeweled desk knife to pry open the waxen seal. Two jagged-edged documents spill out onto the floor. The burgomaster lowers himself to grasp the torn pages. He stares at them: a baptismal registry and marital banns. He looks up at his visitor. "And what of this heretical painting with my daughter portrayed as the Virgin Mary?"

"You will not ruin him; you will protect the studio? And you will not tell him of our agreement?"

The burgomaster cares nothing for Johannes; his rise and his fall are meaningless to him. He plans for his daughter's salvation, as he sees it. So she will go to the highest Calvinist bidder, a wealthy landowner a full four days' ride away.

"That is what we have agreed, Pieter Steenwyck. And I am a man of my word. So, tell me of *The Chrysalis.*"

Johannes runs down the muddy lane, but even so, he arrives late for their rendezvous. The rain has kept him. His arms spill over with bounty for their picnic; he grins at the thought of Amalia's certain delight with the delicacies in the basket. They will have to enjoy an indoor banquet for two on this special day, their wedding day.

The barn is empty. He waits, believing that the rain has kept her as well. In time, he rushes back to the studio; they have but minutes before the marital banns will be read and the priest will expect them at the altar. He hopes that she is awaiting him there, out of the deluge.

Pieter sits on the stoop. He rises to hold Johannes back from entering. Johannes pushes him to the wet ground and races past him, past the kitchen with its broken pottery, past the spill of paint and shredded canvases.

"Pieter Steenwyck, what have you done?" he roars. Instinct tells him whom to blame.

He rushes into the studio, looking for Amalia. Her cape lies trampled on the floor, her wedding veil sits in a dark pool of rainwater, but she is gone. As is Burgomaster Brecht's portrait, which Johannes had set aside as a wedding gift to his new family. As is the Jesuits' painting, *The Chrysalis.*

AUTHOR'S NOTE

During the early days of my tenure at a behemoth New York City law firm, the seed for *The Chrysalis* was planted. After a particularly grueling work-week, my close friend and then fellow associate Illana asked me a question, one posed to her in a law school seminar. Would I ever decline to represent a client on moral grounds, even though the client had a solid legal basis for the position it wanted to advocate?

Over the weeks that followed, her query stayed with me. As I reviewed box after box of discovery documents, I kept asking myself whether such a client really existed for me. After all, like most lawyers, I had the occasional client with a position resting on strong legal principles, though its stance might be tinged around the edges with moral ambiguity.

Then an article describing the emergence of a few cases in which families of Holocaust victims attempted to recover artwork stolen by the Nazis during World War II captured my attention. I began to do some reading and research in my not-so-copious spare time. Sympathy for the seemingly wronged plaintiffs did not translate into superior legal rights; the law did not seem to favor the surviving family members of Holocaust victims. In fact, the opposite was more likely to be true. I had my answer to Illana's question: If I was asked to represent a client in its efforts to keep artwork from a Holocaust victim's heirs, I hoped I would decline, even if precedent supported the client's arguments.

This process yielded the backdrop for *The Chrysalis*, even though its main character, Mara Coyne, does not refuse to represent Beazley's. The legal landscape depicted in the book is largely accurate. Holocaust survivors and their families filing civil suits as private plaintiffs must deal with many of the same issues faced by Hilda Baum. I did streamline the issues, fictionalize the legal precedent, and heighten the difference between the relevant American and European law, both for dramatic tension and to make a murky quagmire of arcane procedural issues more interesting and accessible.

Since I began writing *The Chrysalis*, the topic of who owns artwork plundered during wartime has become headline news. Some courts and legislatures have made efforts to rectify the inequities in the law, injustices that did not anticipate the horror of the Holocaust. Conferences have been conducted; guiding principles established; commissions on looted assets formed; art-loss registers created; legislation considered and, in some situations, adopted. Plaintiffs have filed more and more cases, and some courts have begun to shift the case law. Given that private plaintiffs seeking the restitution of art looted by the Nazis must still leap over many of the same hurdles as Hilda Baum, however, I left those developments unmentioned and unexplored. They will make a brief appearance in my next book.

The idea for introducing a fictional seventeenth-century Dutch artist and painting into this realistic legal setting came mainly from my reverence for the artwork of that time period: the quality of the light, the near-photographic attention to detail, and, most of all, the multifaceted symbolism, which acts as a prism that changes the viewer's initial perception. The full reason is more complicated. Since *The Chrysalis*'s legal issues focus on who owns artwork throughout time, I thought it might be intriguing to make the custodial fate of the painting dictated by its iconography. I became captivated by the idea that the painting's religious symbolism would determine its ultimate destiny—namely, to be acquired by Erich Baum for his personal worship, to be discarded by the Nazis due to its Catholic message, to be welcomed by the Jesuits as a returned treasure, and, lastly, to be sought after by Hilda Baum as a remembrance of her late father. The seventeenth-century Dutch paintings—with the hidden stories that lay beneath their deceptively simple scenes—seemed perfect. But no one existing painting told each of the stories I hoped to share. So, I created Johannes Miereveld. And *The Chrysalis.*

ABOUT THE AUTHOR

HEATHER TERRELL is a lawyer with more than ten years' experience as a litigator at two of the country's premier law firms and for Fortune 500 companies. She is a graduate of Boston College and of the Boston University School of Law. She lives in Pittsburgh. *The Chrysalis* is her first novel.

ABOUT THE TYPE

This book was set in Electra, a typeface designed for Linotype by
W. A. Dwiggins, the renowned type designer (1880–1956). Electra
is a fluid typeface, avoiding the contrasts of thick and thin strokes
that are prevalent in most modern typefaces.